D0950050

FOR ERIN BLACK, MY BRILLIANT EDITOR.
YOUR INSIGHT, ENCOURAGEMENT, AND DEDICATION
BRING OUT THE BEST IN ME AND MY STORIES.
THANK YOU.

THE BRIMSTONE BLEED, INC.
Pandora Assignments, Con't
Contender Cluster C

Pandora: KD-8
Design Type: Fox, Small-Scale
Ability A: Replication
Assigned Contender: Tella Holloway
Code Color: Red

Pandora: RX-13
Design Type: Eagle
Ability A: Invisibility
Ability B: Nautical
Assigned Contender: Harper Shaw
Code Color: Green

Pandora: M-4
Design Type: Lion
Ability A: Flame
Assigned Contender: Guy Chambers
Code Color: Orange

Pandora Identification: EV-0
Design Type: Elephant, Small-Scale
Ability A: H_2O
Assigned Contender: Olivia Finch
Code Color: Blue

***Pandora Identification:** Z-54
Design Type: Cheetah
Ability A: Night Vision
Assigned Contender: Jaxon Levine
Code Color: Green
**Expired*

Pandora: BK-68
Design Type: Pig
Ability A: Hypnotizability
Assigned Contender: Braun Kirkland
Code Color: Green

THE SEPARATION

CHAPTER ONE

I am stronger than I was before.

Six weeks ago, I was a sixteen-year-old girl from Montana whose brother was dying. Nine months before that, I was shopping with my best friend in Boston, picking out the perfect shade of coral lip gloss. I was the girl who loved a chilled Greek salad, hold the onions, who texted my girlfriends every time there was a sale at Express, who had a closet full of glitter — and so what, a girl has a right to glitter.

Before, I figured that when my family was struck with illness, when my brother, Cody, first passed on a second helping of meat loaf with red gravy and started losing weight, that this was the *thing*. This was the tragedy I'd have to deal with in my life — watching my big brother crumble and my family with him.

I tried to be brave, to smile when there was nothing to smile about. To offer a polished joke in the doctor's office so that Cody could cast off the fear in his belly and laugh instead.

Good-bye, fear. Nice knowing you! I won't be needing you since my sister's here.

Now I'm competing in the Brimstone Bleed to try and save his life. I thought the bad hand we were dealt was Cody's being sick. But sometimes a hand worse than illness is the one offering a slippery morsel of hope. That's the thing about life: When you're dealt a crappy situation, you think to yourself, *At least it can't get any worse than this.*

And then life slaps you upside the head for being naïve.

I wasn't cut out for a race across the jungle or to trek across the desert with the sun scalding my cheeks.

But like I said —

I am stronger than I was before.

CHAPTER TWO

Guy Chambers looks worried. And when he worries, I worry right along with him. Of course, sometimes Guy makes it difficult to be anything at all besides lustful. Even in the heart of the desert — the fresh pink scar on my stomach itching like crazy — I could still shove him on a Popsicle stick and slurp him up. *Nom-nom-nom.*

"Tella," he says. His voice is sharp, even urgent.

Though, in my mind, he says my name more like *Te-lllla.*

Guy tilts his head as if he's not sure I'm listening, which I'm not. We've been at this desert base camp for over a week for "rest and recovery." But it's hard to do either when we're counting down the days until the Brimstone Bleed continues.

The Brimstone Bleed covers four ecosystems: jungle, desert, ocean, mountain. Or mountain, then ocean. Two we've completed; two remain. We're halfway. Hoorah! Victory dance.

Except it's hard to feel positive about how far we've come when we're battling one another for the Cure — something that will save our loved ones back home from croaking — and because we've already lost friends along the way. Even worse, the people behind this race are the ones who *made* our loved ones sick, though they pretend to be the heroes. And for the grand finale? The second ecosystem we overcame was harder than the first, which doesn't make me real optimistic about what lies ahead.

Guy's lion, his Pandora, gives a small growl deep in his throat. It's as if he's frustrated that I'm not paying attention to his Contender. My own Pandora growls in return, though it's amusing, considering the sound emanates from a black fox one-tenth the size. I scoop my Pandora, Madox, into my arms and attempt to focus on what Guy is saying.

"What's up?" I ask, hoping if I sound casual, the concern will leave his face.

"I think they're getting ready to move us."

"Move us," I repeat, my brow furrowing. "Like we're cattle or something." My blood burns as I remember that these monsters ordered us to kill other Contenders' Pandoras to qualify for the rest of the race. Sometimes, I can't shake the memory of sliding a blade into Levi's dying Pandora, even if his brother did ask me to do it.

Guy shifts as if he's going to brush away the hair from my face like men do in romance novels. Not that I'd know or anything. Not as if I used to dig those suckers out of my mom's nightstand and devour them while plunging an arm into the graham crackers box.

Before Guy can morph into Fabio, his hand drops to his side. Maybe it's because I hacked my hair off and all that remains to caress is the blue-and-green feather Mom gave me, the same feather my grandmother once wore in her own hair. Or maybe he's being distant again. I thought we were past that, but lately I'm not so sure.

Guy runs his hand along his clean-shaven jaw. It won't be that way for much longer. "I can just sense something's happening. We've been here long enough. It's time." He pauses, bites the inside of his cheek. "Look, Tella . . ."

Te-lllla.

"You should forget about what I said," he continues, voice lowered. Guy musses his dark hair that, after hiking through the jungle and desert, still manages to look *GQ*. "I'm not going to let you —"

"We've been over this," I interrupt. "I have to try and win, for my brother. After that, I'm going to help you destroy . . ." I glance around at the other Contenders, at their exhausted faces and slumped shoulders. I study the Pandoras by their sides, beaten and bruised from helping their Contenders survive. "I'm going to help you destroy the race so no one has to go through this again."

The Green Beret of a dude nods his head, though I can tell he's not convinced. And that in the end, if I'm one of the final five and receive an invitation to become a Brimstone Bleed employee, he might accuse me of cheating so I can't continue. Assuming cheating is even a thing, which it probably isn't.

"Hey-o! Are we packing up? Are the Rambos moving out?" This comes from Jaxon, my friend. He's wearing a blue flag, the kind that helps us navigate to base camps, around his forehead. His blond curls spring up and over the top. Seeing me eyeing the flag, he says, "See, like Rambo." Jaxon holds his arms up as if he's got a machine gun and proceeds to put a round of bullets into Guy.

Guy isn't amused.

Clinging to Jaxon's leg is Olivia, a ten-year-old girl with exactly nine fingers. She'll show everyone who asks those fingers, and anyone else who doesn't. A blue-gray trunk wraps around Olivia's waist.

"Cut it out," Olivia tells her elephant. Though I can tell she secretly adores her Pandora's nuzzling. Jaxon looks at her elephant, EV-0, with longing. He lost his Pandora in the desert when one of our Contender allies turned out to *be* a Pandora and ate his animal companion.

And the people running this race think we can "rest and recover" at base camp.

Please.

"So are we?" Jaxon repeats. "Moving out?"

Guy nods as if he's sure, but I don't know how he can be. Then again, if Guy said our next leg of the race would be on the moon, I'd start looking for the shuttle. He stares into the desert as if the answer is there. "There's been talk."

“Scandalous.” Jaxon’s head bobs, a huge smile plastered on his face.

Guy sighs, and I lock eyes with him. Blue eyes. Not blue like the ocean at high tide or the sky on a summer afternoon. More like the blue of a dead body. A kind of blue that makes you hold your breath and count your blessings and beg for one more. I like when Guy sets his gaze on me. That shade of blue could make the world tremble on bended knees, but I’d happily drown in it.

An enormous hand with polished nails comes down on Jaxon’s shoulder. “He’s going to kill you one of these days,” a surprisingly soft voice says. Surprising because its owner is the size of a planet.

Braun orbits into view, his pig Pandora grunting at his side. “Do we know where we’re going next?”

Guy’s eyes widen. He’s looking over Braun’s shoulder, and I turn to see what nabbed his attention. The two men who work for the Brimstone Bleed stand outside the perimeter of the base camp, an orange flag in each of their hands. They hold the flags by their sides and drag the toes of their boots in the sand, creating a large circle.

I hear it before I see it — the unmistakable *thwump-thwump-thwump* of a helicopter approaching.

CHAPTER THREE

The helicopter is like a crow against a sea of blue. As it gets closer, it seems more like a smudge of black paint, one I could swipe from the sky with the pad of my thumb. And then it seems only like what it is, a beacon of hope. Or one of fear.

Contenders rush from huts, which resemble tepees, out into the open air. They raise hands to their brows and watch as this metal monster hovers over our heads. Sand beats against my skin, stinging. It isn't much worse than the sun's ever-present bite. What limited brush there is flattens against the ground, and I feel myself doing the same.

Someone grabs on to my elbow and yells into my ear. It's Guy, but I couldn't hear him if he spoke telepathically, let alone over the sound of the helicopter's blades whirling. A nervous brown muzzle nudges my arm, and I dig my hand into the bear's dense fur. AK-7 is a grizzly bear Pandora and has the girth and jaws to prove it. But his previous owner did unspeakable things to him, and though I've tried to show the animal he won't be hurt again, he's still skittish. I've adopted AK-7 as my own, for better or worse, but it's hard to not see his former owner — Titus — when I stroke his thick coat, or to forget how Titus died trying to kill me. At least I know he isn't coming back and that the rest of the Triggers have all but disbanded.

To the tune of orange landing flags waving, the helicopter touches down, and the wind dissipates, leaving behind an eerie silence. One of the Brimstone Bleed men jogs over. He opens the door, and at the same time, Guy drags me backward. Braun, Olivia, and Jaxon follow our movements. The Pandoras line up in front of us, and Madox raises his wet nose into the air.

"Not too close," Guy orders no one in particular.

The pilot steps out of the helicopter, graceful as a ballerina. She's wearing an orange knee-length pencil skirt and a stiff white collared shirt. Brown kitten-heel boots adorn her feet, and when she takes a step into the sand and sways, the man who opened her door offers his arm. She takes it with a warm smile and tosses bulky headphones back into the helicopter.

The other man, the tall one with enormous ears and a shortage of hair, reaches into the helicopter and slides a box forward. He lifts it up, putting every ounce of strain on his back, which everyone knows is wrong. The three of them, one with the box in his arms, stride toward the largest hut on the perimeter of base camp, landing flags forgotten. The green-and-blue-plaid blanket that hangs over the entrance is pushed aside, and the crew vanishes from sight.

The sun is setting on the sixth night of our rest week. The fourteen days we were allotted to make it to base camp have passed. No one ever enters the base camps after the fourteen days expire. Not in the jungle and not in the desert. I want to dwell on what happens to the ones who are still out there. But Guy tells me not to. He makes it seem easy to forget, and that worries me.

"We should go to our huts and relax," Guy announces. "They'll be moving us tomorrow."

He speaks with such confidence. It makes me hate him. But then his face turns in my direction, and his strong jawline, his cheekbones, his shoulders — they tell me to ease up. That and he is the single most resourceful Contender in this race. His father told him about the Brimstone Bleed, trained him to take it down from the inside. I regard his mangled left earlobe and the gash through his right eyebrow, souvenirs from that training.

"How about, instead," Jaxon says, "we huddle into one hut and talk all night about why a strange woman appeared at base camp, who may or may not be cougar hot."

"Seriously?" Braun chuckles. "She's one of them."

"She's one of them *now*," Jaxon says, popping his collar.

Olivia rolls her eyes. "Unpop your collar, jackass. No one does that anymore."

Guy heads toward his hut, the one I've shared with him for the last several days, and Olivia, Jaxon, and Braun follow behind. Jaxon continues to chatter about how he can "turn" the woman in orange, and we all ignore the fact that he is still heartbroken over Harper's leaving. We hear the way he tosses her name out in every other conversation and the way he studies the desert at night as if she'll suddenly flicker into view like a lightning bug.

Harper won the second leg of the race. With that win, she received a five-year Cure for her sick daughter. But her daughter died before it could be administered, and Harper gave the Cure to Caroline instead. Before she left the desert base camp, Harper wrote a note. In that note, she explained how she'd return to finish the race — and help me win.

I'm not sure she'll be able to do that, and I wish she hadn't promised something she isn't able to fulfill. Because sometimes I catch myself following Jaxon's gaze, praying her blond hair, green eyes, and brick-house stamina will reappear.

Guy eventually waves Jaxon, Braun, and Olivia away. The three of them huddle near a lit torch with their remaining Pandoras and speak quietly as the sun plummets toward the earth, the relief of night cooling our campsite.

"Inside," Guy says to me, leading the way into our hut. The moment we arrived at base camp, Guy staked claim to this particular hut. It's the one I woke up in after Braun carried me from the formations. The one I woke up in after I helped kill Titus. Other Contenders sleep inside the hut with us, but Guy made it known that the dusk hours were his and mine.

When Guy speaks, people listen. Not because he's abrasive, but because everyone is searching for a leader in this race, whether they'll admit it to themselves or not. And Guy supplies a sense of security when he vocalizes what he wants.

I sit on a single cot, and Guy sits next to me, his arm brushing my own. Goose bumps rush across my skin, and I'm certain it isn't from the sudden chill in the air. "We should tell the others about our plan," I whisper.

His eyes flash in my direction, and my heart clenches. "It would put the others in danger," he responds. "I can't risk that." I sigh, because the last part is really what he means. The part about others being a risk to his plan. Guy's strategy is act alone. One-man show. It's do or die, as long as he's the only person affected. It's why he's tried to talk me out of joining him on his crusade. "I'm going to sneak over to the main hut tonight, see if I can learn anything." Guy studies my face and, slowly, his gaze roams to my mouth. I press my lips together with anticipation. Maybe I'm trying to keep his attention there; I don't know.

Guy hasn't kissed me since the day he told me about his plans for the Brimstone Bleed. I'd be lying if I said that didn't hurt. My priority is Cody, but it was nice feeling as if someone cared deeply about me inside this race.

"You should stay here tonight," Guy says.

"No way, I'm going with you."

"Tella, you have to listen to me if this is going to work."

Maybe it's the distance he's put between us the last few days or how he promised he'd never leave me again, but what he's saying frustrates me. "Why?"

"Because I want to keep you alive, and I don't like you taking unnecessary risks."

"It's not your job to keep me alive."

Guy smiles. "I make it my job."

Madox trots toward Guy and releases a playful growl. Guy suppresses a laugh and stretches his hand toward him. But Madox turns his head, refusing anything but my affection . . . or treats. He'd certainly take a treat from Guy. "Lighten up, fox," Guy tells Madox. "You should love me."

Now I smile. "He should, should he?"

Madox reluctantly offers Guy his right ear for a scratch. "Well, yeah, your Contender would still be back in that jungle if it weren't for me."

The air is sucked from the room, and I flinch from the sting of his words. I know he didn't mean to intentionally hurt me just now. But he did. Guy chuckles lightly and tosses me a genuine grin, and I do my best to return the gesture.

I've spent six weeks with Guy under insurmountable stress, and yet that one sentence he uttered is as hard to swallow as some of the biggest obstacles we've overcome. Is that how he thinks of me? The girl who needs saving? The girl who wouldn't be here if it weren't for him?

If I'm being honest with myself, it's something I've thought a lot about over the last few days, especially since he rescued me from Titus and the Triggers. How would I fare without Guy around? Would I still have a chance at winning, at surviving? I'm not sure why what he said struck me so hard.

Actually, yes, I am.

It's because it's the truth.

"You okay?" he asks.

I nod and pull a calm mask with a fake half smile over my face. "I'll stay here when you look around tonight."

"Good," he says with relief. "That's good." Guy seems for a moment as if he's going to take my hand. But in the end, he simply rises and vanishes through the blanketed door like a ghost, taking my pride with him.

CHAPTER FOUR

Once Guy leaves, I feel utterly alone. Except, that is, for Madox. My Pandora is snoozing on my legs, tongue lolled out onto the blanket, where a quarter-sized puddle of fox drool forms.

Nice.

Almost immediately, I begin rehashing our conversation. Guy thinks I've only made it this far because of him. Which begs the question: What would happen to the mission to destroy the race if he weren't around? The fact that I'm unsure makes me ill. The fact that Guy is probably unsure of my ability to persevere makes it that much worse. I don't even know how to remedy this situation. I need Guy. No, that's not right. Guy is an asset. One I care deeply about. But maybe I need to rely on myself more than I do.

I climb out of bed and pace the hut, stepping over sleeping bodies, which fidget and moan. An older dude tells me to *bring him the corn* without opening his eyes. Out of all the things I'd want someone to bring me in my dream world, corn doesn't top the list, if you can imagine that.

Madox jumps down from the cot and leaps over the sleeping bodies.

"Should we go after Guy?" I whisper to Madox.

My black fox cocks his head as if I'm nuts.

Then I recall that this isn't the way we communicate. *Should we go after Guy?* I think to Madox.

He straightens, and his tail stops wagging. We're communicating now, but that's not exactly a command.

Should I go after Guy? He told me to stay here. Because it's his *job* to keep me alive. Because I'd still be back in that jungle if it weren't for him. Wasn't I just thinking that I was stronger than I was before? How strong can I be if I've followed Guy blindly for the last month and a half?

My lips form a thin line, and I think to Madox, *We're going after Guy. Follow me.*

My Pandora, KD-8, follows me to the doorway and waits as I peek out. As with most nights in the desert, the sky is devoid of any clouds, magnifying a dense bouquet of stars. For some, the brilliant, sweeping stars remind them that a higher being is at work. For others, they put their lives into perspective, make them feel small in comparison to that kind of vastness. Me? I think of the silver-sequined dress my mom bought me: a dress I never got to wear, a homecoming dance I never attended. Yeah, stars make me think of a bombshell dress.

Don't hate.

I'm about to leave when I'm bumped from behind. I spin around and find AK-7, the grizzly bear Pandora, sleepy-eyed and waiting for instruction. He raises his weary head, and I order him back to bed. The bear nudges my side as if he won't let me go without him, but I gently push him backward. He doesn't move an inch.

"You're a touch too big, Monster," I say, using my nickname for him. The name took shortly after we arrived in the desert. I overheard one of the other Contenders referring to AK-7 as a monster. Olivia and I got a good laugh at that, because AK-7 is anything but a monster. "I need stealth tonight." He lowers his muzzle and attempts to make himself smaller. I stifle a laugh. "Next time, okay?" AK-7 huffs through his nostrils and waddles back toward my cot. He collapses on the floor and lays his head upon his front legs. I resist the urge to spend the next ten minutes hugging and coddling the beast. It's a difficult battle to wage when he's looking at me with those chocolate-pudding bear eyes. But I persevere.

Racing across base camp with Madox at my side, I picture myself as invincible. Instead of cargo pants, I'm sporting camo. Instead of stitches in my stomach, I've got a gun holster wrapped around my abdomen, John Wayne style. Guy is probably tied up and gagged, and I'm about to save the day, barrels blazing.

I spot Guy and his lion hunkered down outside the main hut. A smell of roasted meat hits my nose and makes my mouth water. Now I'm more Madox than John Wayne, drooling away. I also detect the sound of music playing, and as I get closer, the lyrics increase in volume.

I sidle right up next to Guy and his Pandora, and I'm incredibly proud that I'm able to get so close without being discovered by the Green Beret or his lion. His head whips around, and at first he seems proud that I'm there. But then his brow furrows, and he takes me by the upper arm and pulls me down beside him.

He holds a thick finger to his lips and points away from the hut and toward our own as if I should follow him. Before I do, I gaze through a space Guy must have created in the grass structure. I spot a quiet fire in the center that's strategically positioned away from the flammable walls. One of the two Brimstone Bleed men spins a roast over the open flame and occasionally sprinkles green flakes across the tight red-brown skin. A battery-powered radio sits to his left, and a crackling radio station drowns out anything the threesome may have revealed. The other Brimstone Bleed man sits near the wall, picking at his teeth.

The woman in the orange skirt, still impeccably dressed, stands before a large sheet of paper strung along the wall, a hand cupping the back of her neck in thought. On the paper, there are names, a series of digits beside the names, and a color written at the end of select lines.

Contender Joseph – 31 – Red

Contender Courtney – 101 – Green

My eyes return to the woman, and I inspect her closer. My breath hitches when I realize it's the same lady from the train in Lincoln. She wore a green dress then, and doled out green pills to me and two other Contenders in our train car. I turn my attention back to the paper, but before I can read more of the writing, Guy guides me away, our Pandoras tailing us. I remain silent until we're directly outside our hut, standing a safe distance away from the blanketed doorway, as if that will help us remain unheard.

Guy presses me against the outer wall until my back itches from the straw poking through my shirt. He takes my face in his hands, his thumbs brushing the sensitive skin beneath my eyes. "Why did you come after me, Tella?" He says it evenly, intensely. But tonight his intensity is off-putting. I can't stop thinking about what he said to me earlier. I think about how he's distanced himself the last few days. How ever since I said I'd help him take the race down, our lips haven't touched.

"I wanted to see for myself what they were up to," I respond.

Guy swallows. His gaze falls to the sand, to our beat-up combat boots. He doesn't say anything for a moment. It's hideously quiet. I pick up the sound of that blasted radio station and wonder how I didn't hear it before from this distance.

I start to add something else. How he's wrong about me.

His head snaps up and his hands fall to his sides. "Tella, when I ask you to stay behind, it's because I think it's safest."

My brows furrow. "I can think on my own without getting hurt, you know."

Guy's lion nudges his fingers, but Guy jerks away. The lion grumbles his discontent and flops down onto his stomach. Madox jumps at the front of his paws, and the lion swipes lazily at my Pandora, annoyed at the fox's late-night enthusiasm.

"Of course you can," Guy says, but his lack of conviction is like a punch to the heart.

I flinch as if he actually *did* strike me. He really doesn't believe in me. And he really does think the only reason I'm here is because of him. But who's to say I couldn't have made it this far on my own? No one can, I guess. Because that's not how this played out. I latched on to Guy in the jungle, looked to him for guidance, and haven't stopped since then.

When is the last time I looked inside myself for answers?

I'm suddenly mortified at how he must see me. Turning away, I realize I'm having trouble breathing. I'm about to walk back to Guy's hut, *my* hut, when one of the Brimstone Bleed men catches my eye. He's striding toward a small dark mass on the ground. When he gets closer, he bends at the waist to inspect it. The mass is an animal — a Pandora, no doubt — sleeping soundly. The man kicks the Pandora, and my jaw falls open to protest. Before I can, Guy wraps his calloused palm around my mouth and shushes me. Before, I would have stood still. I would have let him hold me in place because surely it was best.

I stomp down on Guy's toe and he jerks that foot up, but his hand remains in place. Confusion crosses his face.

The man crouches to a squat, and I notice he has a can in his right hand. I hear a faint clinking sound and then a hiss. The man pats the animal, stands up, and walks away. Guy removes his hold on me, and I lurch backward.

He seems so baffled that I stomped on his foot that I find myself saying, "Sorry, I just . . . I just didn't like you covering my mouth like that."

Guy's features soften, but he folds his arms across his chest. "I didn't want you to do something that would get you in trouble, Tella."

"I can take care of myself," I snap.

A single eyebrow on Guy's face rises in a question. *Can you?*

I storm toward the entrance of my hut but pause before stepping inside. Glancing back, I examine the Pandora on the ground. Without the man blocking my view, I make out that it's a long, spindly reptile, and along its back is a red stripe of spray paint. It seems to be okay, so I turn away.

I catch Guy's gaze and recall what he said. *Still be back in that jungle if it weren't for me.*

As much as I care about Guy, I want to imagine I can prove him wrong. That I can do anything I put my mind to, just like the guidance counselor at Ridgeline High said. And that I can do it all without his help. But I can't quiet the voice in my head.

Can you?

CHAPTER FIVE

The next morning, I wake to a commotion. Half the Contenders staying in the hut with me are gone, and those who remain are getting to their feet. Outside the straw walls, I hear the voice of an older man shouting orders. I glance along the floor for Guy. He'll know what's happening, maybe. He'll know what we should do, definitely.

Then I remember our exchange last night and my throat tightens. Gathering Madox in my arms, I stand from my cot, determined. The fox wiggles in my grasp, stretching upward to lick the bottom of my chin. I wipe the slobber from my skin and lower my arms so he can't reach me. No matter. He just licks my hand instead.

"Come on, Monster," I say to AK-7. The grizzly bear rises on four legs and happily plods after me. "Looks like you could use hibernation," I tell his sleep-laden face. The bear rubs his enormous body against my left side, and I shift Madox into one arm and scratch behind Monster's right ear with my free hand. This elicits a grizzly-bear moan that makes the lingering Pandoras in our hut extremely nervous.

Outside, in the blinding sunlight, a man who works for the Brimstone Bleed stands tall, a small trunk at his feet. My muscles clench as I pull the device from my pocket. It isn't blinking, but I suppose I don't need it to tell me what I already know. This is when we decide exactly how brave we are. Whether we're willing to, once again, risk our lives to save our family and friends back home.

Though it infuriates me, I find myself searching for Guy. My eyes rake over Contenders, Pandoras, and miles of venomous sand. Then I see him. He stares back at me, a proud lion by his side. Guy takes a quick step in my direction and then stops. He seems as hesitant as I feel. Maybe he's still frustrated that I didn't listen to him last night. Well, so what. I'm frustrated that he thinks I need him to tell me when to breathe. Still, I fight the instinct to wave him over. Part of me — okay, most of me — wants to forget about what he said. So what if I lean on him too much?

I care.

Jaxon, Braun, and Olivia and two Pandoras head over. The three of them insisted they sleep in a separate hut at base camp so that we could "do it" in private. Olivia's words, not mine. Though sometimes I doubt Olivia is old enough to know what she's talking about; never mind that I pointed out there wasn't a chance of privacy anyway, not with so many Contenders and so few dwellings.

"Guy was right, I guess," Jaxon says when we're all standing together.

"When is he not?" Olivia adds.

"It's pretty obvious," I snap. "I mean, it's the seventh day of rest."

Braun rubs my back. "Everything okay with you two?"

I sigh and put Madox down. "We aren't a twosome. We're Contenders."

It hurts to speak the words aloud, and I may have said it to feel the sting. Or maybe I said it because my idea of Guy and me as equal partners is splintered. It's more like I'm a child he has to protect. What a disturbing thought.

Braun nods his understanding, and Olivia stays quiet. Jaxon, on the other hand, steals closer. He fingers the blue-and-green feather over my shoulder. "Hey, girl, hey. Have I told you how good you been looking lately? I dig a chick with short hair."

I pull the feather out from between his fingers and laugh. My shorn hair is growing back slowly, but it's still well above my shoulders. I often wonder if I'll keep it this length when this race is over. The moment I cut it off was the moment I got serious about the race.

It's the moment I knew I would take on any challenge to save someone I loved.

"May I have your attention," the big-bellied man booms. "Just like last time, we'll form two lines. If you wish to return home, please form a line to the right. If you wish to continue, move to the left."

Jaxon is always the comedian, but at this, he doesn't utter a word. There isn't anything to say. We've waited over a week for this moment, longed for it, even. Because sometimes, sitting in place is worse than running.

Jaxon glances at Braun and at me, and then he wraps his arm around Olivia's shoulders and guides the two of them toward the man on the left. Olivia's Pandora trails behind them, sending miniature clouds of sand into the air with each elephant step. Already, there is a line of at least a dozen Contenders in the continue line.

Braun places his giant hand on my shoulder and leaves it there for a moment. He searches my face, so I offer him a smile. He lowers his arm and takes off after Jaxon, with his pig in tow.

I stand alone.

"We can do this," I whisper to Madox, even though he doesn't understand when I speak aloud. "We're halfway."

I consider my black fox and brown bear. Out here, they're my family. My comrades.

My gangsters.

"I'm going to make this next leg of the race my biatch," I tell Monster. I hope this sounds thuggish. As if I'm not afraid of the colossal needle Pregnant Man will soon draw from the carved wooden box.

"Right sleeves up," the man instructs.

I tell myself not to look. I echo the thought until I hear nothing else inside my head. It doesn't help. I still turn and glance in the direction I last saw Guy.

He stands solid as a skyscraper, shining like a god in the sun. With pride beaten back, I square my shoulders and head toward the stay line, a Pandora on each side of my body. I hope I appear confident as I march forward. I hope Guy is all, *Oh snap! Look at her go! I've totally underestimated her.*

When I settle into place, I find myself searching for the woman in orange. The helicopter is still here, so she must be also. I locate her at the entrance of the main hut. She speaks quickly to one of the men standing just inside the structure. Her hand waves impatiently before being handed a black notebook. She opens it, inspects what's inside. Closes it.

All the Contenders have chosen their lines, and the man who will hold the syringe lies in wait. His gaze falls on the woman, and she treads toward the two lines, a smile playing on her lips.

"Bring me the box," she instructs one of the men.

He goes inside the hut and emerges with the box I saw them unloading yesterday evening. The woman stops beside the second man as the first places the box at her feet. My pulse quickens when I grasp that something big is about to happen.

I spin on my heel to refer to Guy and find him standing directly behind me, a man of stone. He inspects my face as if he wants to memorize it. I hate him looking at me that way when I know what he really thinks: weak. My jaw snaps together, and I face forward, my question unasked.

"May I have your attention," the woman says, touching a hand to her blond hair and squinting into the sun. The Contenders quiet. "Since you are headed into the third leg of the race, we want to ensure each of you remains as safe as possible."

Bull. Crap.

"One way we want to do that is by marking you," she continues. "This will be entirely painless, just a bracelet around your right wrist. Each color represents a team lead at headquarters, and it's their job to keep track of you. If one of you doesn't make it to the next base camp, it will be their job to find and rescue you, if need be."

I know her words are meant to reassure, but they don't. Because there weren't teams in place for the jungle and desert portions, and if they cared about keeping us safe, they would have stopped us from getting speared or almost drowning in the flooding river or subsisting on nothing but unripe, unnamed fruit in the desert for — was it days? Weeks? So the bracelets must mean something else.

One of the men opens the cardboard box and withdraws a bag of blue plastic strips. The woman takes it from him and references her notepad. "If I call your name and you are in the stay line, please step forward."

The woman announces the first name.

CHAPTER SIX

A man in his late twenties approaches the woman, a swan Pandora teetering behind him. The man is built sturdy — strong shoulders, thick, hairy forearms. We all crane our necks to see what happens. "You'll be on Team Blue," the woman says. Then, to all of us, "That's how you can think of it. Teams. That's fun, huh?"

It's not fun. It's not anything. It's blasted hot outside, that's what it is. And I've got a hankering for a peanut-butter-and-chocolate milk shake. And an air conditioner. And, yeah, I want to know what color team I'll be on.

The woman asks the guy to hold his right arm out, and she zip-ties a length of blue plastic around it. The man produces a pair of scissors from the box and comes at the guy. The guy jumps back.

Smart guy.

"Don't be afraid," the woman says through a laugh. "He's only going to cut the excess."

Sure enough, the man does just that. The twentysomething dude and his Pandora return to the stay line. One down.

After that, several more Contenders move forward to receive their wristbands. When Olivia's name is called, I almost step out in front of her, though I don't know what I'd be protecting her from.

I glance at the line across from mine, heart thumping wildly. There are only four people leaving the race. They seem more than pleased with their decision to bail, considering this new turn of events. One of the guys leaving is someone I recognize — a Trigger. He meets my gaze before turning away. My stomach rolls as I remember his ex-leader tumbling from the side of a cliff.

The next round of Contenders gets a green bracelet. Both Jaxon and Braun collect one of these before returning to the line. The woman holds up a bag of orange plastic strips, and after a few Contenders are named, Guy gets called. He strides toward the woman as if he couldn't care less, a powerful lion at his side, and I envy the ease with which he accepts unknowns in the Brimstone Bleed. Finally, the last round is called: reds. Two boys and an older woman are ordered forward. And then —

"Tella Holloway." The woman must try and fight it, she must, but the hint of a smile still tugs at the corners of her mouth. I march toward her, my hands sweating. Behind me, Madox and Monster whine, but I shoot them a firm, reassuring look that says to stay put. The woman asks me to hold out my right arm. When I do, she wraps the red plastic bracelet around my wrist and zips it tight. The man snips the excess off the end as if he's working a carnival booth.

I can't stop myself from staring at the woman. Caught in her gaze, I feel as if I'm standing before a speeding train, horn blaring for me to move off the tracks. But there's beauty in being so close to death, knowing you can hurl yourself out of its path at any moment. Waiting until the very last moment to leap.

"You may return to your line now," she says.

I decide I hate this woman.

When I get back in place, she announces a few more names and then makes her retreat. As she paces toward the hut, her kitten heels digging into the sand, a hesitant voice rings out. She spins around, and the beauty I glimpsed before vanishes. In its place is something a bit darker. "Did someone say something?" she asks with a tight-lipped grin.

A man in his late forties raises his hand. He's in the stay line, six people back from where I stand. "Not all of us got assigned colors."

The woman lays a hand against her chest, fingers brushing the sky-blue blouse she's wearing. "Oh, I'm so sorry," she says. "I should have explained. The last team is flesh colored. No need for a band at all." The woman grips her chunky gold-and-white necklace in the palm of her hand, squeezing. Her eyes flick back to me for a moment, and she smiles warmly before striding away.

This woman likes me. Or maybe it's that she prefers me over the others. She looked at me as if she knows me in some way, has found favor in me, perhaps.

After the woman has disappeared behind the blanketed door, one of the Brimstone Bleed men bends to open the trunk at his feet. The chest is the same as before — carved wood with a latch that glitters emerald. From inside the box, he withdraws a mammoth syringe filled with green, swirling liquid.

Ah, old friend. How I detest you.

I roll up my sleeve and wait for the sting as those in the leave line watch. The man reaches me quickly, too quickly. His breath smells like cigarettes, and he plunges some of the blasted green liquid into my arm. I want to tell him about Altoids. Or York Peppermint Patties. Or Bubble Tape. Before I can, my mind begins to spin, and the back of Braun's head blurs.

A noise behind me steals my attention, and I whirl around. Now the two Brimstone Bleed men are rounding up stray Pandoras that the Contenders leaving won't need anymore. The first guy hooks a rope around the Pandoras' necks and secures it to stakes in the ground. The other man reaches for the creature he tagged with red spray paint last night, an iguana. He secures a rope around its middle and begins dragging the creature away from the others. What is he doing with that one? What are they doing with any of them?

My skin tingles, both because of the serum and because I'm terrified for the iguana Pandora.

I'm not even sure what I'm going to do when I say, "Wait."

My voice sounds like I'm hearing it played back to me on a recorder. It's a strange sensation that's chased with a desire to ask, *I don't really sound like that, do I?*

I say it again, louder. "Wait!" Contenders gawk at me, and the man who had the syringe tells me it's too late to change lines. But I don't care about that. I care about where the Brimstone Bleed man is taking that Pandora. Even though it must be 110 degrees, I'm chilled to the bone thinking about it.

He shouldn't drag the Pandora behind him like that. He shouldn't be taking it somewhere we can't see. And I'm certain the Pandora's back shouldn't be marked with a haunting red stripe.

I stumble in the Pandora's direction, my steps labored, boots catching the sand. It's hard to walk, hard to stand, but I have to do something.

"Get back in line," the man pulling the iguana orders. His voice sounds funny, too. So does the one coming from behind me. It sounds like Guy's voice. Well, he can eat it. I'm a girl on a drug-infused mission.

I reach for the rope, and the man yanks it away. "Let me keep it," I plead.

The man scoffs, and my eyelids grow heavy. Madox leaps around beside me, and every once in a while his paws knock the outside of my knee. He weighs next to nothing, but right now it's almost enough to take me down.

"Let me keep it," I repeat. "You guys have let other Contenders take Pandoras before." It's true. At the end of the jungle base camp, Titus and his Triggers took Levi's ram Pandora, among others, and the two men working the race did nothing to stop them.

The man seems as if he's considering it, though I can't be sure. His face swims in and out of focus. Madox barks, and it sounds like it comes from a giant hellhound instead of a baby fox. I catch sight of a large brown mass waddling toward me. AK-7.

"No," the man says with finality.

I lunge toward the rope. I don't know what I'm doing. Or maybe I do. Maybe I should have lunged on someone, anyone, long before now. Maybe I needed something to dull my senses before I could think clearly. These people ordered us to kill one another's Pandoras. This race isn't just about giving us a chance to fight for those we love. It's about their infecting those we love, ordering us to risk our lives, and giving us sadistic objectives along the way, like murdering innocent animals. It doesn't matter if Pandoras are genetically engineered. They bleed and hurt like real animals. They care for their Contenders as pets care for their humans. And they risk *their* lives for *us*.

My fingers are numb from the injection. My words slur together, but I gather that I'm screaming, prying the rope from the man's hand, running. Someone grabs me around the middle and tackles me to the ground.

"Hush now," he says. "Remember Cody."

Fox tongue against my cheek. A grizzly bear on his feet, roaring a warning. An iguana flat on my stomach. I don't have much time before my thoughts are gone from me. So I fill my lungs, and I think of Caroline. And Dink. And of Ransom and Levi and all the friends who aren't here for one reason or another. I think of Harper, too, of whether she'll make good on her promise to return and help me win.

I squeeze my hands into fists. I close my eyes. And I whisper my brother's name inside the folds of my mind: *Cody.*

Cody on the last day I saw him well. He was drinking pickle juice from the jar and wincing from the sourness. Has he always liked pickle juice? I can't remember, but I want to see him drink it again. I want to see him drink *anything* without the use of a straw and small sips. I want to take back every bad thing I've ever said to him and replace it with this: *I look up to you.*

The woman appears. She says something. She's holding something. She lifts her slender arm into the air to show the men her prize.

I narrow and widen my gaze, trying to see past the drug's fog.

And then I know exactly what she's holding.

It's a life jacket.

THE TIDE

CHAPTER SEVEN

I could sleep forever to this sound. It's a lullaby I wish I could bottle. Place the glass jar next to my ear and give it a shake whenever I wanted. *Whoosh, slurp, whoosh, slurp.*

My eyes open slowly. The sun is stiff midsky, overeager as always. Though I'm warm, a subtle chill rushes across my exposed skin, and when I breathe in, I'm greeted with the satisfying kick of salt in the air. I'm being rocked side to side, gentle as my mother's arms.

I sit up to find myself on a moving boat, Monster to my left, Madox on the right. I'm not sure Madox has done much in terms of adding body heat, but the bear certainly has. When he rolls to one side like an oversized Labrador, groaning, cool air whips across my cheeks, whispering of early October days.

There's a blue squishy pad beneath me, and even more spread along a wooden deck, studded with sleeping Contenders. Some Contenders are fully awake, standing against a cream-colored railing with their Pandoras nearby, staring into the distance. The two men working the race are on the other side of the boat, arms crossed. No one ventures in their direction.

The boat is massive, big enough to handle dozens more Contenders and their Pandoras, too. There's a Noah's ark joke somewhere in here. I'll have to work on that later. Behind me is a glassed-in area, and above that are white poles and cords I know nothing about, though I bet Guy does. I have to stop myself from looking for him among the Contenders. I *won't* look for him.

I remember at once the scene I made at the desert base camp. I'm surprised they didn't send me packing. My eyes scan the area in my direct vicinity, but I don't see —

And then I do.

The iguana.

I get to my feet, relief coursing through my veins. The creature cocks its head in my direction as I near it. Gingerly, I reach out and stroke the animal's side. It closes its eyes to the touch of my hand. I inspect the red streak on its back; the streak's not going anywhere, I suppose. "How you doing, girl?"

The iguana's eyes open, and her thick pink tongue darts out, tasting my skin, smelling me. I lift her back leg and then the other before I find what I'm searching for. *FDR-1* is tattooed in black ink on the underside of her clawed foot, so small I can hardly read it. I'm overjoyed at finding her here. It's a victory I never expected.

And that makes me incredibly nervous.

"Tinker Bell, you're awake."

I abandon my new Pandora and turn at the sound of Braun's voice. He's standing along the railing with his pig, BK-68, and the other Contenders who have woken. I sidle toward him, and when Madox pads after me, I mentally ask him to stay put. He whines but lies back down. I don't want to leave FDR-1 alone quite yet, and God knows Monster isn't waking up anytime soon. Judging by how sleepy both — er, all three — of my Pandoras look, I decide the men who work the race must have injected them with the swirling green serum after they did the Contenders.

Frustration burns the rest of my grogginess away as I reach Braun. But when Olivia swings out from beside him and offers her hand, I can't help but smile.

"Slap me one," she says.

Come again?

Olivia wriggles her fingers. "Lay your skin on my skin, woman."

I give her a high five or, in this case, a low four. She grins a wide toothy grin and claps me on the back as if we're old pals. The gesture is very un-ten-year-old-like.

She and Braun are both dressed in the same thing I am, a black wet suit of sorts. The wet suit has a matching short-sleeved top and shorts that end at the knee. On the right breast of the shirt is a pocket depicting a coiled gold serpent, tail rattling. I pat the pocket on my shirt and feel a small bulge — my device, no doubt. On our feet, we sport black wet shoes that make bowling shoes seem fashionable. No joke.

"You have to admit it's beautiful," Braun says.

I realize that he doesn't mean the outfit or the shoes. For the first time, I turn my face to the sea.

The blue swallows everything. It stretches out before me like an open palm, and the sky embraces the tide like a lover. There aren't any clouds overhead, as if the sun scratched his chin and said to himself, *Not today, today we let the great ocean shine.*

Waves roll across the surface, and as they crest, one after another, it almost seems as if the sea is moving. I mean, I know it *does* move, incessantly advancing and receding from the shore. But the way I see it now, it's more like a herd of purple stallions barreling across the earth, covering ground, searching for something beyond the horizon. It's enough to make you reach for a saddle and reins.

"It's beautiful," I say, and in my peripheral vision, I catch Braun nodding.

But maybe I claim it's beautiful because that's what I've been taught to say. Because when Mom and Dad took Cody and me to Long Island every summer and we gazed out at the water, that's what we said. *It's beautiful.*

In actuality, Cody and I were holding our breath, wondering how much longer we had to stare at the water before Dad said we could go get lobster rolls and sweet-potato chips. As soon as he turned his back to the water and grumbled that *we might as well go eat because his children will never properly appreciate God's gifts to humanity,* Cody and I would pump our arms and hiss, *yes!*

Now that I see it as a Contender, with the sun acting like a spotlight, my mind ticking through the challenges the ocean will bring, I think I may have been wrong before.

"Actually," I whisper, "the ocean is terrifying."

Olivia holds her arms out to her sides. "What have I been saying this whole time, Braun?"

I glance at Olivia, and in a rare moment, I see the little girl behind the bold words and fast talk. I try to reach for her, to reassure her it'll be okay, but she brushes off my attempt. So I turn and search for Guy instead, proud it took me this long to look for him.

I spot him across the deck, sitting on his spongy blue pallet, his lion lying nearby. He's got one knee cocked, and he's resting his tanned forearm upon it. And he's talking to Jaxon. He doesn't notice me watching, which also means he isn't searching for me.

Once more, I find myself gazing into the distance, searching for a girl with blond hair and a bombshell body. Searching for Harper. She isn't out there, and my heart cracks just a little, because I'll be going these two legs of the Brimstone Bleed without her. If she had shown, it would have given me hope. It would have told me there are rules to be broken, and that if she could finagle the system and return, then anything could happen.

But disappointment is part of this race, and I have to accept that and plunge onward.

The scuffle of feet moving draws me from my thoughts. The Contenders are rising from their pallets and walking toward the back of the boat. A shiver works its way down my spine while I watch them and realize the boat is no longer moving. Olivia takes hold of my hand and her elephant, who made her way over moments before, swishing her trunk with agitation. A few Contenders move aside, and I finally see what everyone else does. One of the Brimstone Bleed men is holding his right hand up and out.

A device is in his palm.

And the red light is blinking.

CHAPTER EIGHT

I find myself looking to Guy without thinking. He's looking at me, too. Twenty feet separate us. It isn't much.

It's enough.

He extracts the device from his pocket and places it into his ear, and all around us, Contenders do the same. Madox and Monster sense a change in the air, and they make their way toward me.

Don't leave FDR-1 behind, I think to my fox.

Madox cocks his head like, *Seriously, the damn iguana?*

When I shove a hand on my hip like a strict mama, Madox glances at Monster, and their eyes meet in understanding, though that can't be right. A moment later, the grizzly bear groans and lowers his muzzle to the iguana. He takes the lizard's middle between his jaws and tosses the smaller Pandora into the air.

"AK-7!" I shout.

The iguana lands shy of the grizzly's back but manages to grab hold with her claws and crawl up. With the iguana on his back, AK-7 shuffles toward me.

I stand frozen at what I witnessed.

Did Madox speak directly to the bear with his mind? No way. No *freaking* way.

Braun clears his throat, and I realize he and several other Contenders are studying me as if I'm crazy. They must not have seen what happened. If they had, they'd be gawking at my Pandoras instead.

Guy is watching me, too, an impatient tilt to his head, the hint of a smile on his mouth. Even remembering his lack of faith in me, I still smile back. After all, maybe I haven't earned his faith. He's not intentionally trying to hurt my feelings when he tells me what to do. But that doesn't change the fact that it's enabling my reliance on him. It's also not enough to make me hate him. I can't imagine a world in which I'd hate him.

Though I can certainly imagine one in which I tell him to bite me.

When my three Pandoras reach my side, I put my own device into my ear and scratch behind AK-7's ear. Madox yips, so I bend down and scratch him, too, never letting go of my hold on Olivia's hand.

As soon as the device is in place, I hear static, followed by the incessant clicking. Everyone now has their device in, and I wait while the woman delivers her speech. She always does this: makes us wait, forcing our minds to run rampant with fear.

She begins.

"Contenders, if you are hearing this message, then you have advanced to the third leg of the race — the sea. We, at headquarters, are extremely proud of your individual efforts, and we are proud of your Pandoras', too. Those of you who have lost your devices have been issued replacements, but it's extremely important from this point on that you keep track of them. Also, by now you've all been sorted into teams so we can better ensure you are safe and accounted for. You can take comfort in that."

I glance down at the red plastic band around my wrist. When I flip my hand over, I see the faint outline of a serpent I hadn't noticed before.

"Six weeks ago, one hundred and twenty-two Contenders entered the jungle to compete in the Brimstone Bleed. Three weeks ago, seventy-six Contenders entered the desert to do the same. And today, sixty-four remain to tackle the final two legs of the race."

These people infected Cody and Guy's cousin and Harper's daughter. They brought us here to a race only one person could win. They sent hunters to kill us and made us kill one another's Pandoras, and yet they pretend to be the good guys. They are not the good guys. They are the monster under the bed, a slippery shadow in the corner at midnight. They are the thing you didn't think to fear until it was too late.

"The prize for the jungle portion was monetary, enough to afford the best doctors for your loved one. The prize for the desert portion was a small supply of the Cure, enough to ensure your loved one lived a minimum of five years. For the sea portion of the race . . . there will be no prize."

My heart sinks. I despise this robotic woman and her self-assuredness. I despise that I was hoping for a ten-year Cure. Something that could help Cody see his twenty-ninth birthday. The Contenders grumble their disapproval, but they don't do much more than that. Neither do I. We're too afraid to lose the chance to save someone back home.

For me, though, it's more than that. My mission remains the same: Finish the Brimstone Bleed in first place; save Cody; earn an invitation to work at headquarters; take down the race. This plan is based on Guy's information, which I'm hoping holds up.

"In a moment, you will each break into groups of eight, and each group will board a vessel that you'll navigate through this leg of the race. Anyone not on a boat will be sent home. Only the Contenders in the first six boats to arrive at base camp will be allowed to continue in the race, and the first person from each group to reach base camp will count as the whole of the group. The rest of the Contenders in the remaining two boats will return home."

Contenders' heads turn, murmuring to one another, already scouting the strongest, the smartest to partner with. Olivia drops my hand. I glance down at her, my mouth gaping. She twists her palms like Caroline, our old Contender comrade, used to do. At first, I believe she's stating that I'm too weak to team with. But then I notice the way her head droops. I grab her hand forcefully and squeeze. She lights up with relief before turning her attention to her baby elephant in embarrassment. I look from Braun to Jaxon to Guy, but their attention is diverted.

"Remember, you only have to follow the flags to arrive at base camp. And you will have two weeks. As always, we, at headquarters, wish you the best of luck. At the end of all this, one Contender will win the Cure to save the life of their loved one. We wish we had enough to give everyone this gift, but we take comfort in knowing we will at least save one."

The Contenders silently calculate their odds.

Six boats out of eight will make it.

Forty-eight people.

"And now, Contenders, it is time to race."

As soon as she speaks those words, commotion splits the ship like an earthquake.

CHAPTER NINE

The two men working the race wave us over to their side of the boat, and we rush forward to see what they're referencing. Contenders are still calling to one another, working out teams, strategizing. Even the Pandoras seem to size one another up.

Olivia has let go of my hand and is tugging on Jaxon's sleeve, her mouth moving without cease. Jaxon is agreeing, scrunching his nose, agreeing some more. I don't see Guy anywhere, not that I'm looking for him.

A hush falls over us as we gaze out across the ocean. In the distance, bobbing like sprung jack-in-the-box heads, are eight enormous boats. They're smaller than the one we're on now, but still large enough to hold eight Contenders and their Pandoras. Each of the boats is different. There's one built like an expensive yacht and another that resembles an old red-and-white steamboat. On the far right side, there's a vessel that appears in every way like the party boats I've seen on TV, all Christmas-light decking with little cover, and across from that there's an ancient sailboat that reminds me of a pirate ship. Next to each boat is a flat platform that slopes toward the water on one end.

Something catches my eye, and I realize a Contender has hurled himself off the side of the ship. The dude has dark hair, an incredible body, and a quiet confidence I'd kill for. A moment later, a lion tumbles end over end after him.

As soon as Guy and his lion hit the water, others begin to jump in. Guy didn't wait for me. He didn't tell me which boat to go to or when to leap. Why?

Because he assumes I, and the others, will follow him anywhere.

I hesitate long enough to send Madox a message to follow me and to tell AK-7 to bring the iguana. Then I run to the edge and climb to the top of the railing. I tell myself to jump. *Jump!* But my body won't listen. The height is incredible, and maybe it reminds me of the way Titus fell to his death. Maybe it reminds me that I helped kill a human being.

Other Contenders cling to the railing also, too afraid to let go. When I look back at the sea, though, and glimpse Guy's athletic body shredding through the water, my fear vanishes. In its place is resolve born from frustration.

. . . still be back in that jungle if it weren't for me.

I jump.

My arms pinwheel, and my stomach lurches into my throat. The world rushes by, and for an awful moment I believe I will hit the water too hard and die. I've heard it's possible. That when you're falling this fast, hitting the water can be like belly flopping onto a parking lot. I instinctually suck in a breath, and then I crash into the ocean.

Dark.

Cold.

Wet.

Rational thought slips away, and I become a machine. Get to the top. Keep swimming up. Keep going. Kick, kick, kick. I can't believe how far down I plunged, how long it's taking to get to the surface. Don't look around. Don't panic. Swim. Swim.

When my head breaks the surface, I gasp for air. It feels so good filling my lungs, I could sing. I want to get out of the water. I don't want to be where something can get me. Every shark movie I've ever seen rushes back to me in an instant. I've never been particularly afraid of them, but that was before I was swimming in the middle of the sea, wondering if that's a fin I'm seeing. I think of all the creatures that could be in the water with me and in the water near me, and if I wasn't already icy cold, I'd have goose bumps.

When I look up, I see two twin grizzly bears climbing down the side of the ship with their extendable claws. AK-7 can extend and retract his claws so he's able to climb or descend almost any surface, and Madox can change himself into any other Pandora. One of the grizzlies has the iguana in his mouth. The lizard lets this happen without struggle, like she's already lost all sense of dignity, so why not ride in a bear's jaws into the ocean?

As soon as I see my Pandoras are okay, I swim fast and hard toward the eight boats. Even from here, I spot Contenders climbing aboard one vessel or another; though other Contenders still haven't found the courage to leap off the main ship. It makes me feel proud that it didn't take me as long to dive in as it did for others, but I can't help wondering if I jumped only because Guy did.

Doesn't matter. I'm front-crawling my way toward the closest ship, and I'm thinking about tossing in a butterfly or a breaststroke to show everyone that I know what I'm doing. I once got a green ribbon (third place, but still) at a swim meet when I was Olivia's age. That's something right there.

I raise my head from the water and inspect the boats. Madox and Monster dog-paddle next to me, and the iguana clings to Monster's back, amused at their efforts. Madox is back in fox form, and he yaps like I should make a decision already.

Most of the Contenders are clamoring over one another to get to the yacht with the vast front deck. If you're going to race for base camp, why not do it in luxury? I grit my teeth, seeing Guy standing aboard the yacht, a hand to his brow, gazing across the water. When he glimpses me and my three amigo Pandoras, he waves me forward eagerly. Now it's obvious what he was doing by jumping into the ocean without talking to me beforehand. He was going first. Scouting the boat out and deciding whether it was the best one to travel aboard. Now the decision is made, and he wants me to follow that decision.

If Guy is on the yacht, then the yacht is the best place to be. He knows it. I know it. The iguana probably knows it. But I find myself hesitating. Why am I hesitating?

Contenders are now physically fighting one another for the yacht, pulling one another off the boarding platform. The yacht must be the fastest. It's certainly the sleekest. Other Contenders abandon hope and swim toward the steamship or the party boat or the fishing boat.

The point here is speed. We have two weeks, and I can't waste time fighting Contenders for a vessel when I could be racing across the ocean. More than anything, more than the best vessel, I want the right teammates. And I don't see Braun or Olivia or Jaxon aboard any of the boats, which means they're still in the water. That means we still have a chance to work together.

Guy waves his arms frantically, but I count at least seven people — all who are not my people — already aboard the yacht. I'd have to give up the others to join Guy on the yacht. It may be the best decision. It probably *is* the best decision.

But it's not *my* decision.

I turn and swim toward the boat no one wants, my pulse pounding, and when I arrive at the boarding platform, I tread up the slope that meets the waterline. My Pandoras follow me, and together we board the ship we'll call home for the next several days.

I shake the water from my cropped hair and ensure my feather is still firmly attached. Then I walk to the edge of the rickety pirate boat and search for Olivia, Jaxon, and Braun. My legs feel weak beneath me, and my head spins. What am I *doing*? I just abandoned my best chance at tackling the Brimstone Bleed. My feet pace the wood decking, and I'm wondering if any of the others will follow me, and hoping beyond reason that they — and even Guy — will choose to continue together.

But why would they? I certainly chose the least glamorous boat. I mean, it has sails, for crying out loud, and tattered red flags hanging limply from their masts. I remember squeezing Olivia's hand in reassurance, but maybe she'll evaluate my decision and find me seriously lacking in the sanity department.

But no.

There she is now.

Grinning like heaven is here with me.

Her baby elephant plods up the boarding platform, and once the twosome are even with the boat, they step on.

"Where's . . . ?" I begin to ask.

"Here," Braun says. "I'm here." He huffs and puffs, and, my God, I think he's going to blow someone's house down. His pig oinks with every step it takes, clearly displeased.

The smile on my face is so wide, it hurts. But I can't help it. Braun is here, too! Though if I'm honest, I was actually inquiring about Jaxon, not Braun. I'm surprised Jaxon wasn't by Olivia's side when it came to jumping off the mother ship. Ever since I met the twosome at the start of the desert race, they have been inseparable, like siblings, or maybe even like father and daughter.

I hear a splashing sound and spot a girl, younger than Olivia, at the foot of the platform. She gazes up at our boat, at me, and her bottom lip quivers. Her blond hair is plastered to her thin face, and her green eyes hold a question in them. The girl can't be any older than eight, and I can't believe I never noticed her before this. She's a beautiful child: smooth skin; red cheeks; long, dark eyelashes. The girl tucks hair behind her ears, and I notice how much they stick out. Even that imperfect feature grants her an endearing quality.

"Did you want to come up?" I ask.

The girl doesn't hesitate. She strides up the platform and steps onto the boat. Then she sits down a short distance away and crosses her legs. I note her orange wristband.

"What's your name?" I ask.

"Willow," she answers, her gaze lowered. "And I want to stay."

"No one is going to make you leave," Braun tells her, and I agree.

"Where's your Pandora?" Olivia asks Willow.

The youngest girl raises the hair from her neck, and out crawls a white rat with red eyes. The rat raises its nose in the air and sniffs. Then it hunches over on Willow's shoulder and starts cleaning itself by running its pink-clawed paws over its face.

"This is C-90," Willow explains. "It's a girl."

The rat's gender does nothing to disguise the revulsion on Olivia's face.

"Damn ocean," a man's voice mutters. Braun and I lean over the edge to inspect who else has arrived. The first things I notice are his bald spot and potbelly. The second thing I notice is his blue wristband. The guy tries in vain to sweep salt water off his wet suit, which does nothing to flatter his figure. "I'm coming up," he yells.

As the man gets closer, I notice he has an extraordinarily wide mouth and doughy lips, giving him a fishlike appearance. He must be in his early fifties, and I'm not saying he walks like a penguin, but I'm not saying he doesn't, either.

Behind the man is an alligator, toothy grin and all. When the man steps onto the boat, he references his alligator and says, "This here is V-5. Blasted Pandora can't swim. Had to shove him off the side of the ship when he wasn't paying attention. Then I had to hold the thing's head above water the whole way over."

Madox races over to the alligator and flicks on his green eyes. He's about to record the Pandora's abilities so he can use them in the future. I brush my fox back and tell him to mind his manners, though I know he'll just do it later while everyone sleeps. Fine by me. This is a race, after all, and we need to win. But there's no reason not to be polite about it.

"When are we going to move out?" the man booms. "Let's go already."

"We only have five people," I respond. "We need three more."

"We don't need anything. The woman on the device didn't say we have to arrive with eight people, did she?"

Sixty seconds. That's how long it took for me to dislike this guy.

"We're waiting," Olivia says.

Braun and I tell him that's right.

The man gruffs and waddles over to Willow. His alligator stays put. "Name's Mac," he all but screams at her. "Mr. Larson to you."

"Who's the new guy?" a familiar voice says. I spin around and find Jaxon with his arms open like he's waiting for a hug. "Hey-o! The party's here."

I go to embrace Jaxon, my heart bursting with happiness, but Olivia beats me to the punch. She throws herself into his embrace and then punches him square in the gut. "Don't lose me like that again."

"Room for one more?" a different voice asks.

The hair on the back of my neck prickles when I see who it is.

CHAPTER TEN

The guy on the boarding platform stands over six feet tall and is built like a Roman gladiator. His hair is so black, it's almost blue, and his eyes are light brown. He reminds me of Guy in a way, but he isn't Guy. This dude is more unnerving. I mean, Guy Chambers is as unnerving as they come, but not in the way that makes you think he might kill you in your sleep.

A black bull stomps up behind the new Contender, the heavy ring in his nose dragging against the metal platform. The bull is massive, built of brute strength and agility. Madox goes absolutely crazy with excitement when he spots the new Pandora. My fox leaps from side to side, and as soon as he's able to, he races over to the bull as he would a new friend.

The bull snorts forcefully through his nose and sweeps his head to the side as if he might make a shish kebab out of Madox with his horn. My Pandora jumps back in time, but the near attack does nothing to lessen the fascination he has with the bull.

The Contender stops at the top of the platform. He's older than Guy: maybe midtwenties, whereas Guy looks more like nineteen. "May I come aboard?" He speaks slowly, as if he's weighing his words carefully, and his eyes don't leave mine for a second. "It seems your Pandora likes my Pandora."

"Not sure the feeling is mutual," I say.

The guy smiles, and my discomfort toward him melts.

"Leave the fox alone, Y-21," he says, without looking away.

"You're welcome to join us." I wonder when I became the person to ask. Do I look like the captain?

I'm totally the captain.

The ocean air nips at my skin as New Guy steps aboard, directing his bull, Y-21, toward the other side of the boat. "My name's

Cotton," he says as he strides away. I didn't really ask, but I'm glad to know. Before I turn back, I check his wrist — orange band.

Jaxon makes a big production of counting the Contenders before exclaiming, "Seven."

It's only taken about ten minutes to nearly fill our boat, but already two of the eight boats are sputtering, their engines turning. One begins to navigate away — the yacht — already the leader in this race.

I turn my face away to hide my disappointment, and my heart plummets. I'm not sure what I was thinking. That he'd follow me instead of the other way around? Despite the desire to stand on my own two feet, I don't want to be without him.

As it is, I'm having trouble breathing as I imagine him leagues ahead of me. My face already forgotten in his mind.

Then I hear our last Contender marching up the platform. I'd know that confident stride anywhere. My head whips in his direction, and cold, hard blue eyes meet my soft brown ones. He's dripping wet, and his black hair is matted against his head. The wet suit clings to his chest, his abs, his thick thighs. He looks like a king. He looks like a savior.

He looks like he's waiting for me to explain myself.

"You're here. Good." I try to disguise the relief in my voice and act confident in my decision. I'm not sure it works.

Guy opens his hands as if awaiting my excuse.

"There wasn't enough room on the yacht for the team," I say.

He stares at me for a long time, as if I'm playing a joke and he's trying to figure out the punch line. Then Jaxon shakes Guy by the shoulders and Braun flings water on him. Guy breaks eye contact with me and heads to the sails, the long, lean muscles in his back straining as he works them.

I inspect the area and recall every pirate movie I've ever watched that featured an archaic boat. If memory serves, there should be an anchor around here. I find it, and Braun helps me drag it from the sea. When we're done, we grin at each other, proud that we accomplished a task. No sooner than the anchor is freed from the sand does the ship start moving.

Guy heads straight to the back, takes the wheel in his hands, and cranks it to the left. The boat lurches, and when he straightens the wheel, I notice that the other remaining seven boats have already begun to pull away. I suppose that doesn't surprise me, since our boat probably took the longest to fill and is much harder to operate.

The race has officially started. As the boat groans to the left, I think to myself, *Here we go.* I can't help the joy flooding my system. Everyone is here, and Guy chose us over the faster boat. Now I have to pray my decision was a good one.

"Woo, boy!" Jaxon cries out, his arm around Olivia.

But before Guy can straighten the wheel, a strange sound reaches my ears. "What is that?"

"I heard it, too," the young girl Willow says.

The sound comes again. It's a thrashing, a yelling, and it's coming from behind our boat.

Guy meets my gaze, and I wait for him to tell me what to do. Because, you know, that's what he does. Guy instructs. When the noise comes again, I grow frustrated. It sounds like someone is struggling, and if it's a Contender in the water, I won't leave them behind. "Stop this thing."

"No way," Mr. Larson says, waving a chubby finger in my direction. "Keep going."

Braun comes to stand beside me. It's a bit like standing next to a soda machine. "We can't leave someone out there."

"Like hell we can't."

But Guy is already dropping the anchor. I try hard not to celebrate knowing I'll get to watch him pull it up, with his sexiness and such.

The boat more or less stops, and the thrashing grows closer. Guy searches until he locates what he's looking for. He throws an aged yellow ladder made of dense rope over the side. All the Contenders aboard move to see who's climbing up, but Guy holds an arm out, stopping us.

Finally, a hand whips over the side.

Harper's head appears.

"Harper!" I yell, rushing over to help her climb inside.

She's dripping water, and there are dark circles under her eyes, and she's visibly thinner than she was before. But she's here! She said she would return, and she did.

I try to embrace her when she's on her feet, but she pushes me back gently. Then she places her two pointer fingers in her mouth and lets out an ear-piercing whistle. RX-13, her bald eagle Pandora, bursts out of the water and lands on the boat's railing, shaking herself dry like it's only natural for an eagle to swim beneath the surface of the ocean.

Harper wears a green wristband like Jaxon and Braun, and there's a navy blue strap hooked over her chest. Behind her is a bag that must weigh as much as she does. "Harper," I begin.

She walks past me to Guy and unloads the bag onto the ground. "Took this from one of the other ships. It was all I could carry."

"How?" Guy asks, all business.

"Slipped into the water while the rest of you slept. They transported me from home straight to the boat." She holds her wrist up. "Gave me this band. What does it mean?"

"We don't know," I answer, trying to cut Guy out of this conversation and remind Harper I'm here. That I care about her and hate that her daughter died, and how is she even standing through the grief? It seems that if Harper's goal is to return to help me win, she thinks Guy is the key to that goal. Can't say that doesn't cut deep.

"See now?" Mr. Larson says. "I like this girl."

Harper starts to respond but stops when Jaxon slams into her. "Don't try and fight it, darling," he says. "This is right."

Harper doesn't smile, but she doesn't push him away as she did me. Jaxon lets go of her, and Harper's gaze darts across the boat, taking in the other Contenders. She stops cold. Her right hand twitches by her side. Her nails are chewed to bits. It must drive Braun nuts. Everyone turns to see what captured Harper's attention.

Willow.

The small girl who looks so much like Harper must have as a child. My stomach revolts as I realize what Harper must be thinking. Harper takes a step in her direction. Pauses. "Let's get going," she orders no one in particular. "We have a race to win."

Her eyes stay on Willow.

Her eyes stay on Willow as Olivia tries in vain to garner Harper's attention.

Her eyes stay on Willow as Guy works his magic and the boat races forward like a racehorse tearing down the track.

CHAPTER ELEVEN

Cotton is the one who finds our supplies. He descends below the main deck and into what Guy says is the hold. There he finds supplies that could easily last us a month at sea. Olivia locates a notepad and pen in the crew's quarters and makes a list:

(10) Pallets of plastic water jugs
(8) Pallets of canned food
(8) Eating-utensil setups
(3) Large yellow duffel bags
(2) Small red duffel bags
(1) Pair of binoculars
(1) Can opener
(1) Flashlight w/ batteries
(1) Flare gun
(1) Compass
(1) First-aid kit
Toiletries

I feel indomitable with all these supplies. But then my brain starts ticking. This leg of the race will likely be harder than the two that preceded it, so why give us this advantage? "Why do we have all this?"

Guy leaves the hold and goes above deck, back to where our Pandoras remain. The rest of us stand and stare at our loot buried at the bottom of the ship. Willow holds the flashlight on the stuff, and I remind myself that I'm not claustrophobic. I'm not. And I enjoy the mildew smell that climbs the wooden plank walls and seeps into my wet suit.

“There must be challenges worse than finding basic survival requirements,” Cotton ventures.

“Genius, that one,” Harper mutters.

Cotton glares at her.

“Don’t worry, bro,” Jaxon tells Cotton. “She’s spicy. That’s why we make a great couple. I like my women with a little . . .” He shivers to emphasize his point.

This is the part where Harper negates Jaxon’s point about their being together. But she doesn’t. She just exits the hold in silence. I have so many questions for her. Like how she talked the people running this race into letting her back in when they knew she had no one to fight for. And what happened to RX-13 while she was away.

“It was a good question,” Cotton says to me. My gaze finds his, and he holds it. There’s something behind his eyes I can’t quite reach. A mystery I want to unfold in my hands like an origami flower.

“Thanks,” I say.

We trail above deck, and Madox meets me with a slobbery kiss when I pick him up. With the fox in my arms, I spin in a slow circle and inspect the ship. Two tall masts jut into the sky, and connected to those are black-as-decay sails that roll up and down and can make us go faster when the wind is right. At the very top of the masts are oval perches Guy calls fighting tops, but I’d prefer to call them lookouts since I’ve had enough fighting. Netted ropes stretch from the deck to the lookouts and form a ladder.

Right now the sails are lowered. Guy says it’s a stroke of good luck that the wind is at our back. I say, *How in the heck do you know so much about a pirate ship?* I don’t actually say that aloud. Because I know the answer. His father trained him and his brothers in case they were the ones chosen to enter the race. He was prepared for this sea. He was prepared for anything. That's why he says I can't win. Because he knows the things I don't. And that, my friend, is called cheating. Not that I worry much about that. As long as he's on this boat, helping get us safely to the ocean finish line, then I'm cool with whatever insider information he harbors.

The boat moans softly as it plows through the water, and a slight breeze picks up, causing the red flags at the tops of the masts to snap in the wind. It's colder than I expected it to be, but with the sea mist spraying lightly across my face and my Pandora and Contender friends alongside me, I am optimistic.

I set Madox down when Cotton hands me an opened can of preserved peaches and a fork. I thank him as heat rushes to my cheeks. I didn't notice before, but Cotton's eyebrows are nearly blond. It's a striking contrast to his blue-black hair and brown eyes. Guy's head turns in our direction. His jaw tightens before he returns his attention to the helm, which steers the boat.

"Why are we staying near the other boats?" Mr. Larson waddles toward to the front forecastle deck and points a pudgy finger at them. "Shouldn't we pull away?"

Harper takes a step in his direction. Her eyelids are half closed, and I want to tell her to sleep. I want to thank her for returning and never stop thanking her. I want to tell her I'm sorry, but I don't know how. "We're sailing between a cluster of islands," Harper says. "Some are to the right and some to the left. We're choosing to go left. So are the boats around us."

I put my hand out, and Harper gives me the binoculars she's holding. Sure enough, there are two other boats in the distance. The others must have gone right. I wondered how we'd ever find flags out here, but now I realize they must be on the islands.

"Harper?" Willow says. I lower the binoculars. The little girl stands near Harper, looking up and into her face as if Harper is the mother she never had. "I'm hungry."

Harper's face contorts with pain.

"Leave her alone," Olivia tells Willow. "Get your own food."

"Olivia, watch yourself," Harper snaps. Her Pandora flaps her eagle wings, agitated that her Contender is upset.

Olivia shrinks into her elephant's side, hiding her face.

"Olivia didn't mean anything," I say quietly, trying to explain on the girl's behalf.

Willow takes Harper's hand and smiles like she won a game I didn't know we were playing. Harper relaxes into Willow's touch and guides her below deck to get something to eat.

"Harper is being weird," Jaxon says, eyeing my iguana Pandora.

"Her daughter died," Guy says. "She can be whatever she wants to be."

"Damn." Cotton's sturdy shoulders dip. "I didn't know."

"We're all going to be dead if you don't speed this boat up," Mr. Larson says, his alligator shuffling nearby, claws scratching the deck. "Why I got on this thing, I'll never know. And what about dinner? We've been sailing for hours. If you ask me, we should be sitting down to a meal. Plenty of girls to help with that."

"I beg your pardon?" I say.

"Dinner is a good idea," Guy says. "But we all need to help, understand?"

"Listen, boy —"

"Don't." Guy's voice rumbles like a volcano threatening to erupt. "Just . . . don't."

Mr. Larson rolls his eyes like we're all a lost cause and disappears below deck.

I'm about to follow behind to ensure Harper doesn't kill him when I notice Jaxon sitting next to FDR-1. He's running his hand slowly over the spikes trailing the iguana's back. The Pandora closes her eyes against Jaxon's touch. I nibble my bottom lip, remembering that Jaxon no longer has a Pandora. How hard that must be.

"That Pandora needs someone to watch after her," I announce. "I can hardly care for the two I have."

Jaxon's brow furrows with confusion. And then, slowly, understanding dawns. "I could do that. I mean, I'm good at watching after stuff."

"No giving her back if she gets out of hand. You'd have to basically name her your Pandora and call her as such."

Jaxon's head bobs. "She *is* my Pandora. What are you even talking about? We've been partners since the dawn of time." He's making a joke, but I don't miss the grave expression on his face. The one that tells me this Pandora means he's back in the race to win.

Braun chuckles at Jaxon's speech, and I open my hands like it's settled. When I turn to head below, Guy meets my stare. The faintest of smiles touches his lips. Gone before it fully forms. "We should eat the canned meat for dinner," Guy says to me. "We have a lot of it."

"Why are you telling me? Do I look like a servant to you?"

Guy laughs. It's a short, sharp sound that rises above the ocean's ever-present hum. He wipes his calloused palm across his mouth to suffocate the emotion. But it's too late. He's revealed a secret. He's happy here with us. He may not think I can win. He may think he's better, more trained than the other Contenders on this boat, but everyone wants someone to call a friend. Guy Chambers is no different from the rest of us.

I beam in his direction even though I despise his disbelief in me. Though his hand still covers his mouth, I spot the crinkles beside his eyes. The ones that say his grin may very well be bigger than my own.

"Hey, Tella, if you want, you and I could make dinner together." Cotton stands near the hatch that leads to the hold, his black hair tied back into a low ponytail, blond eyebrow raised in a question.

"Yeah, okay," I answer too quickly.

As Cotton holds the door open for me, and our bodies grow closer, I notice how much older he is than me. At least eight years, I'd guess. Too old, and yet young enough for me to admire the single dimple in his left cheek — a sharp contrast to his angular face.

Right before I descend, Cotton touches a hand to my lower back, and a feeling I can't name rolls through my body. I recognize most Contenders at this point, at least somewhat, and their Pandoras, too. But I don't remember Cotton or his bull. And Cotton has a body worth remembering. Where did he come from? Why did he choose this boat? Everyone on board has a reason. We know one another, or we were too young to fight for a better one, or too old. But when Cotton touches me like this, the way Guy hasn't in days, I find myself not caring what his reasons are.

Overhead, though the sun is shining, thunder sounds somewhere in the distance.

It whispers a wicked promise.

CHAPTER TWELVE

Cotton and Harper reach for cans of potted roast in brown gravy, because that's what Guy said to eat. But if there's one thing I know, it's food. Did Guy spend the last three summers trying to flatten his stomach before swim season? Doubt it.

With Guy watching on, I say to Cotton and Harper, "Let's eat the chowder instead. There's less of it, but it'll keep the fat we have on us. Our bodies work harder to burn calories from protein than they do carbohydrates, and we're going to need every ounce of energy we have to work this boat and gain an advantage."

Guy waves his arm. "I already told them to eat the roast."

"And I'm saying we should eat the chowder."

Guy's face contorts like I'm making a big deal over nothing, which I am. But it's time I state my opinions. It's time we all did. This is a race, after all, and we need everyone's minds at work if we are to win. No more relying solely on Guy.

Harper and Cotton look back and forth between the two of us, and then Harper reaches down and grabs the can of potted roast. Traitor!

Cotton follows her lead.

I shrug and grab the same thing, then stride away. While I'd be lying if I said I didn't feel a little betrayed that Harper followed Guy's lead, it's canned food we're talking about. Not a life-or-death situation. And as I stated, it's more important that we're all thinking on our own, regardless of what we ultimately choose. As a team, we should present options, and as a team, we should make a decision. And apparently, a decision was made that I don't know what the hell I'm talking about.

So here we are, spooning roast onto tin plates and filling our ceramic mugs with lukewarm water. Willow finds two candles nestled into holders and lights them with matches from the single kitchen drawer.

We're in the crew's cabin, which sits even with the main deck and directly beneath the quarterdeck. In the front of the crew's cabin is a cramped dusty room with a round table, eight chairs. There's a sink, but no running water, and a glass porthole that can be covered in bad weather. Right now it's open, but each time the thunder barks, I eye the porthole.

Is it time? No.

As long as we don't have to cover the porthole, then there isn't any danger. This is what I tell myself.

Cotton and Harper argue about the best way to lay the plates out. Or, more accurately, Cotton suggests a certain way to do things, and Harper does the opposite to spite him. She clearly infuriates him, but he doesn't snap. He doesn't even raise his voice. Jaxon ignores the twosome working side by side. He's too enraptured with his new Pandora, who he's named Rose.

"FDR-1?" he'd said when he saw the tattoo. "Seriously? A Roosevelt fan?"

The other Pandoras dislike Rose. They pick on her the same way they did Madox. My fox doesn't partake in the abuse, and Monster is too lazy to care either way. But the others harass the helpless animal. I don't know what the Pandora's abilities are, but if she doesn't show them soon, she's going to have a difficult race.

Mr. Larson yanks a chair away from the table and drops his weight into it. The chair protests. The boat does, too. "Finally," the man says, reaching for his plate. "I'm starving."

"You're on cleanup," I tell Mr. Larson.

"I'm not on anything," he replies. "Right now I'm eating. Then I'm going to go through that there door to the bunks and lay my bones to sleep."

"You need to help," I insist, my face burning.

"Shush your mouth, girl. I'm trying to enjoy my supper." He drives a fork of shredded roast into his mouth, wipes the gravy from his plump pink lips, and shoves in a second bite.

"You'll help clean up," Guy says from the doorway.

The man turns in his chair. He doesn't stop chewing, but he doesn't respond, either. Guy doesn't threaten him. He doesn't need to. The man grunts and turns back to his meal.

Guess who's doing dishes tonight? The Penguin!

I'm happy Guy backed me up again, but it's also infuriating. I need to learn how to do what it is he does. He chose this boat to sail upon. But what if he hadn't? Who would lead? Harper? She's too lost in her head except for the moments Willow calls her name.

Braun strides into the room like a mountain that's come to say hello. "Can I help with anything?"

"Just sit," Harper says.

Soon, we're all seated at the table, except for Jaxon, who is now manning the wheel. Willow dives into her food, and already Mr. Larson is grumbling about needing more to eat. We mostly ignore him. We also try to ignore the boat's incessant rocking. It's better when we're seated, but when I stand up, I have to grab hold of something to keep from stumbling. The waves are growing choppier as the storm approaches, and inside my chest, my heart is pounding.

Guy Chambers chews silently, one hand fisted on the table. His eyes raise and meet my own. My stomach flips, and I grit my teeth against my body's reaction. The way he's staring at me, it's like he's trying to figure me out.

I can't stand the silence any longer or the thunder growing closer outside the glass-covered porthole, so when Olivia speaks, I'm thankful.

"This thunder is disturbing, but it was just as scary at the start of the jungle race, remember? We'll adjust." She seems to be trying to soothe herself as much as making conversation.

Braun laughs deep in his belly. "They put us in those boxes in the jungle."

"Shiver me timbers," Olivia says like a pirate. "What about the first time we got to base camp? It's like, *So* this *is the luxury retreat we get after trekking through the jungle for two weeks?*"

"At least they allowed us a letter from home," Mr. Larson whispers.

All heads turn in his direction. He doesn't add anything else, and my contempt for the man falters. Mr. Larson is here to save someone he cares about, perhaps his child or his wife. He can't be such an awful man if he's willing to put his life on the line for their own.

"I remember the first time I saw the device." Braun leans back in his chair. "First day of school, in my locker."

"You know what I'll never forget?" Willow asks. "The desert sun."

Everyone groans.

My gaze lands on Cotton. He seems to be avoiding our conversation. "What about you, Cotton?"

"Don't want to talk about it," he says. "Nothing worth reminiscing about."

Harper sits to his left, and when he says this, she glances at him like she's seeing him for the first time. "You know what I want to know?" she says. "Why we don't just attack the people running this race? Hold them hostage. Demand they make enough Cure for everyone."

Everyone stops talking. Even the thunder seems to hold its breath.

"Do they expect us to really believe they can only make one dose?" she continues, her voice almost a growl.

Cotton places his hand on her wrist. I don't know why he does it. He should know not to touch her.

"Take your hand off me," she snarls.

"You're angry because you lost someone you loved," he says. "But you can't sacrifice other people's chances by launching a revolt."

Harper jumps up from the table, her chest rising and falling rapidly. Her green eyes rage in the candlelight, and outside, the rain starts to fall. "I have one last question." She faces Guy. "How do you know so much about this ship?"

Guy puts his fork down and straightens in his chair. He is silent a long time. "My father used to sail. Took me and my brothers —"

She leans over the table. "Bull. Shit."

Then she's gone, marching out and into the rain. The door slams behind her. I get up to go after Harper, but Braun tells me I should give her space. Guy and I exchange a look, and I know we'll be talking later. Harper needs to know that our plan is to take down the race from the inside as employees, and maybe our other Contender friends should know, too. Guy says it will put them at risk, but we can't make the decision for them any longer.

I open my mouth to tell him we need to talk while I'm feeling decisive, but I don't get the words out before Jaxon rushes into the crew's quarters, dripping rainwater, the enormous iguana draped over his shoulders. "Follow me. Hurry!" he tells Guy. "I think something is happening to the sails."

We leap up at once. Before we trail out, I catch sight of Braun dropping the cover over the kitchen porthole.

Outside, the rain is torrential, and Pandoras are screaming into the night as if they're arguing with the sky. I immediately search for Madox and Monster to no avail, ashamed that I hadn't checked on them before now.

Waves crash against the boat with unbridled fury, and a massive black cloud hangs overhead like a coffin. It was harder to tell from inside the comfort of the crew's quarters, but now I know for certain — the storm is upon us.

CHAPTER THIRTEEN

Darkness swallows the sea. The only light we have is from the moon and the stars, and even those are drowning in the storm. Hours ago, we teetered inside a delicate glass snow globe, the sun shining. But someone took our artificial world into their chubby hands and shook to watch the chaos unfold.

I can hardly see where I'm going, but my voice rings out, calling for the Pandoras I pray are still aboard. *Madox, find me. Please.*

A whining by my heel steals my attention, and when I spot my fox wet and shaking and looking up at me with scared canine eyes, I sweep him into my arms. *Where's Monster, Madox?*

Madox turns his muzzle toward the bow of the boat, and I race forward. I find Monster huddled in a ball near the railing. "Monster, this is the last place you should be." I coax him to follow me, and he does. Contenders breeze past, calling out for their own Pandoras. Even Mr. Larson appears terrified that his alligator, who can't swim, has somehow gone overboard.

We should have had a plan. We knew the storm was coming, and we didn't do anything to prepare. The boat moans with such magnitude that I'm certain it's a living being, crying out for its mother, for a lost child, for liberation from the sea. The front mast, the *fore*mast, makes a horrible cracking sound, and lightning licks the salted waves.

"Guy!" I scream. "Guy, where are you?!" I run, Madox now by my side, Monster on the other. "We have to take down —"

I crash into Cotton. His arm encircles my waist, and his hand cups the back of my head. He towers over me, his chest, shoulders, and neck a stretch of dominance that has no end. His eyes seem to flash in the darkness, and he looks at me with emptiness. There is nothing inside him, nothing that I can see. I try to pull away, but he has a firm grasp on my neck and around my body. I panic. I don't know why. My heart races, and the rain curtains around our bodies, and I yank his black hair.

He releases me.

I break away from him and continue my mad search for Guy, unease over how Cotton looked at me swirling in my stomach, knowing I must forget it for now. Finally, I spot Guy at the helm. I stumble through the storm, past Harper shielding her eagle and Braun holding his pig.

"We have to take the sails down," I yell at Guy.

Lightning tears across the sky, and waves slap over the side of the boat. Water catches a length of rope and drags it along the deck like a plaything. Guy's lion chases the rope like this is the most fun the animal has had in his genetically engineered life. Remembering his Contender, the lion breathes a ball of fire to provide sight for Guy, but the flame is quickly smothered by the rain.

Guy's arms strain against the wheel as he tries to steer the boat out of the storm's way. *Oh, you wanted to stand here? Pardon me! I'll move. No bother.* His shoulders tense, and his knuckles whiten, and as lightning once again sets the world ablaze, Guy is silhouetted in the rain. He is beautifully masculine in the light, hard lines against a hard sky.

"Get everyone below," he hollers. "I'll manage the rest."

"No, you can't steer and tackle the sails. We need to work together."

"Just get them out of here, Tella." He opens his full lips again as if he'll gift me a spell to calm the winds. But then his jaw snaps shut, and he stares ahead.

Anger fires through my veins, and thunder explodes overhead. The ocean is a great, churning beast, and we may all be eaten alive. And we're supposed to huddle below deck and leave our fate to one person? No way.

I race toward Braun, and this time I don't ask what we should do. "Take all of the Pandoras into the hold. Then return here to help me take down the sails."

Braun scans the boat frantically as if he's searching for someone. His pig squeals in his arms.

"Braun, go!"

He hears me at last. He runs.

Willow notes where Braun is headed and follows him inside, her white rat clinging to the top of her head. I order Olivia to do the same but secretly hope she stays with her elephant instead of returning.

I spot Mr. Larson next and start in his direction, moving as quickly as I can along the swaying boat. I know I need to take my own Pandoras below. But I also know they won't go unless I am with them. When the mast cries out again, I look up, hardly able to see through the falling rain. The sails can't be taken down, I realize. They must be rolled up. We can do that. And once the sails are rolled up, they won't catch the wind, and the pressure on the masts will subside. We'll get the Pandoras below; we'll save the mast. Everything will be okay.

Someone screams.

A tidal wave arches over the boat, coming down like a swift hand on a bloated mosquito. I only have time for one thought.

Cody.

The water hits me with a force I have no words for. My back slams into the deck, and I'm sliding, sliding. I feel teeth clamp down on my shoulder, and I scream. It stops me from sliding farther, though, and so I'm thankful for Monster's jaws buried into my flesh and his supersized nails digging into the deck, holding us in place. My throat tightens as I search for Madox. He's a few feet away, running in our direction, already taking AK-7's shape. He lies down on my other side, and the two form a barrier for my body, pinning me so that I'm not taken by the sea.

A new voice rings out. It's male. Older.

"The girl is in the water!" Mr. Larson yells.

My mind sifts through who it could be, and when I find the answer, I struggle to sit up. Monster's jaws retract, but it takes much longer to convince the animals to let me stand. In the end, I must leap over Madox's head and his glowing green eyes to run to Mr. Larson.

"Where is she?" I yell.

He points fifteen feet from the boat, and I spot her blond head. Where is RX-13? Harper's Pandora can swim. It could save her. I scan the boat and don't spot the eagle. Braun must have managed to get the animal into the hold. What was I thinking, telling him to do that?

I'm about to call out reassurances that we'll rescue her, when Jaxon shoves me out of the way. He has a white rescue tube in his hands, and he's eyeing the sea. Confidence rolls through his thin body. He pushes his long blond hair from his eyes, grits his teeth, and throws.

The tube lands twenty feet from where Harper swims. It's like he never meant to throw it to Harper at all. Understanding crashes over me.

Someone else is in the water.

CHAPTER FOURTEEN

The sea lights up as if the sun itself just emerged from a watery grave. The illumination is coming from one particular place, and when my eyes adjust, I make out who it is. Or rather, *what* it is.

Jaxon's new Pandora, Rose, swims toward the rescue tube, her body glowing like she's radioactive. She doesn't have to swim far; Jaxon's aim was impeccable. The iguana's long tail navigates her through the waves like a swallow's wings would the sky, and before long, she has hold of the tube.

"What are you doing?" I scream. "Save Harper."

Jaxon shakes his head and tugs the life preserver toward the boat with the attached rope, moving efficiently, hand over hand.

I try to pull the rope away from Jaxon's grasp and when that doesn't work, I glance back out at the ocean, heart pounding. I don't see Harper. *I don't see Harper!* My body demands I go in after her. And so I do. I climb the boat's short lip and over the rope railing. Madox and Monster go nuts, each trying to pull me toward them, but also afraid to push me overboard.

I am yanked backward by a Contender. My left side, the one Monster bit, slams into the deck. Pain explodes inside my wounded shoulder like the freaking Fourth of July.

The person who pulled me away dives into the ocean. I run to the railing, but I don't see Harper or the person who went in after her. And then they appear, Harper sputtering water and Cotton with his arm around her chest. Harper's head lies on his shoulder, her face tilted toward the sky. I rush to find the ladder Guy used earlier today, and with Jaxon's Pandora lit up like a glow stick, I'm successful. I toss it overboard and yell for Cotton to grab hold of it.

He does so, and slowly, as he holds tight to the bottom, Harper begins to crawl up. The waves reach black fingers toward her slim body, intent on keeping their flesh offering. Twice, she slips in the pouring rain, but Cotton is right behind her. He touches a hand to her upper thigh when he needs to, reassuring her that he's there.

Finally, she reaches the top, and I'm there when she does. "I've got you," I say. She takes my hands, and I guide her over the rope railing and onto the main deck. Cotton crests the boat a minute later.

I hear Guy hollering. He's barely hanging on to the wheel, but he's yelling my name. It doesn't matter. We have to get the sails rolled up. I grab Harper and order her to get below deck. She doesn't argue. I go to tell Mr. Larson the same thing, but he's already gone.

I grab Cotton's arm as he coughs up water. "Are you okay? Can you help me with the sails?"

He coughs once more and staggers toward the masts. I jog after him, and Madox and Monster stay close by. Braun appears and tells me he's gotten most of the Pandoras below, and that, no, it wasn't easy. That Cotton's bull and Harper's eagle in particular have been going nuts.

The three of us tug on the lines until we figure out what we're doing. Eventually, the black sails roll upward toward the yards. Almost immediately, the mast stops creaking. We race to the other mast and do the same thing with the sails there. The boat seems to breathe a sigh of relief, and though the storm still rages, a sense of collectiveness settles over me.

"Braun, take my Pandoras to the hold," I instruct. Braun hesitates, eyeing the two grizzly bears. "Don't worry. They won't hurt you."

As I expected, Madox and Monster refuse to budge, but after everything that has happened, I'm insistent. If the other Pandoras must be separated from their Contenders, then they do, too.

"Go!" I yell.

Go! I think.

The two grizzlies waddle after Braun, and I think for a moment how the hardest part of being their Contender is making them do things for their own good that they don't understand.

I find Jaxon sitting outside the captain's quarters. He's huddled against the door, and Rose is in his lap, though she hardly fits. I grab him by the upper arm and pull until he gets to his feet.

"What were you thinking?" I hiss. "She could have died."

"That's why I had to save her," he mutters.

"I meant Harper."

Jaxon crouches down and picks Rose up. She pours over his arms, and I can tell he's laboring from her girth. He clutches the iguana close and doesn't respond.

"You should have saved Harper first, Jaxon."

"And lose my chance to save my baby sister?" he screams suddenly, his face contorted. "That's who I'm here for. My little sister. She's only eleven years old, Tella! I thought I was screwed when Dink killed Z-54, 'cause how could I win the race without a Pandora? Remember how killing one was part of the last leg of the race? I do! And now I have this Pandora that can help me. . . ." His head drops so that his chin rests on his chest.

I don't know how to feel. We're all here to save someone we care about. But Jaxon saw Harper in the ocean; he saw how she struggled to stay above water; and he threw the rescue tube to a Pandora because he believes she will help him win the race. This is what the Brimstone Bleed does to people. Makes us choose between lives. Makes us less human and more animal, desperate to protect our pack mates above all else.

"Take Rose into the hold," I tell him. "I'll be down in a sec."

Jaxon marches away without another word, his Pandora's tail dragging behind him.

I stride through the rain toward the crew's quarters. I need to grab the candles and matches before I visit the hold, in case Rose stops glowing and we're left in the dark. When I open the door, I find Harper and Cotton scowling at each other from across the room, as if they are one heartbeat away from manslaughter.

"What's going on?" I demand.

"This idiot thinks I need saving," Harper practically screams. "That's what's going on."

Cotton taps his temple like Harper is crazy. "Correct me if I'm wrong, but you were *underwater* when I found you."

"If I'd had my Pandora, it wouldn't have been an issue." Harper swings her attention to me.

I flinch from the sting of her words, because she's right. When I'd made that call, I didn't know if it was the right one, only that someone had to do something for the animals. "I need you two to get in the hold."

"Who put you in charge, Tella? Whoever it was must have been blind, because so far your *orders* have been crap." Harper pushes past me, and Cotton follows her out. I turn to check that they're heading toward the hold, then I lean against the doorway and let my head fall back, thankful that the rain hides my shame.

I allow myself one moment of guilt before chasing after Harper and Cotton. I want to ensure that everyone and all the Pandoras are safely below. Then I have to think of a way to get Guy off the deck. He can't be out there in this storm. We may believe he's indestructible, but I know better, and he shouldn't be expected to steer our vessel while we seek shelter.

I enter the hold and watch as Olivia spots Harper and her eyes fill with tears. She rushes forward to hug the Contender, but before she can, Willow throws herself into Harper's arms. Willow pulls on her until Harper kneels on the ground and whispers in the child's ear.

"I told them what happened," Braun says.

"Glad the girl is okay," Mr. Larson adds, though he certainly didn't stay and help.

"Is everyone here?" I ask, patting Madox and Monster assuredly. "Is anyone missing their Pandora?"

When no one answers, and I feel satisfied that they'll be safe, I turn to fetch Guy, as if he is the type of dude who needs fetching.

I stop short.

Guy is standing at the foot of the stairs, the top to his wet suit gone. Rainwater races down his chest, tracing firm muscles before free-falling to the floor. Dark hair is plastered against his forehead, and his long, wet eyelashes do nothing to soften the fever in his eyes. He takes a step toward me. Another.

He grips my wrist and pulls me toward him. "Come with me. Now."

CHAPTER FIFTEEN

Guy drags me behind him, and I struggle every step of the way. Underneath it all, I am still the girl who loves strawberry cheesecake and lavender pillow spray (it totally helps you sleep), and I am still the girl who would rather Guy be present than fumble with how to survive this race on my own. But I won't be led through the rain like a stray dog without fighting.

He drags me inside the captain's quarters and slams the door. I yank my wrist free and go to slap his cheek, because if my brother were here to see this, that's exactly what he would do — but with a fist instead.

Guy dodges my slap, which I find wildly insulting. I turn to leave, not sure where I'm going but knowing I don't want to be anywhere near him after he manhandled me in such a manner. Before I get beyond his reach, he grabs me by the waist, spins me around, and takes two quick steps so that I am forced against the back of the door.

He is everywhere at once, filling up the small space with his bare chest wet from rain and his blue eyes that paralyze me in the most infuriating way. His body presses against mine, his lips so close, I could weep. My pulse races, and my legs grow weak, and wasn't I just angry?

"What were you thinking out there?" he asks, his voice dangerously deep.

I raise my chin. "I was treating them as equals. I was acknowledging that our team members are an asset, not a liability."

He strides away, and I glimpse the pink scars hugging his rib cage and the hawk tattoo over his right shoulder. "Why are you going against everything I say? You did *everything* wrong out there."

"Excuse me?" I say, hardly able to contain my anger.

"What were you thinking, climbing onto that railing?" He turns around and points an accusing finger in my direction. "I saw you. I saw what you were going to do."

"Harper was in the water," I yell.

Guy mumbles something.

"Speak up, Chambers."

"I said, *I don't care*!" he roars.

He's shaking, though from the cold and the rain or from what he's saying, I'm not sure. "Do you have something to say to me?"

His urgent steps swallow the distance between us, and suddenly his hands are grasping my face. His eyes search mine, and his nostrils flare. He doesn't say anything. He never *says* anything.

"Why don't you trust me?" I whisper. "You said I'd still be in that jungle if it weren't for you. Do you find me that helpless?"

Understanding and hurt flash in Guy's eyes, but they're gone so quickly, I wonder if I imagined them. He releases me. "I came here to save my cousin's life," he says. "And now I can't think beyond keeping you safe. The only way I can do that is if you do what I say, when I say it."

My hands curl into fists. "You may know the best way to survive this race, Guy Chambers, but you know nothing about working as a team. How can I trust you once we get inside headquarters if you don't trust *me* to think for myself?" I tilt my head to the side, give him a chance to redeem himself. "Tell me you trust me. Tell me you don't see me as someone who needs saving."

He sighs and runs his hands through his hair. "Destroying the race was never meant to be *our* plan."

I step past him, crushed at his response.

With Guy silent behind me, I inspect the captain's quarters. The area is the same size as the crew's quarters, which seems unfair since it's built for one person. There's a sturdy mahogany desk near a wall of windows, and outside, I note that the rain isn't falling as severely as it once was. In the corner stands a queen-size bed with a deep red comforter that looks velvety to the touch. And overhead, a green glass candleholder dangles from the ceiling, lit from within by a thick candle.

To my left is a door that must lead to a latrine. Why have we been sharing one latrine all day when there was a second one in here? What's more, who will sleep here tonight? Will Guy claim this room as his own while the rest of us share a cramped space? I'm about to pose these questions, but when I spin around, Guy's face suddenly opens with alarm. "What happened to your shoulder?"

Pain ignites in the puncture wounds when I recall the injury. "I'm fine. AK-7 did what he had to do to keep me from going overboard."

"I'll get the first-aid kit," he says, as if he's relieved to have something to do.

"Don't bother. I don't need your help." I brush past him, open the door, and stride out into the dying storm. Each time I'm around Guy, I'm conflicted. One moment, he makes me feel protected and cared for; the next, he's undermining my ability as a Contender in the race. He said I did everything wrong, but as the rain relents and the thunder once again grows distant, I wonder if that's true.

We survived. Every last one of us and our Pandora companions, too. The ship made it through intact, and we have food and water to last us the rest of the journey. I can't help thinking that at least one group of Contenders out there was not as lucky. Maybe I didn't make the calls Guy would have tonight, but I went with my gut and didn't cower when the storm was on top of us. In short, the girl I am tonight is a far cry from the girl I was six weeks ago. I believe if he saw me now, I would make my big brother proud.

After I open the hatch door, I descend the stairs and find most of the Contenders and Pandoras lying on the floor. Relief is etched into the lines on their faces, because even down here it's easy to tell the worst has passed. Though the storm lasted a little over an hour, it feels as if we battled it all night.

"It's safe to go up," I say. "I think the girls should sleep in one place, and the guys in another. That way, we can maintain some privacy. We can leave the hatch door open, and the Pandoras can go above and below deck as they please in case it starts raining again."

Mr. Larson grabs three cans of tuna and two bottles of water as if he's preparing for something. For what, I have no idea.

"You girls should take the captain's quarters," Cotton says.

When no one argues, Harper leads Willow upstairs, and Olivia follows behind, but only after hugging her baby elephant good-bye. Soon after, the boys trail upstairs. Cotton is the last to leave. I grab him by the arm and jerk him toward me. When Jaxon's skinny butt disappears through the hatch door and it's only me and Cotton left, I push my face close to his. Or as close as I can, considering I have to stand on tiptoes to even pretend to be threatening.

"What were you doing out there? Why did you grab me like that?"

His full lips form a tight line.

"Answer me."

"I didn't want you to get hurt," he says.

"So you thought you'd pin me in place and just stare at me like a creeper?"

Cotton grinds his teeth and continues to avoid my gaze.

I sigh, fingering the blue-and-green feather over my right shoulder. "Look, we all panicked to some degree, but don't touch me like that again, understand?"

From the corner of the hold, a large, dark figure emerges. The hair on my arms rises. It's Cotton's bull, and apparently, he doesn't like the way I'm speaking to his Contender. Cotton holds his hand out to stop Y-21, and the bull complies. When I glance over my shoulder, I spot Monster and Madox eyeing the bull, a challenge in their stances, though Madox seems a bit more hesitant about the potential face-off than AK-7.

"Tella," Cotton says gently.

When he doesn't add anything, I grow uncomfortable. I don't know how to feel about Cotton. He's much like Guy in his cool, quiet mannerism, but he's older, and a darkness seems to cloak his broad shoulders. He saved Harper, but I can't forget the way he looked at me out there as lightning ripped across the sky.

He opens his mouth, hesitates. "You remind me of my little sister."

"Oh." I clear my throat, and my cheeks burn. "Is that who you're racing for?"

He shakes his head. "No, my sister . . . she was murdered years ago."

His words hit me like a wrecking ball to the gut. Here I was, judging him, after everything he'd been through. No wonder he's peculiar. If Cody had been killed, I'd be a walking zombie.

"I'm here for my father," Cotton adds. His forearms tighten. "I *have* to save him."

What he doesn't say is that he can't lose somebody else, and I empathize with that. I'm working out the right thing to say to comfort him when the sound of someone descending the stairs stops me.

Harper stands staring at us, a blanket wrapped around her shoulders.

"You should be in bed, Harper." I go and wrap my arm around her shoulders, and this time she accepts my embrace. "Come on. Come with me."

I turn back to Cotton. He plays with something invisible on the hem of his wet suit top. "I'm sorry," I murmur. Before I lead Harper away, I notice black hair dye dripping down his neck. I wonder if he has a closet full of black clothes back home, too. Some may mistake Cotton as an emo kid, but sometimes black is a fashion statement, and other times it screams of sorrow. Still, as a girl who knows a good dye job, I'm impressed by his lack of roots showing after six weeks in the Brimstone Bleed. If I ever make it out of here, maybe I should ask him for some style tips.

I hug AK-7 good night and scratch beneath the bear's chin, and then I do the same for Madox. Though Harper prides herself on being detached from her Pandora, I see the way she smooths the eagle's feathers before turning away.

Be good, sweet boy, I think to Madox.

He wags his tail.

As I walk Harper back to the captain's quarters, my mind works its way through everything that happened tonight. More than anything, I cling to the exchange Guy and I had. He wants to destroy the Brimstone Bleed alone, but that mission became my own the moment he told me the truth. Guy says telling anyone else about what's really going on will put them in more danger. But these days, I'm thinking for myself, for better or worse.

"Harper, wait." I inspect the deck to ensure we won't be heard. The soft, lingering rain will help smother our conversation. "Before we go inside, I need to tell you something."

CHAPTER SIXTEEN

I tell Harper the whole story. I tell her how a dangerous man named Santiago ordered genetic engineers to create mutant animals for profit and how the anxious engineers burned down the facility to destroy their work. I tell her how Santiago's daughter was inside the burning building and how she died at the hands of an accident.

I tell her the rest, too. How Santiago created the Brimstone Bleed as punishment for those who killed his daughter. How, today, people related to the original engineers are chosen — one to be injected with a virus, one to race, and one to create those same mutant animals that may help their chances of survival.

"Today, the genetic engineers are called Creators. The animals are called Pandoras, and the Cure is simply the antivirus." I don't know what I expect Harper to do when I tell her what I know, but it isn't to walk away. "Where are you going?"

She holds up a finger as if I should stay put and returns with a white box. "Let's go inside."

I follow her into the captain's quarters, and we find Willow already asleep in the bed, her white rat curled on her chest, even though I'd said to keep the Pandoras outside so that it was fair to everyone. Olivia sits at the desk, her eyes widening ever so slightly when we come in. She opens her mouth to say something but stops.

"Sit there." Harper points to a chair in front of the desk, ignoring Olivia entirely.

I do as she instructs, because quite frankly, it feels good to have someone tell me what to do after such an exhausting ordeal. But then I remember Harper in the ocean. Harper vanishing from sight. "You should be lying down." I start to stand up, but she guides me back into the chair.

"Take your top off so I can dress your wound." Harper sets the white box, the first-aid kit, onto the desk and pops it open.

I tug my top off and cover my bare chest as best I can. I remember a time when I would have been embarrassed to flash a ten-year-old. Those were the days.

"What happened?" Olivia whispers.

I smile in her direction. "Nothing major. AK-7 got a little excited in his enthusiasm to protect me."

She grins, but I note the fear in her eyes. "Wish we still had DN-99. Remember how that raccoon could lick Ransom's wounds and make them heal like —" She snaps her fingers. Then, slowly, her smile begins to fade. "I wonder where they take the Pandoras they don't use anymore."

"Probably back to a retirement area," I answer quickly. "Bet they spend the rest of their days playing with each other and just being lazy."

Olivia's face relaxes, and this time there's no lingering worry. As Harper rubs a cool cream over my left shoulder, I tell the girl, "Why don't you go get in bed with Willow? There's room enough for both of you."

Olivia's upper lip stiffens.

"Don't be difficult," Harper says. "Do as she says."

The girl turns her face away so that Harper can't see the hurt she inflicted, but I catch it all the same. My eyes snap up to Harper's, and I know she can read the message I'm sending her.

You don't have to be so tough on her.

Harper shrugs and continues slathering cream on my shoulder. She takes a roll of gauze in her hands and wraps it around my shoulder, secures it with a metal fastener. "You'll need to change this out often, but the salt water will help it heal." She tosses the blanket she had around her own shoulders earlier toward me. I use it to cover up and thank her for the help. "My mom is a nurse. Not that it helped matters."

With her daughter, that's what she means. I wait a beat and then say, "You should go easy on Cotton. He's experienced loss, too." She shakes her head like I'm ridiculous. I consider telling her about Cotton's sister so that the two may find common ground in each other, but I decide it's not my story to tell.

"Your device okay?" I ask.

She pats her pocket twice in response. *Right here.*

I clear my throat. "It's my fault you went overboard, Harper. Guy told me to get everyone below deck, but I thought it'd be better if we worked together to get the boat's sails down quickly. I should have listened to him. You could have died out there."

Harper's nose scrunches. "Guy told you to get us all below deck, but you went against him?"

Harper seems to think about this for a moment. Then she opens a cabinet door and retrieves another blanket. She lies down on the floor and closes her eyes. I lie nearby, rethinking my idea to separate the girls and boys, because surely they have free cots in the crew's quarters we could use. I also think about Harper's daughter and what it must feel like to lose a child.

"Hey, Harper," I whisper. "Thank you for coming back. It means a lot to me. But . . . sometimes I wish you wouldn't have. I hate thinking that you're risking your life for my sake."

She balls the edge of her blanket and lays her head on it. Her eyes stay closed. "You helped me win in the desert. So I came back to help you win."

It doesn't take long for Harper's breathing to grow heavy. I didn't tell her what my plan was regarding the Brimstone Bleed, and she didn't tell me what she thought about everything I revealed. But her kindness toward me said she's thankful for the information. Perhaps I need to consider who I should tell next.

As my body relaxes, I replay the decision Jaxon made, how he saved his new Pandora instead of Harper. She didn't mention it, but it must have hurt terribly. What I hate most about the whole situation is that I understand Jaxon's decision. I made him think I didn't, but I do. He wants to save his baby sister. And I would have wanted to save anything that could help save Cody. It's more than that, though. Each Contender is paying a price for something our ancestors got involved in, but the Pandoras are innocent in all this. I can't say I was furious when Jaxon pulled that animal from the sea, even if I want to pretend I am.

I roll over, hating myself for this internal admission. Hating that I've grown attached to these creatures when I *should* focus on how they can help Cody, my brother. My brother, who once took the fall when Mom discovered I'd stolen a glass unicorn figurine from a tourist shop and who spent the next few weeks talking about a unicorn's prowess to drive the point home when we all knew . . . he was a dirty liar and I was a thief.

I think about how, for my birthday, my then eleven-year-old brother dragged my ice cream cake from the freezer and into the car, and when it melted, said my dad must have forgotten to bring it in. Cody was mad at me because I told Mom he got in trouble at school when I swore I wouldn't, so maybe I deserved it. When I wouldn't stop crying over my melted cake, Cody attempted to make me a new one and nearly burned the house down. He never said he was sorry, and neither did I. We didn't have to.

I wonder what Cody would say to me if he were here tomorrow. What would he say to his little sister, who has blood on her hands, who's commanding Pandoras and navigating a deadly sea and trying to survive an impossible race?

What would my brother say to me on my seventeenth birthday?

CHAPTER SEVENTEEN

I tell Olivia the next morning that it's my birthday. Why, I will never know. Maybe because she's wearing a frown like it's the hottest thing on a fashion week runway. Maybe because she insists on skipping breakfast. Or maybe it's just to get her out of bed, period.

"Get out of bed, Olivia."

"No."

"Get out of bed or I'll push your elephant into the sea."

"Go ahead."

"Please get out of bed? For me?" My gaze slides to the ceiling, and I sigh. "Get out of bed because it's my birthday?"

She sits up, cautious that I'm toying with her. "Is it really?"

I grin, and she immediately jumps to her feet and begins bouncing up and down on the mattress. "It's your birthday! We'll have a party!"

"What? No."

Mr. Larson waddles into the captain's quarters. "Need to use the restroom. Other one is full."

"Hey, Mr. Larson," Olivia sings. "Guess what? It's Tella's birthday."

I protest as the girl runs through the open door and tells everyone within earshot that it's my birthday. Mr. Larson humphs and disappears into the latrine.

Standing in front of a foggy mirror, I run my hands through my short curly hair and try to rub some life into my seventeen-year-old face. After Mr. Larson gets out of our bathroom, I use some of the toiletries we found in the hold to brush my teeth and wash the salt from my skin. I give myself a full twenty minutes to groom, feeling a bit like an archaeologist, like I've scavenged some lost luxury.

I remember thinking it was strange that the people running this race equipped us with so many tools to survive this leg of the Brimstone Bleed, especially toiletries. After last night's storm, I now believe it was a decoy. They wanted us to feel safe, to throw us off guard, so that the storm they probably knew was coming blindsided us. I can picture them bending over oceanic weather forecasts, watching a delicious storm cell develop not too far from where they were planning to drop us.

Take them here, one of them would have said. *And make sure they feel cozy before that storm rolls over them.*

I shake my head. Maybe they didn't know. Maybe I just want a reason to excuse our lack of preparation.

When I finally appear in the doorway, Monster pushes me onto my back and Madox leaps onto my chest and licks my face. So much for my makeshift bath. Braun appears and pulls Madox off me, though a part of me doesn't want him to.

"Hey, Tinker Bell, it's your turn to keep watch."

I'm not sure what he means until he shoves the binoculars into my chest. "For flags?"

"Yep. You'll do it from up there."

Braun points to the lookout near the top of the largest mast and hands me a can of pears and maraschino cherries with a fork stabbed into the syrupy pulp. He pulls once on my right ear for whatever reason.

"You all right?" I ask. "Look a little green around the gills."

He touches a hand to his stomach. "Seasickness. It'll pass, hopefully."

I touch the hand covering his stomach sympathetically and then turn to climb the ratlines. I realize when I've reached the top of the mast that I left my breakfast on the deck, not that I could have climbed with it in my hand anyway. My belly grumbles as I hold the binoculars up and gaze out across the water.

I'm not sure what I'm looking for beyond a blue flag. There's so much water, so much sky, that I can't imagine finding anything amid the preexisting blue. It seems as if the flag would blend in with its surroundings. Harper said we were sailing between a cluster of islands, and I figure since the flags must reside on them, we might have to eventually disembark to explore. I guess my job should be to search for which island to try first.

Below me, the Contenders shuffle across the deck: chatting with one another, unfurling sails, instructing their Pandoras. At one point, a ball of fire shoots from M-4's jaws, and then Monster sprays a gust of wind from his paws to offset the blaze. The Contenders laugh at this. I lift the binoculars and inspect the happenings on the ship's deck closer.

Jaxon's Pandora, the iguana, has several red gashes across her back from the other Pandoras' abuse. Even now Willow's rat scurries toward the iguana, nips her, leaps back, and then repeats the bullying. FDR-1 huddles in a corner and flinches each time the rat gets close. I wave my arm above my head and call out to Jaxon, trying to make him see that his iguana needs him. He spots what's happening on his own and rushes to Rose's side. With the toe of his shoe, he kicks the rat away.

I lower the binoculars, my heart heavy from the exchange. When I glance up, I nearly stumble over the side of the lookout. Harper's Pandora is perched on the rope ledge, cocking her eagle head at me. My hand flutters to my chest in surprise, and I laugh.

"Hey, there," I say, nerves lilting my voice. Pandoras are loyal only to their own Contenders, and if they believe you're a threat, they'll respond accordingly. I back away from the regal bird, and for the second time nearly tumble over the side to my death. Perhaps that's the point of this visit.

When the eagle doesn't do anything rash, I try conversing with her again. "Um, thank you for always helping Harper . . . bird."

RX-13 cocks her head in the opposite direction, much the way she would when eyeing prey. I spot the longer, forward-facing talon on her foot and decide it must be two inches long. And sharp, very sharp. I swallow.

The bird opens her wings in the salted air and flaps them. I find myself reminiscing over seeing a bald eagle at a zoo for the first time. Mom had brought me by myself. It was a girls' day, she said, and I could go wherever I wanted. Well, I knew Cody had wanted to go to the zoo, so that's where I picked. You know, so I could rub it in over dinner that night.

Sibling love: It's complicated.

The way I remember it, I think I looked at the bird for about two seconds while Mom explained that it was the national bird, blah, blah, blah, before asking, *Where are the tigers? You said we could see the tigers.*

Now that I gaze upon RX-13, I decide it must be horrendous for a bird to live in captivity. Not able to soar into the sky and hunt. I can't remember a single hour on this boat, except during the storm, when the eagle hasn't floated above us. I gingerly reach my hand out, holding my breath as I do so, and pet the eagle's velvet feathers once. Then I jerk my hand back and look for missing fingers. Wouldn't Olivia be excited if I joined her nine-digit club?

When I realize the eagle may not be here to commit premeditated homicide, I reach out a second time and stroke the bird on her back and her head and beneath her intimidating beak. "You know she loves you, right?" I tell RX-13. "She just has a hard time saying it. You're a good Pandora, and she needs that right now."

The eagle accepts my affection for a bit longer before she takes flight. I gasp at the bird's power when she takes to the sky. For a few seconds, I watch as she flies into the distance, so far away, I can hardly see her. I wonder where she's going, maybe to hunt for fish or maybe simply to explore. I raise the binoculars and watch until RX-13 becomes invisible, literally. A moment later, the invisible eagle splashes into the ocean. Doesn't seem like a fair fight to the fish.

My brow furrows when a question occurs to me. Where does she eat the fish? I didn't see her return to the boat with a catch even once yesterday, which means she's eating it elsewhere. Since I don't spot the hint of land in the distance, I decide there must be something else. My muscles clench with excitement as I return to my binoculars. I search everywhere but don't find what I'm looking for. Still, I have an idea, and that's more than I had before Harper's Pandora showed.

When I let the binoculars drop, I'm startled to find the eagle hovering above me. Something is in her talons. She drops it before I can recognize what it is. A startled scream escapes my lips, and I cover my head. Wetness splashes my shins. I glance down and see pear and maraschino cherries splattered on the floor of the lookout.

A grin overtakes my face. "You brought this for me?"

The bird dips her head toward the spilled food like she's waiting for me to pluck some off the dirtied platform and eat it. When I don't, the eagle hops onto the floor and gathers a pear quarter into her beak. Then she jumps back onto the lookout's ledge and stretches her neck over my head like she's about to . . . to . . .

"Oh no. No. You cannot baby bird that pear to me, RX."

She shoves her beak closer to my mouth, but I jerk my head to the side, laughing.

"It's not that I don't appreciate the gesture, but that's simply not happening."

The Pandora squawks until I pet her, communicating that it's nothing personal. Then she steps off the ledge and free-falls toward the deck, landing an arm's length away from Harper. I can't stop the warmth spreading through my body. Though the morning carries an unrelenting chill, I barely feel it through the joy. With my heart full, my mind glides easily back to the question I'd been puzzling through. It occurs to me then, and the answer is so obvious, I don't know how I missed it.

My family went on vacation to Florida once, and in order to arrive at our destination, we had to ride a ferry. We threw bread to overzealous seagulls, and as we got farther into the ocean, I spotted a fat sleeping seal lying on a buoy. My dad inclined his head and said, "Those are markers for ships. They help them navigate safely."

"Does that animal help, too?" I'd asked.

My dad laughed from somewhere deep in his stomach and scratched his short beard. "Yes," he said, "the animal helps, too."

I snatch the binoculars and press my face against them, renewed hope blossoming in my gut. Wind whips through what little hair I have as I peer across the horizon. I look long past the moment I realize there are no buoys to see. When Jaxon crawls up the ratlines and says it's his turn to search for flags, I'm still hesitant to end my hunt.

I tell him my plan and add, "I think you can find anchored buoys closer to land. So even if we find one and it doesn't have a flag, at least it'll tell us we haven't navigated too far from the islands."

"You think base camp is on an island?" he asks.

"I do."

"Tella, do you think Harper will ever forgive me?"

I help Jaxon into the lookout before I answer. "I think she's already forgotten it."

He fills his lungs and releases a heavy sigh. "You know that isn't true."

I'm not sure why I do it, but I find myself pulling Jaxon into a hug. He's so much taller than me that my head smashes into his armpit. It's not a pleasant experience. "You didn't see the iguana in the water last night, Jaxon," I say quietly. "You saw your sister."

He releases me. "That's right. You have to tell her that."

I climb over the side, and Jaxon holds on to my arm, ensuring I have hold of the ratlines before letting go. "I'll do my best."

Jaxon smiles and retrieves the binoculars from the floor. "What's with all the fruit, T-Pain?"

I laugh and descend the rope ladder, proud that my hands don't sweat as much as they did on the climb up. When I reach the main deck, a pair of arms wrap around my middle, throwing me off balance. I barely regain my stance before Olivia circles around me, throws open her hands, and exclaims, "Welcome to your birthday celebration, Tella Holloway!"

A drum starts beating.

CHAPTER EIGHTEEN

A booming opera-style voice lifts over the rumble of the drum and into the midday sky. Braun grabs my wrist and guides me away from the ratlines and into his arms. He raises my right hand into the air and places my left at the base of his neck.

"Am I hurting you?" he asks, referring to my shoulder.

I tell him he's not.

Cotton beats on an overturned rain barrel, a thousand-watt smile on his face, and Mr. Larson raises his voice to a new level of awe. He sings a quick, foot-tapping song, and Braun spins me in circles so that the world blurs.

"What's he saying?" I ask, referencing Mr. Larson.

Braun shrugs. "Beats me. Said it was a celebration song. It's Italian, I think."

I run my left hand quickly over Braun's shaved head as I would a dog, and he rumbles with laughter. His smile is a nice one, and he's not a bad dancer, either. "When is your birthday, Braun?"

"Summer baby," he replies.

"If I were to get this summer baby a gift, you know what I'd get him?" I ask. Braun tilts his head. "A day at the spa. Get those nails a real once-over."

The tractor-sized dude feigns shock and puffs his chest out. "I don't care about my nails, Tella. I'm a man. Men don't care about such things."

"You keep telling yourself that."

Braun dips me low. "You know what I'd get a fall baby for her birthday?"

"What's that?"

"A dance with an amputee."

Braun swings me out, and Olivia grabs hold of my palm. Now I'm dancing with the girl, and as I skip around the deck with her, Mr. Larson makes a fist and places it at his stomach, really getting into the lyrics. There's emotion in his eyes I've never seen before, and it reminds me that he's a human being with layers, even if he only shows us the crabby one.

Harper sits along the railing, RX-13 next to her, and M-4 lies on his back a few feet away, lion belly to the sun.

"I have a surprise for you, Tella." Olivia's hair is wild from the open air, and her round face becomes even rounder as she beams up at me. "Wait here."

Olivia lets go and turns to retrieve this surprise, but stops short when Willow appears from inside the crew's quarters, a cake in her hands. Olivia's face falls, but she tries to maintain a smile through her disappointment.

"This is your birthday cake," Willow says. "We made it for you."

Olivia opens her mouth to object, then closes it. I hug the ten-year-old close and kiss the top of her head. With Madox and Monster shuffling behind Willow, I take the cake and hold it up. Mr. Larson stops singing his opera song and a new song begins. One I've had sung to me for sixteen years. Now seventeen.

Happy birthday to you, happy birthday . . .

The cake is made of packed meats, and slimy gravy is drizzled over the top. A lit candle as big around as a magic marker is plunged in the center, and the whole thing sits on a flimsy, round dinner plate. It's the worst birthday cake I've ever seen. It makes me so happy, I could burst.

"Make a wish," Harper says from the railing.

Madox cozies up to my bare calf, and Monster stands on hind legs and makes everyone nervous. Cotton's bull snorts, and Olivia's elephant raises her trunk, and all the Contenders watch me with kindness.

I raise the cake a bit higher. I want to wish for all of our loved ones to heal and for Cody to have never gotten sick and, okay, maybe I wish for a spa day with Mom, who I miss so very much. But since it's my birthday — and I want to believe in the power of wishes — I hope for something that might actually come true:

I wish that Cody is happy today.

The small flame swooshes out, and Mr. Larson instantly breaks into a new, even livelier song. Contenders clap along, and Madox barks. I swing the fox into my arms and dance one-handed with Olivia. Later, Olivia tries to dance with Harper, but she shrugs her off. Even Braun and Willow can't get the Contender to her feet. Eventually, Cotton calls Braun over and shows him what he's doing on the drum. After Braun takes over, Cotton stretches his tall frame and strides in my direction. A knot forms in my throat as I'm remembering what he told me about his sister, wondering how awkward it would be to dance with him now.

But he bypasses me and squats down to speak with Harper in a hushed tone. She shakes her head vehemently, so Cotton does what he must — he slides one arm beneath her knees and the other beneath her arms, and he carries her out onto the deck. She beats his chest and yells at the top of her lungs, but it's no match for Mr. Larson's seasoned vocal cords.

Braun is barely able to continue his drumming, he's laughing so hard, and I'm laughing, too. But I'm also wondering where Guy is. We argued last night, and this morning I saw him only from a distance at the helm. Is he so upset with me that he won't even attend my birthday celebration? Not that I care. Birthdays happen every day for people across the world. And Guy? He's just a dude with a handsome face. And a sick body.

A half hour later, Braun climbs the ratlines to relieve Jaxon, and I offer the Pandoras my birthday cake. They rush at it like they've never seen food a day in their lives. I remember Titus once saying in the desert that his bear hadn't lost an ounce of weight while he himself was shriveling away. But that doesn't mean the Pandoras don't need to eat from time to time or that they don't enjoy it.

The iguana doesn't try to compete for the meat cake, and so I bring her a taste instead. She flicks her tongue toward it and then eats a small bit. I sit down and stroke Rose's back, avoiding her injuries from the other Pandoras. It breaks my spirit to see the creatures hurting one another this way, and I wonder what it is she can do that causes them to worry.

I spot Madox leaping around Cotton's bull, trying to engage him, but the bull wants nothing to do with my black fox. Madox doesn't give up easily, though, and when I glance over again, I see my Pandora offering Y-21 the last piece of birthday cake. The bull snorts like the smell is revolting.

My fox has certainly gained confidence over the last several weeks. I still remember when he first hatched. I was asleep by the fire Guy's Pandora lit, and in the dead of night, I heard the first crackle of his eggshell. Madox came out covered in green slime, and I sang to him, hoping he would recognize my voice. He spent that first night asleep in my lap, and the next day fleeing from chimpanzees with me by his side. As I watch him now, tongue draping from the side of his mouth, I think about what Olivia asked.

I wonder where they take the Pandoras they don't use anymore.

I've often dwelled on what happened to Ransom's raccoon, DN-99, after Ransom left for home. One day the raccoon was there, and the next he was gone. Perhaps I'm being naïve. Maybe I know exactly what happened to DN-99. The people running the Brimstone Bleed certainly don't care about our lives, so why would they treat the Pandoras any differently?

My eye catches on the red spray-painted stripe down Rose's back. I remember the way that man dragged her away like she was disposable. Surely they've marked other Pandoras when we weren't paying attention, and I can't forget how they asked us to kill one another's Pandoras to enter the desert base camp. So the question remains: What happens to our Pandoras after the race?

Nothing good, that much I know.

BK-68 plods over and stares at me, breaking my sudden glum mood. "Are you going to hypnotize me?" I ask.

"Don't let it do it," Braun yells down from the lookout. "Blasted pig mind freaks me all the time."

"Is that right?" I ask the pig.

The pig grunts as I scratch under its chin. Something tells me it can only hypnotize someone when the Contender it's targeting is off guard, otherwise we'd all be on our knees petting the Pandora and declaring it the Pig King.

BK-68 nibbles on my red wristband, and I pull my hand back, laughing. "Haven't you had enough to eat, pink pig?"

"Have *you* had enough to eat?" a low voice asks.

I find M-4 sitting behind me, panting. Beside him is Guy.

"The cake vanished before I could get any," I say. I continue petting the pig until a wide, strong hand lowers.

"Dance with me?"

CHAPTER NINETEEN

My stomach flips. I'm furious with him, and yet if I show my anger, it'll only prove how childish he must think I am. Also, his hand looks clean and warm, and I want so badly to feel it in my own.

Before I accept his offer to dance, I get to my feet and rub my hand through his lion's mane. I want Guy to know I'm not in any rush to dance with him and that maybe his Pandora is more interesting. M-4 jerks his head back and shows his teeth, but I don't miss the way the big cat's eyes soften.

"Blow me a hot-air balloon, won't you, cat?" I coo to the lion.

The Pandora gazes up at Guy like I'm crazy. Guy nods his head, and the lion roars. When he does, a flame ball shoots from his jaws. The fire is comforting in a strange way. It makes me feel alive. I don't believe I'll ever see the day when watching a Pandora do something extraordinary doesn't turn my world upside down, however briefly.

I take Guy's hand.

He leads me to the deck, and Mr. Larson softens his voice, bringing an upbeat song to a close. The bulbous man mutters something to Jaxon, who's now on the drum, and then straightens his back. This time, when he sings, his words open like a rose to the sun. I don't understand what he says, but it feels like strolling through a field of despair, like finding true love on the other side of the world and never holding that person in your arms. It makes my chest ache in a maddening, uncontrollable way, and if Guy weren't holding me so close, I might not find the will to stand. I never knew music could affect me in such a manner until this moment.

Until Guy's cheek caresses mine.

Until his hand spreads across my lower back and his thumb traces the ridges of my spine.

I'm not sure what the other Contenders are doing. I don't know if Cotton has released Harper or if Jaxon is watching the two of them sway with a heavy heart. But I know that the dark stubble along Guy's jaw has returned. I know the Pandoras have quieted and that if there was such a thing as an apologetic embrace, this is it.

As we dance, I think back on that silver-sequined homecoming dress I never wore. I envision it on my body now, with a delicate pink corsage decorating my wrist. I put Guy in a tux and a disco ball over our heads. My best friend, Hannah, is there, and all my other friends, too. After this, Guy will take me to a party. I'll spend every second of this entire night with him because for the very first time, Mom said nervously, "No curfew."

My feet follow Guy's, and I smile when I realize he's humming along with Mr. Larson. There's no way he knows this song, but it tells me he likes this kind of music, full of torture and loss. Guy Chambers told me on a dark night in the jungle that he has three younger brothers. He told me he has a cousin who loves the smell of lemon and that he himself likes the way a newspaper crinkles when the pages turn.

I know he wants others to think he doesn't care about his appearance but that in actuality he's embarrassed of his mangled left earlobe. Guy enjoys the quietness that settles over his house in Detroit right before dawn. He likes building things with his hands, even though he's not terribly good at it, and he prefers a freshly sharpened pencil over a ballpoint pen any day.

I know these small things about Guy, but the music is new.

Guy's hand slides up my side, grazing my rib cage and tickling the skin beneath my wet suit. His fingers caress my neck, and my head pulls away from his chest. My arms stay upon his shoulders as he takes both hands and wraps them around my face. He doesn't tell me happy birthday. He doesn't offer a cake made of meat or a song sung in an Italian tongue. He simply closes his eyes and breathes out. In that exhale, I hear the pain he holds inside. It seems to match Mr. Larson's lyrics, and I suddenly understand why he hums along.

"I'm stronger than you think, Guy Chambers," I whisper. "Strong enough to handle whatever it is you're keeping from me."

The muscles in his shoulders tighten, and he licks his lips. "Tella . . ."

Guy opens his mouth to say more, but there's no time for that.

Harper screams.

Mr. Larson quits singing, and Jaxon stops beating the rain barrel drum. Overhead, I hear Braun calling out, asking what's happened. It's Cotton who gets to her first, but Harper shoves him away much harder than necessary. I rush to her side and see what has her worried.

Her eagle has the iguana cornered and was no doubt antagonizing the creature yet again. This time, though, the eagle appears to stumble as if dazed. Somewhere behind us, Olivia's elephant blows through her trunk and startles us all. Harper rushes toward her Pandora even as Cotton tells her to stay back.

RX-13 dives toward the iguana, upset at something the iguana must have done. This time, we don't miss the exchange.

The moment the eagle's beak snaps over the iguana's back, the oversized lizard arches her side. Rose's long, powerful tail whips across the space between them and pops into the eagle's side. It sticks there for a second before falling to the deck. Rose's mouth hangs open, and the heavy pink beard under her jaw puffs out.

Harper reaches the eagle and pulls the bird to her, but the eagle is furious and wants revenge on the iguana who finally learned to stick up for herself. The eagle tries to take to the sky to hover over the lizard, but she crashes back to the deck and shakes her head, disoriented.

"What's happened to her?" Harper cries. "Why is she acting funny?"

Jaxon scoops the front half of Rose into his arms. "Your Pandora deserves whatever happened to her."

Harper's fists clench, and she gets in Jaxon's face. "Why? Because she threatened the Pandora that Tella *gave* you? How about me? Did *I* threaten your Pandora? Is that why you left me in the ocean?"

Jaxon's cheeks redden.

I pick up the iguana's tail gently and inspect it. The tail has a tiny spike at the end like her back does, but I know it doesn't belong there, not on an ordinary iguana. I push the side of the spike with the pad of my thumb, and soapy white liquid oozes from the tip.

"Rose has injected the eagle with venom," I announce.

Harper laces her hands over her head and watches RX-13 stumble around the deck. "What will it do to her?" She looks at each of us, frantic, and then reaches down to comfort her Pandora. "I can't lose her. I can't."

What happens next is like a thin white line dividing two parts in time. There's before, and after. There's the brittle security of a ship beneath our feet, and then there is the wild, unpredictable churning of the sea.

It goes like this:

Harper is reaching for her Pandora.

Cotton is reaching for Harper.

Jaxon is turning his shamed face to the deck, and Olivia is touching a four-fingered hand to his arm.

Guy is striding toward a wheel that's been long neglected, and I'm holding an iguana's tail.

Mr. Larson and Willow are out of sight and may very well be in the hold.

Braun is above us all, so he must have the best view. He must capture every millisecond of pandemonium when the ship explodes, and debris fly into the air, and water comes rushing in as if to say —

I shall finally claim that which is mine.

CHAPTER TWENTY

The first thing I do when the blast goes off is to hurry to the hold. We're going down; there's no question about that, and we won't be able to access any food or water once the ship sinks. So I run.

I find Mr. Larson inside the hold, but not Willow. He's on his back, blood oozing from his right ear, but it doesn't take long to get the portly man to his feet and up the stairs. Water blasts into the hold, and already much of our equipment bobs in the current. I reach the dry side of the hold, where some of our supplies are untouched, and my mind races with what to take and how.

I fumble over everything, touching each item in turn, trying to decide what's important. A tickling sensation shoots up my ankles, and when I spin around, I find that the water has already reached this side of the hold. The sound of the water pouring in is deafening, and I wonder what Titus would say about his beloved ocean if he were here to see it now. Hammerhead, his father called him.

I grab the first large yellow bag I see and unzip it, thinking this will work perfectly to fill with food and water. When I feel the sticky, rubberlike material inside, I realize I've happened upon something even better — a life raft. I search the area and locate the other two yellow bags. I grab those and the two red bags, too. Almost everything is floating in water at this point, which is the only way I keep hold of it all. I berate myself for not searching the bags before now. We've only been aboard the ship for twenty-four hours, but we should have been more meticulous. I bet Guy knows what's in them.

As if he read my mind, Guy blows down the stairs. "Tella, where are you?"

Fingers of fear climb the rungs of my spine when I realize the water is to my hips. "I'm here. We need these bags."

Relief floods his face. He leaps into the water and powers through the tide. "I'll get them. Just get above deck. You can't be down here."

Some of my fear dissipates when I spot Madox jog down the stairs. My fox hesitates before choosing to take the shape of Guy's lion, which is in the water next to Guy. My Pandora, now dressed as a lion, swims toward me.

I place the red bags' handles into his jaws. *Take this above deck. Show them to Harper.*

Guy snatches another one of the yellow bags and drags it after him. He tries to grab me with his other hand, but I jerk out of his grasp. "Now's not the time!" he snaps.

I don't know what he's talking about, but I do know we have to get the other two life rafts. "M-4, take this bag above deck," I instruct. The lion paddles next to his Contender without making the slightest move in my direction. "M-4, *please*."

The lion swims forward and takes the bag's straps in his mouth. I wish I had a camera to photograph the surprise on Guy's face. No, I'd like a chalk drawing. An old, Dutch master–style oil painting, with half his face in dark shadow. Maybe a gaudy frame to hold my prize.

As the water gushes higher, I spot Monster tripping down the stairs. I want to tell my grizzly bear it's too dangerous to be down here. It's the same thing I should have told Madox when the water was still waist high. But I won't have the arm strength to pull the third yellow bag up the stairs, especially when it's soaking wet. So I call for my bear as Guy hollers at me to come on. As soon as I get the straps of the third bag in Monster's jaws, I take hold of his back and hang on as he pulls me toward the steps with ease.

Sunshine burns through the open hatch with such cheery enthusiasm, instilling a false sense of confidence.

What bad thing could happen in daylight? the child in me asks.

Cotton is at the top of the stairs. He sees Guy swimming toward him. He sees me hanging on to Monster's back, and he sees the water gushing into the hold with unstoppable hunger. He sees all of this, and he backs out of the hatch and disappears from view.

The lion makes it to the stairs and bounds sideways up them, dragging the yellow raft bag behind him. Guy reaches the stairs, too, and stretches an arm toward me as if he can somehow will Monster to swim faster. I grab any canned items I can with one hand and gather them to my chest.

We're almost there. Monster's claws brush the remaining exposed stairs, and he fumbles for footing. I spy Madox in the hatch, a pleading look on his face. I'm already ticking through the Contenders and their Pandoras, forming a plan for how we'll get everyone into the water and onto the rafts safely, when I hear the splashing.

The surging water makes a constant static noise as it impregnates the hold, greedily devouring anything it can find. But this sound is different. It stands out from the background like a red-headed woodpecker along the trunk of an old oak tree. My ear has slid over the sound time and again, but now that I've heard it, I can't *un*hear it.

"There's something in the water," I yell to Guy.

His eyes widen with panic when he sees that I'm hesitating. "Just come up the stairs, Tella. We can look from here."

I turn back to the water.

And then I see exactly what it is I've been hearing.

CHAPTER TWENTY-ONE

An alligator thrashes in the current, his short front legs clinging to a pallet of sliced mandarin oranges. *Margo's Mandarins: In their own juice!*

Mr. Larson left his Pandora behind. He knew the animal couldn't swim, and he left him anyway. I push away from Monster without a second thought and swim toward the alligator. I'm almost to him when I spot the ivory teeth protruding from his jaws and pinching the tight green skin around his mouth. I wish I had an alligator treat or something to lure him toward me without actually having to touch him. What do alligators eat?

Oh.

I tread water for a second and pull in a deep breath. Guy yells from across the hold, and from the sound of it, he's already leaping back into the water. The sea is rising rapidly inside the hold, and it's cold, much too cold to tolerate for long. So I do what I must — I make a grab for the alligator.

The beast snaps at me, and I scream. Then I bite down, knowing I can't waste time, and grab for him again. He must know I'm his only hope, because this time he allows me to grab under his neck. I hold his head as high as I can and whisper soothing words into what I hope is his ear. For good measure, I also whisper a few *please don't death roll me, please don't death roll me* requests, too.

I swim toward the stairs, propping the Pandora's shockingly heavy head over my shoulder, using the water to bear his weight. When Guy tries to take the animal's head from me, V-5 snaps at him and not in the way he did me. My snap was a restrained warning — Guy's was a death certificate.

Guy swims aside, and I continue using the water to pull the mammoth creature to safety. As soon as the Pandora's legs touch the stairs, he scrambles up. Monster roars at him as he passes by, as if he's not happy this creature threatened his Contender's life. I grab hold of a stair and climb up, the extra cans of food forgotten.

"Into the sea," Guy yells when he steps onto the deck.

"Set up the lifeboats," I yell at the same time. We exchange a glance, but I quickly recover. "It'll be harder to figure them out with the waves knocking us around."

Olivia's brow furrows as if she's uncertain, but Harper doesn't hesitate for a moment. "I'm with Tella. Let's inflate the rafts now." She gives me a silent nod, and I recall our conversation from the night before. How surprised she seemed that Guy wanted to send her into the hold during the storm.

"We need to worry about getting off this boat first." Guy spots the water gurgling from the hold, and doesn't wait for further resistance. He grabs the first yellow bag and tosses it off the side of the boat. Braun and Mr. Larson glance back and forth between us, and in the end, they help Guy move the other two rafts off the boat as well.

Guess the conversation is over.

My blood boils under my wet suit.

Olivia looks to me for direction, God love her. I sigh and wave her toward the ladder. Mr. Larson steps in front of Olivia and grabs hold of the rope. Then he swings his girth over the side of the boat and climbs down. I ask Harper to go next because I want her in the water in case one of the girls needs her. She obliges, but not without ensuring her Pandora is well enough to take flight.

Within minutes, we're all in the sea. Mr. Larson holds his alligator's head above water, and I remind myself to make time to berate the man later. The rest of our Pandoras can swim, even the iguana, as we found out.

Guy tugs on cords inside each of the life raft bags, but he's not having any luck since he can't get traction bobbing in the waves.

The water is freezing, and my heart is thumping rapidly in my chest. I can spot the worry on Guy's face. His eyes flick toward me for only an instant, but it's enough. He's admitting he miscalculated.

Braun looks back at the boat and then reaches over to help Guy. "We should have done it on board, I guess. We had time."

"I'm so cold," Willow says as her teeth chatter.

"What the hell, Guy?" Harper snaps. "If you're going to underestimate everyone else, you better be sure of your decisions."

Guy growls and makes several more attempts. Willow's head vanishes below the surface, and Harper has to dive after her. She wraps her arms around the shaking, sputtering girl and glares at Guy.

Finally, mercifully, the first life raft bursts from its bag like a mushroom cloud. There's a small rope ladder over the side like there is on the ship, and the Contenders use that to pull themselves aboard the inflated raft. It isn't easy, and it takes Mr. Larson about a hundred and one tries before he manages.

We decide to put the Pandoras in the second and third life rafts after Guy gets them working, and many of the creatures we have to help pull on board. There's also the issue of sharp nails, but the creatures seem to instinctually know to lie on their sides, or in Monster's case, to retract his claws. When Cotton opens one of the two red bags and finds a length of rope, we use it to tie the three rafts together. After that's settled, Willow curls up against Harper's side, and RX-13 comes to land on our raft, holding her talons a centimeter above the rubberlike material.

Each raft has a side that's covered by a tarp, which I'm guessing is for protection from the sun. Braun pushes the tarp back to make room for the nine of us to spread out, and in doing so, finds three pieces of a paddle. Guy screws them together, plunges them into the water, and begins thrusting our three boats away from the sinking ship. Cotton finds a second set in the third life raft, and mimics Guy's broad strokes.

As we move slowly but efficiently through the water, our heads turn back toward the ship. Only the bow of the boat is visible, along with the long, pointed bowsprit at the front. It's hard to believe the thing lasted only a day — twenty-four hours above the sea, one twisting in a storm. Now we're here, our pride wrecked. I thought when they equipped us with supplies that they wanted to make us feel invincible before the storm. But that wasn't the twist. The twist was they equipped us with everything we'd need to survive the ocean, and then they blew it all to kingdom come.

"It was some sort of explosive, huh?" Braun's face is so flushed, I wonder if he's going to be sick.

When Guy doesn't respond, I tell Braun, yes, that's exactly what it was.

A silence settles over us as we grasp what this means. We're going to be stuck in rafts for days, maybe weeks. The ship provided distance from the ocean, but not anymore. Even though there's a massive boat sinking in the distance, it doesn't make a sound. That is, until the last of it disappears on the horizon, then there's a long, deep belching sound.

Jaxon sits up straighter. "Did the ocean just burp?"

Olivia giggles, and he tickles her mercilessly. Harper sees their exchange, and she punches him in the shoulder.

"Ow!" Jaxon flinches.

"You're an idiot," Harper says.

"You love it."

I hold my breath as the smallest of smiles crosses Harper's face. But it's gone the moment Jaxon says, "I'm sorry, Harper."

"Shut it, freak show," she says. "I'm working on my tan."

My gaze finds Guy, and though he'd never admit it, there's relief etched into the tiny crinkles around his eyes. Hit us with a storm, fine. Blow up our ship, great. But strife between Contenders? Nightmare.

I consider telling him something that will help his bruised ego. *No one besides you could have steered the ship through that storm*. Or *I'm only able to think clearly knowing you're here if I fail.*

But I decide to let it rest. After all, it's not a big deal. He made a call, and I did, too. The problem is he didn't consider my option for a moment. But maybe I didn't consider his, either.

"I think I see something," Willow says.

All eyes swivel to the small girl, who looks more like a cherub than anyone should.

"You brought the binoculars?" Olivia asks, admiration in her voice.

Willow nods until Braun steals them away. "They were around my neck when everything happened. It was sheer luck."

He stares through the binoculars, and when he pulls back, his jaw is hanging open. "It's a flag."

Cotton holds his hand out, and Braun gives him the binoculars. Cotton looks through them. "Yep, flag," he says. "It's on a buoy."

CHAPTER TWENTY-TWO

Mr. Larson wants to remove the blue flag from the buoy. Apparently, he's reclaimed his youth and wants to tie it around his enormous bicep like all the cool kids do. I'm adamant, though. This race is hard enough, and I hate the thought that removing the flag could deter other Contenders from finding base camp.

"You think they'd do us the same courtesy?" Mr. Larson has a finger up his snub nose, digging. He doesn't care that we're all watching him.

I shrug. "It doesn't matter. In the jungle and the desert, it was easier to survive."

Olivia barks with laughter.

"Easier than this," I modify.

Mr. Larson gives up after Cotton threatens to hit him overboard with his paddle. I smile in his direction, and Cotton returns the gesture, but it feels forced on his part. Maybe it is on mine, too. Cotton saw Guy and me struggling to rescue our supplies from the hold and did nothing to help. That will be difficult to forget.

For some reason, I recheck his wrist for the colored band and the other Contenders' wrists, too. I don't want any more unexpected people Pandoras springing up on me. And Cotton . . . he feels off, even if he did supply a reason as to why.

My mind slips back to that night with Dink. It was I who found the young boy in the desert crouched over Jaxon's cheetah Pandora, blood on his mouth, Pandora guts lacing his teeth. That was mere seconds before he lunged at me. Minutes before Guy drove a blade into the child Pandora's heart. The difference between Dink and Cotton is that Dink never had a device, and Cotton does. So I don't believe he's a Pandora. He's simply strange.

Madox barks from the next raft over, and I give him a reassuring look that all is well. Then Braun brings out the rest of the supplies and announces that we have six bottles of water, three protein bars, clear wire, a bobby pin, and a knife. Mr. Larson reaches for a protein bar and unwraps it.

"Fat bastard," Harper says. "You can't help yourself when there are limited supplies."

"Let him," Guy says.

"Screw that." Harper lunges for Mr. Larson, and in the scuffle, Willow slips a bottle of water under her wet suit.

"I'm the oldest. It's my right!" Mr. Larson grunts between Harper's grabs for the protein bar.

"My daughter *died*, prick, and I'm still playing fair."

Guy shakes his head. "This is what they want us to do."

"Stop!" Jaxon yells suddenly. He points into the distance. "I see another flag."

"Already?" Cotton asks.

Jaxon hands him the binoculars, and Cotton mutters, "Already."

"Let's not get our hopes up," I say. "It doesn't mean we're close. It only means we're headed in the right direction."

Guy and Cotton exchange a look and start rowing faster. When the sun has begun to fade, we reach the second buoy. This one is smaller than the first, but no matter, there's our blue flag. This time, Mr. Larson doesn't fight us to keep it.

Braun takes over Cotton's rowing, and when Guy refuses to relinquish his spot to me, I see Harper whispering to her eagle. There's a flutter of wings as the eagle takes to the sky. A second later, the bird dives into the ocean, but something is amiss, and the bird returns soon after, shaken.

"What's wrong?" Harper asks her Pandora. "Go and fetch us something to eat."

It's Olivia who figures it out first. "Maybe Jaxon's iguana messed her up."

Harper's face contorts with confusion. "I don't understand."

But I do, and so does Jaxon. He jumps to his feet, leaps into the raft holding his iguana, and pulls Rose into his arms as if anticipating Harper's attack.

"Harper . . ." Braun begins.

"No," she says, holding her finger up. "No, my Pandora is fine. It'll wear off. She'll be able to swim again. I bet she can still become invisible." Harper laughs once, as if it isn't a big deal, but she doesn't test her eagle's abilities further, and it's a long time before any of us says anything. Harper's Pandora was the best chance we had at finding food, and we all know it. Madox tries once to replicate the eagle's abilities while no one is paying attention, but he can't pull on her invisibility, and so I know he can't swim deep underwater, either.

It's much later, when the sun has set and FDR-1 is glowing softly to grant us light, that we learn a second hard truth — Olivia's elephant Pandora cannot pull clean water from the sea like she did from the sand in the desert. Theories fly, the most popular being that EV-0 can only pull existing water from the earth, and since the earth is so far below the ocean, that's now impossible. So we are without adequate food. We are without adequate water. But chin up, because we've found two flags in one day.

Madox is resting near Cotton's bull when I check on him. The bull looks none too happy about it, but I also note that for the first time, the bull isn't shooing him away. "Maybe we should tell each other what our Pandoras can do," I say quietly. I don't know why I'm being quiet. Maybe because it's unfathomably still, and I'm afraid if I speak too loudly, the storm will return, and this time there will be no hope of surviving.

Willow goes first, but instead of telling us, she shows us. "C-90, come here. Quick!"

One second, the white rat is on the other raft, and the next she's in her hands. Willow's Pandora, C-90, just teleported across space like a ninja. I'm seriously impressed.

We all clap like we're at a magic show and wasn't that something?

When it's Cotton's turn, he asks Braun to be a volunteer. After he positions himself in front of Y-21, looking like a human parade float, Cotton tells his bull that Braun is a threat. In response, red smoke appears from the bull's nostrils and encompasses Braun's body. About ten seconds later, Braun hits the raft. "Don't worry," Cotton explains. "He'll wake up in an hour or so."

"That was wicked cool," Jaxon says. "And kind of mean."

Cotton laughs.

All eyes land on Mr. Larson. "I don't like this. We're competitors, right? So why should we share our Pandora's abilities?"

"For the love of all that is holy," Olivia mumbles, and Harper looks dangerously close to putting our single knife to good use.

"Maybe your Pandora can't do anything at all," Jaxon ventures, laughing.

"If you only knew what he could do!" Mr. Larson says this too loudly, and with too much force. That's what gives him away. It makes me understand why he was so quick to abandon his Pandora in the hold, not that I would have done the same thing.

"I'm sure he'll prove more than capable in the end," I say gently.

The large man doesn't respond.

With the waves rocking us like a babe in the cradle, we settle down to try and sleep. I don't think I'll ever be able to find peace, not while being so close to the ocean. There are still moments in time when I think back to my life before the race and wonder how any of this is possible. Mostly, I remember the way I was before I became a Contender. Competing in this race is like becoming a drug addict. One small slip leads to another, and before you know it, you find yourself in an impossible situation and can't fathom how your life has spiraled so far from what it was.

CHAPTER TWENTY-THREE

When I open my eyes, the stars hang lazy in the sky. Something has startled me awake, and when I see what it is, I jerk backward against the raft. Mr. Larson's alligator is beside me. Well, he's partly beside me. His tail is in his own raft, his belly is draped over the two raft humps that press against each other, and his head and front legs are nuzzled firmly against my side.

I stay completely still, afraid I'm about to be the creature's latest meal. But V-5 is fast asleep, so I clench my teeth to still my racing pulse, and I touch a hand to the top of his head. When I rub the flat expanse between his eyes, the alligator snuggles closer. I smile at this great and powerful reptile, and decide that if I were this Pandora's owner, I would call him Oz.

For several minutes, I continue petting the alligator's thick skin. Then I settle back down. My eyes are already slipping closed when I notice that Guy is awake and that he's been watching me. His full lips are parted, and he's tracing circles on his thigh with his thumb. He seems to be deep in contemplation, and his face is aglow with reverence. I hold his gaze for as long as I can, trying to keep my lids open. But my body betrays me, and I fall back asleep with Guy's expression burned into my mind. It's an expression that asks something of me, though I don't know what. Maybe forgiveness. Maybe understanding.

Screw both.

CHAPTER TWENTY-FOUR

Over the next three days, we survive the sea inside a life raft. Bonus points for finding more flags on increasingly smaller buoys. We're definitely headed in the right direction, and to be honest, it wasn't that difficult of a trail to find or follow, which means we know that's not the real threat. The threat is the ocean itself.

We take turns paddling, though Guy never requests a break. Unlike every other time he's been a martyr for our sakes, his sacrifice takes a worrisome toll. Dark circles form under his eyes, and over the last seventy-two hours his face has slimmed. His skin blisters, and he grows white around the jowls. We haven't had anything to drink for two days, since we finished the last bottles of water, and I don't remember if Guy had any of the bottles we started with. For someone who is only here to save his cousin, he sure seems to make a lot of sacrifices for the rest of us.

I've never been so thirsty in my life or as hungry. In the jungle, and even in the desert, we were rarely without food and water for more than a day. Here it's been almost three. My body cramps like it did when I had the flu. My throat feels like it's on fire, and my head spins, and my heart is going for the gold in the Boston Marathon.

We stink, the lot of us, and urinating in the ocean has leached any sense of pride we had left. Though we can't think of a single way to get water, we did try fishing for food. It was an epic failure without proper bait. Our Pandoras can't help, either. The alligator can't swim, the eagle still hasn't regained her Pandora abilities, and the iguana and grizzly bear can't dive low or fast enough to catch anything.

But last night, I formed a plan.

My stomach turns thinking about it, and I gag on the cold ocean air. What choice do I have, though?

When no one is looking, I reach into a red bag, grab the single blade, and slide it next to my thigh so that it's hidden. Cotton says it won't be long before we begin hallucinating, and maybe I already am. Maybe I've lost my damn mind, and this is what happens when you rob a human being of the things that make them human.

I look at the Contenders, hoping they'll understand.

Then I look at the Pandoras, hoping they will, too.

This must be done.

I raise the blade high, and it catches Olivia's eye. She must note the frantic look in my eye. She must.

"What are you doing?" she shrieks.

Harper lunges for me. Of course she does. She came here to ensure I finish this race, but what the hell for? I'm going to die anyway. Unless . . .

I bring the knife down, and before Harper can rip it away, I gouge a chunk of flesh from my calf. I'm not quite successful; the chunk hangs on by a stubborn thread. The pain is immediate and intense, and more blood gushes from the wound than I'd expected.

Madox leaps over to my raft and goes nuts, jumping in a circle and whining. Even my fox thinks I'm an idiot.

"Have you lost your mind?" Harper screams.

Guy takes his wet suit top off and presses it to my leg. But before he does that, he takes the knife from my hand and cuts the thin flap of skin that holds my flesh intact. He touches my cheek briefly and says, "Don't do that again." His eyes are sunken into his head, and his voice sounds shaky. For some reason, his deteriorated appearance scares me more than anything else we've faced.

Ever the Green Beret, Guy understands immediately what I was doing. He takes the thin flexible wire and the bobby pin, and fashions a fishing line. Then, carefully, he uses my flesh as bait and ties more string around it so that we don't lose it on the first try.

"You cut yourself so that we could fish?" Jaxon's eyebrows nearly touch his hairline. "That's so Rambo, dude."

I laugh, because I don't know what else to do.

"So if we catch a fish and eat it, does that mean we'll be eating a piece of you, too?" Braun poses.

Olivia recoils. "Disgusting."

"It was a fine idea," Mr. Larson says in all seriousness. "It's exactly what they wanted us to do — use ourselves or our Pandoras. You solved the puzzle."

My cheeks warm. I'm flattered by his praise even if he is a jerk; though his flattery does little to wean the throbbing in my calf.

It takes Guy over three hours to catch anything, but once he does, we rejoice as much as our dehydrated bodies will allow. The fish is a good size, silver with a fine blue stripe down its middle. We slice it into small pieces to share, ensuring we leave enough for more bait. For my troubles, I get the head. Guy tells me the eyes have the most moisture, and I try to act gracious. The sushi jokes abound, and only one of us — Braun — upchucks over the side of the raft.

We catch another fish right before nightfall, and when the sky opens and salt-free water collects onto the raft covers, we dance. Willow gets on her knees and pretends to pray to the sky, and we all follow suit, giggling hysterically. Jaxon takes my hands and bows to me like I'm his queen, and I grab my chest and feign modesty. Mr. Larson sings to appease the rain gods at Olivia's request, and amid the celebratory clapping and hip shaking, I find myself in Cotton's arms. For the first time, the strange look in his eyes is gone. In its place is wonder, like he never expected to feel happiness again.

I wish I could see a picture of Cotton's sister. I bet he has one where she has a gooey brownie held to her lips and a Tiffany lamp shade on her head, one her mother paid good money for. I bet when she smiled, the world smiled with her and when she cried, the sky wept as it does now. This is the way I imagine the baby sister he lost.

Cotton looks at something over my shoulder, and very slowly, he releases me. When I turn to see what distracted him, I meet Guy's gaze. Judging by Cotton's reaction, I expect Guy's features to burn with emotion, but they don't. I expect Guy's hands to clench into fists, but they hang open, relaxed. In fact, the only thing that's startling is his posture. While the rest of us sing and dance and open our mouths to the rain, Guy stands unmoving, eyes locked on my face. They flick toward Cotton for a heartbeat, and then the moment is broken. Harper grabs Guy's hands and shakes her butt at him, and Braun takes my hands, and all is forgotten.

And so we end the sixth day with our shrunken stomachs full and our thirst quenched, dancing in circles in a yellow raft, floating upon a sea of bitterness.

CHAPTER TWENTY-FIVE

When I wake on the seventh day, Guy is paddling toward the next buoy. Everyone else is asleep, and the sun is not yet visible. Purples color the sky, promising that it won't be long now. I reach for one of the bottles we filled last night and take a very small sip. We don't know how long it will be before we see fresh water again, so we have to ration.

"Want me to take the other paddle?" I whisper.

He nods, so together we row. The bleeding from my calf has stopped, and it feels good to exercise after spending six idle days crammed into a small area.

We work in silence until the sun makes its appearance. And then, as if the light has given him confidence, Guy clears his throat and says something I never expect, "You're a good person, Tella."

I roll many responses over in my mind before settling on, "Just not a good Contender, is that right?" I don't put anger in my words. It's simply a question.

"You surprise me."

I stop paddling. "Are you saying you might have underestimated me?"

"The others respect you. They listen to you, more and more. And not for the same reason they listen to me."

I feel as if Guy is telling me something, but Braun is rolling over, mumbling, and it won't be long before everyone is awake. I decide to be direct. "Say what it is you want to say to me."

Guy swallows and then flinches as if what he's about to admit pains him. "You're the most amazing person I've ever met."

Now I'm confused, because what he said isn't exactly an apology for treating me like a child. Though I guess part of the fault is my own. It was I who followed him in the jungle, I who did what he asked in the past without question. Maybe we both slid into those roles — with him leading and me silently following — without intention. And we both got comfortable. But I had hoped that when I started voicing my opinions, he'd be relieved.

I'm about to add something else when one of the Pandoras, the pig, starts bounding toward the iguana. I think that the iguana is getting picked on again until I realize that the two are playing.

Maybe FDR-1 isn't a threat anymore. Maybe she can only inject a Pandora once, or maybe the pig knows Rose does it only when she's threatened. Either way, they're having a good time, and it brings a smile to my face. I turn back to Guy, and his grin matches mine, and just like that, we aren't Contenders fighting to save family members. I'm a girl from Boston, and he's a guy from Detroit, and don't we make a fine pair?

Jaxon sits up like a novel thought has occurred to him. "Hey, you know what I was thinking? What is *W*'s deal? I mean, all the other letters in the alphabet have one syllable. But look at *W*. *Double youuuu*. Why's it got to last so long? Right when you get to the end of the alphabet song, there's *W* screwing things up. Am I right?"

"Go back to sleep," Harper groans.

Jaxon gazes at Harper sheepishly. "Maybe if I could snuggle up —"

"Don't even think about it," she responds without stirring.

There's a loud splash, and I spin around to find the pig swimming in the ocean. Y-21 is on his feet and sniffing at the water, looking very guilty.

"Good one, Y," I say. "You may be a bit too big to play with the smaller Pandoras." I cross into their raft, laughing when the bull snorts and hides his head shamefully. "Let's get our pig from the water, shall we?"

My blood turns to ice.

My heart stops beating.

A shark fin breaches the surface. It's there, and then it's gone.

"Guy. Guy!" I lunge back to the first raft without waiting for him to respond, and grab my paddle. Then I leap back to one of the Pandora rafts, the one closest to the swimming pig. BK-68 is a dozen feet from the raft. Not because Cotton's bull knocked it that far, but because the pig started swimming nervously, not sure how he ended up in the water.

"The pig is in the ocean," I hear Cotton shout.

"Shark!" Jaxon yells.

I shove the paddle as far out as I can, but it isn't far enough. The shark reappears, dorsal fin parting the waves. It swims close to the raft, bumping it, and I notice odd stripes hugging its flank. I fall back, hyperventilating. If it bites the raft, it'll deflate. What if it bites all three? The pig squeals, and I throw myself forward again.

"What's going on?" Braun asks, his voice sleep laden.

The shark circles to the other side of the raft, away from the pig, and I lean ever closer to the Pandora. This is my only chance to save it. Guy slaps the water on the other side to draw the shark's attention away from BK-68. My muscles lock so hard, it's difficult to maneuver the paddle, and I'm certain I haven't taken a breath since the beast appeared. I can't let the pig die. Not like this. Not while the rest of us watch.

A second, larger splash reaches my ears. I look over, and everything in my body clenches. Tears spring to my eyes, and I scream like I never have before.

Jaxon is in the water.

CHAPTER TWENTY-SIX

Jaxon is swimming toward Braun's pig, and Braun is yelling something I don't know what, and Cotton is holding Olivia because she's hysterical. This isn't happening. One of our own Contenders can't be twenty feet away from a shark that looks a lot like a tiger shark, and isn't that the most aggressive kind?

"Jaxon, grab hold of my paddle," I holler.

But he won't. Not until he has Braun's Pandora. His blond hair is matted against his head, and his lanky body thrashes toward the pig. I wish he'd swim quieter. There's no telling what he sounds like to the shark. Cotton races to Guy's side and smacks the water, trying to keep the shark's attention diverted.

Jaxon is a hand away from BK-68. His fingers practically brush the pig's skin.

A second, larger shark appears from nowhere.

It takes the pig in its jaws.

Both shark and pig disappear beneath the water, and Braun releases a cry of anguish. My soul shatters into a million fragments that will never piece together the same way again.

"Get him out of there," Harper screams. She means Jaxon, and she means me. It's my job to get Jaxon back to safety. Harper jumps onto my raft and takes hold of the paddle. All we need is for Jaxon to grab it. Then the two of us will pull him toward us with everything we have. Behind me, the Pandoras howl. They understand what's happening, and they're wild with fear. The iguana races back and forth along the lip of the raft, seemingly deciding whether to jump in after her new Contender.

The pig has only been gone a moment when it reappears. Braun yells even louder, and I notice the pig is alive. The sea fills with red, and I glimpse the deep, oozing gash in the pig's head. But

BK-68 is alive and blissfully close to the Contender raft. Mr. Larson reaches out, and together with Olivia, the twosome pulls the pig to safety.

Above the Pandoras' racket, I hear Willow scream.

She's pointing to a third fin.

We are surrounded. If there are three sharks visible, there's no telling how many lie hidden. Jaxon grabs hold of the paddle at last, and we pull him toward us, my muscles burning. Even as my throat begins to open, realizing we'll rescue Jaxon in time, my mind buzzes over what will happen to Braun's Pandora. Over what the sharks may do to our rafts to relish another taste of sweet, living meat.

I lock on to Jaxon's elbow with one hand and his wrist with my other hand. There's a shark swimming toward him, but I've got a hold on my friend like a vise, and I'm not letting go. I pull so hard that the puncture wounds in my shoulder and the still-pink scar in my stomach shoot daggers of pain throughout my body. But it doesn't matter. I have him! I've pulled Jaxon on board, and he's safe, and —

Jaxon slips from my hands.

No, not *slips*. He is *ripped* from my hands. There's a horrible, surreal moment in which Jaxon screams. His face twists with bone-rattling terror, and I understand something in that instant that no one ever should: There is the fear of knowing you're going to die, and there's the horrifying, hell-on-earth fear of knowing you're about to be torn apart and eaten.

The world falls away. I don't smell the musky scent of Jaxon's copious blood or hear Contenders screaming like their bodies have been consumed by fire. I don't see the sharks glide through the water, ravenous, toward their find. These things happen, but they don't register. Not really. I can block them out. I can lean into someone who must be Guy, and I can pretend this isn't happening. But there's one thing I can't escape.

The feel.

The feel of the raft jerking as sharks bump against one another, vying for the best piece of Jaxon. Is it his left arm? His hip bone? His mischievous green eyes?

I scream.

I scream and kick and struggle against Guy. It's my fault. I should have pulled Jaxon in faster. I should have jumped in after him. Somebody should have *done* something. It happened so fast. Jaxon was here; Jaxon was gone.

Jaxon — who cared for Olivia like he would a sibling, who lost his cheetah Pandora in the desert, who crushed on Harper as if she were the most entrancing girl he'd ever met, who came to save his sister but is now in pieces beneath our feet.

Harper is holding Willow as she cries. Cotton is staring into the distance as if he doesn't understand how he got here. Olivia is crying; she's crying so hard and so loud that her elephant Pandora is frantic. Guy whispers in my ear. What's he saying? I don't know. Jaxon is dead. Mr. Larson yells and points to the water. He wants us to paddle away from the sharks, I suppose.

Fuck Mr. Larson.

Braun is the only one who breaks through the fog feasting on my sanity. "It's in its head," he's saying. "Should I pull it out?"

My enormous friend isn't crying. In fact, he's the epitome of calmness. It's like when Jaxon vanished, Braun shut down and all he can do now is spout gibberish about his pig's head. Willow retches, and chunks of partially digested fish gut splash over her chest. At first, I believe her sickness is from the sharks stirring beneath us, fighting for every last bit of our friend. But then I see Braun digging his pointer finger into his pig's skull.

"What are you doing?" Cotton barks.

"It's okay," Braun says with no emotion. "It's dead."

Olivia sobs harder.

I can hardly see through my tears, so when Braun holds up a blinking contraption, I decide that it must be his device. But when I wipe my face, I see that it isn't that at all. It's a silver chip with a green light blinking on and off the same way the red ones do on our own devices.

"It was in my Pandora's head," Braun explains. "What is it?"

"Oh, Braun," Olivia whimpers. She throws herself into Braun's arms, and suddenly the Contender's face darkens.

"Where's Jaxon?" Braun asks, his mouth agape.

Guy tightens his hold on me. Both arms are entangled around my waist, and his cheek is pressed against my cheek. Wetness dampens my shoulder, and I pretend I don't know what it is. I won't turn and look, because seeing Guy Chambers crying means it's over. It means this race was never meant to be a chance to save one single loved one among the rest, or even an opportunity to seek revenge on the relatives who killed Santiago's daughter in the way of trials and tribulations.

If Guy is weeping, it means he may be thinking what I am: that the Brimstone Bleed was created so that we, all of us, die in the worst of ways.

Mr. Larson holds his hand up. He's comparing his device to the chip Braun pulled from the pig's skull. My head drops to my chest, and the tears come faster, hotter.

Because the red light on the device is blinking.

CHAPTER TWENTY-SEVEN

Each of us stares at the device in Mr. Larson's hand. We don't know what the chip Braun's holding does, or if the same things have been implanted in our own Pandoras. We just know the red blinking light means more: more information we don't want, more challenges we're too crippled to face.

Mr. Larson's fear has made him resilient, though, and so he shoves the device into his ear and listens, his head tilting this way and that as if he's searching for a radio signal. When his hand falls to his side and his eyes widen, Guy loosens an arm from my body and searches for his own device.

The sharks have barely quieted and are still circling our rafts. And we're supposed to listen to a message from a robotic woman we've never met? No.

"Don't," I whisper to Guy.

"We must." He plucks my own device from my pocket and places it in my ear. Some of the other Contenders follow his lead. Others don't.

My body shudders uncontrollably, and I shake my head, not wanting this anymore. I want to go home. I want to be in my bed and hear my mother's footsteps padding down the soft carpet, coming to tell me there are pancakes in the kitchen, and, yes, Dad made sausage, too.

My mind snags on the thought — sausage. I gag until I can hardly breathe, and Guy rubs my back. Over and over, Jaxon's death replays in my mind until I believe I'm truly and utterly losing it. There's no time for grief inside this race. Only for more dread, more loss.

A clicking sound fills my ear, and then static.

The message begins.

"Contenders, we have learned that some of the boats we loaned you for the race have malfunctioned."

If I were up to it, I'd roll my eyes. I'd roll my eyes, and I'd snort.

"We provided each boat with three rescue rafts for Contenders and their Pandoras, but we never anticipated that the need to utilize these rafts would arise. Unfortunately, that has not been the case. What's more, we've learned that many of the life rafts themselves have formed spontaneous leaks."

Willow gasps and clings tighter to Harper. All eyes fall to the water. To the sharks.

"Here at headquarters, we're working hard to ensure this glitch doesn't arise in future races. Remember that we have marked each of you with a colored wristband for your personal safety, so while there is no need for panic, we would implore you to move as swiftly and efficiently as you can toward base camp.

"As a consolation for your trouble, we've decided to reverse our earlier decision and instate a prize for the ocean portion. We realize these unforeseen circumstances have been taxing, and so whoever is the first to step foot upon the third base camp will win a ten-minute phone conversation with the loved one they've come to save. We hope this will serve as an additional encouragement to push onward."

The message ends, and we all stare at one another. The prize for the first leg was money to afford better doctors. The prize for the second was a five-year supply of the Cure. In comparison, the ocean prize sounds small.

It's anything but.

After everything we've been through, it's what we're desperate for — a chance to hear Cody's voice. A chance to ask how he's feeling and to assure him (through lies the Brimstone Bleed men will surely feed me) that I am okay and will come home soon. And, no, Cody, I won't tell you where I am. Just take care of yourself. And know that I miss you. And I love you.

Mr. Larson grabs the paddle from where he sits and dunks it into the water. Guy does the same from one of the Pandora rafts, where I remain seated. Together, they begin maneuvering us toward the next buoy and, we hope, away from the sharks. We don't say what we're all thinking. That we're leaving behind a Contender who died in the worst of ways, and that if our raft forms a *spontaneous leak*, we may endure the same fate. Or that we want that phone call so badly, we can taste it.

We move silently through the water until at some point, Cotton gazes directly at me and says, "My dad knows about sharks. He told me about them."

I shrug, like, *What does it matter?*

"They shouldn't have been circling us," he says. "Not in a shiver like that. Not without blood in the water."

That night, as stars drill holes into the sky, Harper curls up in the spot where Jaxon slept the night before, and she cries. I don't know whether it's him she's mourning, or if the tears are for her daughter. I only know they come from a place no one can touch. Her eagle lands near her shaking body, and dips her head in solace. And later, once Harper has quieted, Braun slips his pig's limp body into the black tide, whispering words I can't make out.

The rest of us cling tight to our Pandoras and await the nightmares sleep will bring.

The next morning, Braun nudges me awake. Apparently, I'm the last one still asleep, and the rest of them have been watching me toss and turn, including my drooling fox. The iguana is curled up on my left side and has her tail wrapped around my waist territorially. I wonder how Madox and Monster feel about that.

"We've spotted two other rafts." Harper's voice is hoarse, and her mouth is downturned in a deep grimace. She is beautiful, far more fetching than the lot of us, but even she looks weather-beaten and exhausted.

Willow points toward the horizon, reminding me there are two flawless females aboard this raft, and that her physical appeal holds up better than the former's. "Both are behind us, but not by much. One is a set of green rafts; the others are orange, I think."

Pandoras plod around inside their two rafts, as if they can smell change in the air. Guy points out the birds in the sky and the driftwood floating in the water, and says that means we're close to land.

Land. After eight days riding a salted roller coaster, it sounds like a dream.

Guy is right, of course, and after a few more hours, we discern land in the distance. It's so far, I can hardly see it save for a gray blemish. We're encouraged, and Cotton takes over for Mr. Larson. Together with Guy, the two move the raft even faster toward our goal.

We're making good time — if you can make good time in a raft on an ocean you can't name — until Olivia holds her hand up. Always and forever, we're checking our devices. It's become a nervous tic ever since that first day in the jungle. So we usually know when a message is awaiting us. Out of our group, someone will catch it. Someone will be checking their device when the red light starts blinking. This time, it happens to be Olivia.

We put our devices into place, and I don't have to fight the urge to tear my hair out as I did yesterday. I lost a lot of that fire as I slept. So I sit there — legs crossed, hands on knees — and wait like a good monkey for the woman to begin speaking.

"Congratulations, you have nearly reached the ocean base camp. As you approach the island, you'll find two runways marked by the small round buoys you've become familiar with. The one to the left

will have eight buoys across the entrance, and each will have an attached colored flag. The flags are color coordinated to the rafts Contenders have resorted to. When you reach these flags, you may choose to pull one. If you do so, the rafts that match the colored flag you have retrieved will sink. If you pull more than one, your own rafts will sink. Of course, if someone pulls your colored flag, your rafts will sink as well."

"Oh my God," Olivia cries. "What about the sharks?"

This was my first thought, too. But we haven't seen sharks since Jaxon died, not that it bestows me with confidence. We hadn't seen them before Braun's pig was knocked into the ocean, either.

Olivia crawls toward Harper for comfort, but Harper recoils from her touch.

"One final note before you begin your journey toward the island: You must choose one person from your group to swim to shore unassisted. With a little fortitude, this swimmer can get to base camp and stake claim for your group so that you are one of the six clusters allowed to proceed. The chosen swimmer should use the runway on the right to enter the island."

My scalp tingles with the realization of what she said. The island is much too far away. There's no way anyone could swim that distance. Anybody who attempts it will surely die.

And they'll die because we chose them.

CHAPTER TWENTY-EIGHT

Cotton stands up. "I'll go. I can swim well enough, and it's my fault Braun's pig . . . and Jaxon . . ."

He's talking about his Pandora's hand in the two deaths. I didn't know if he realized it was Y-21 that accidentally knocked the pig overboard.

"No," Harper practically shouts. She seems to gather herself, realizing she spoke too quickly. Harper shoots a death glare at Mr. Larson. "Seems to me it should be the person who's done the least amount of work."

"The weakest," Willow says quietly, looking at Mr. Larson. She squeezes Harper's hand in agreement.

The red-faced man puffs his chest out. "No way, I can't swim that far. I say Cotton should go. He volunteered."

"I bet Willow could make it," Olivia whispers.

"Olivia," I bark, because naming anyone for this death sentence is beneath her. She doesn't mean it, though, and her face flushes with embarrassment to prove the point.

Madox, come here. My fox jumps into the Contender raft and into my lap, and I press my lips to the crown of his head. I hold his small body tight and allow his wriggling to comfort me. Then I gaze at AK-7, my bear, and FDR-1, the iguana who's been through hell. Finally, I look at Guy. He's inspecting his hands as if a solution may materialize from the cold ocean morning and nestle itself into his open palms. He shouldn't worry, because I already know the solution. Because I can't sit back and watch anyone else die.

"I'm going," I announce. "I'm the strongest swimmer."

"You can't possibly know that," Harper says, rising to her feet.

Some of us argue for the chance to go ourselves, while others shout names of people they want to shove overboard. At some point, I turn and find Guy slipping a leg into the water.

"No," I yell, racing across the raft and gathering his wet suit into my fist. "You don't get to make this decision for the rest of us."

He stands up. "I'm good at things like this, Tella. Besides, the Contenders I leave behind will need guidance."

"Who needs guidance?" Harper counters.

Guy touches my hand. His fingers linger on my skin for only a second. "You know this is the right decision."

"I don't know that at all."

"I can swim farther than you can, and faster. It will take me longer to arrive at base camp than it will for the rest of you, but I *will* get there."

"You were stronger when you trained before," I say under my breath.

A shadow passes over his face. "You know nothing of how I trained."

I don't know what I expect to happen. One of us must go, and deep down, I understand that he has the best chance. None of the Contenders behind me has contested his going. They know he's right, and I know he's right. So why can't I let go?

Because even though he doubts me, he makes me feel safe.

Because I'd rather swim to shore knowing he'll be there, than paddle to shore hoping he is.

Tears sting my eyes, and I wrench him away from the edge of the raft. "I'm sorry. I can't let you do this. Not this time."

Guy grabs my shoulders, and his face comes within an inch of mine. "Damn it, Tella. You know this is the right decision. You know I'm stronger than you. Think of your brother. Use your head." He swallows and breathes deeply, drops his gaze. "You want to make your own decisions, fine. But make sure you're choosing the right ones. Especially now."

I jerk away from him, stung by his words. It takes only a moment to recover, to remember Cody, and all the other Contenders behind me who are competing for people they love. Guy is right; I can't make decisions based on what I don't want to lose. I have to remember what I stand to gain: my brother getting out of bed on Sunday morning and tugging on his favorite yellow sneakers for a run; my brother getting his GED and heading to college, his childhood stuffed animal tucked into the bottom of his duffel bag because he couldn't leave it behind; my brother smiling; my brother laughing; my brother well and happy with a long life to fill with mundane adventures.

I snatch the binoculars from Braun and eye the oncoming rafts. Then I tell Guy, "Take a bottle of water with you, but leave M-4. The woman said you must swim unassisted." I turn to the Contenders. "Braun, take the front paddle. Cotton, you take the back. The rest of you need to sit down and stay still. Remain quiet as Braun and Cotton paddle, and be alert for any changes. I'll gauge the rafts behind us. I don't know how many Contender groups have gone before us, so we have to assume we're in sixth place."

Guy is still in the raft, head tilted back. He watches me like he's never met me before. As if I'm someone he'd like to get to know.

"What did I say?" I yell. "Get your ass in the water!"

Guy grins, and for good measure, I shove him off the side of the raft. My heart leaps into my throat, terrified I made a mistake. I wait for the sharks to come, but they don't. I wait for him to curse me, but he only laughs as he reemerges.

"You will make it to base camp, do you understand?" I say.

Guy nods, the water making his eyelashes clump together.

I glance to Cotton, who eyes me with a look I can't place. It could be that he wants to kill me; it could be that he wants to buy friendship bracelets.

"Paddle," I tell him, and he does.

It's the hardest thing I've ever done, but I don't allow myself to search for Guy. I keep my eyes on the island straight ahead, and occasionally, I locate the rafts behind us. It seems like days before we reach the water runway on the left, outlined on both sides by buoys. In actuality, it's probably a few hours. Already, I must drag my thoughts away from Guy and his plight of trying to make it to land. If it took us hours with rafts and paddles, I can't imagine how long it will take him.

Just as it was explained to us, there are eight taller buoys across the entrance, each holding a different-colored flag.

"The rafts behind us are orange and green, right?" Mr. Larson asks. "Which is closer?"

I understand immediately what he means. He wants us to pull a flag and sink a group of Contenders.

"Listen to me carefully, Mr. Larson," I say. "If you take one of those flags, I'll let AK-7 loose on you." As if to prove my point, AK-7 stalks toward the Contender raft, muzzle lowered, jaws agape.

Mr. Larson humphs. "That's nuclear warfare. You sic your Pandora on me, and I'll sic mine on you. We both lose."

Mr. Larson and I study his alligator for signs of aggression. The reptilian Pandora opens one sleepy eye and closes it.

"If we don't pull their flag, they'll pull ours." Mr. Larson reaches toward the green flag.

His hand is all but on it when I yell, "Mac, you sit your ass back down in the raft and keep your mouth shut. We've carried your weight this far, but as God is my witness, I will kill you myself if you touch that flag."

Mr. Larson plops down on his large, flat rear and grinds his teeth.

We're still half a mile from the coast, and there's no telling what might be in the water. I don't know if my decision to leave the Contenders behind us unperturbed was the right one, but with Guy gone, I'm determined to make swift decisions.

Our three rafts, still bound together by rope, float between the taller buoys and toward the island. I watch through the binoculars as the next set of rafts, the green ones, halts by the colored flags. My breathing becomes shallow in my anticipation of their decision.

The people running the Brimstone Bleed want us to destroy one another. Maybe they sorted us into groups so that when we turn on one another, no one person is to blame.

It was a group decision. So I won't put that on my *conscience.*

This activity teaches us to attack groups of Contenders instead of individuals. But we didn't succumb to warped temptations. Now the question is whether the green rafts will follow our lead.

The Contenders pause at the flags for a moment longer. They are fighting among themselves, that much I can make out through the binoculars. In the end, though, they glide between the buoys without pulling a single flag.

I clap my hands and throw my arms over my head. "They didn't do it," I tell the others. Mr. Larson almost seems disappointed that we aren't sinking.

It isn't until the orange rafts reach the flags that I start to sweat again. At this point, we're two football fields away from shore. Close enough to swim with ease, though I still don't want to chance being in the water, not after what happened to Jaxon.

The Contenders stop next to the flags. An arm reaches out.

And three distinct popping noises spring from our rafts.

"I knew it," Mr. Larson hollers.

As our rafts deflate, Contenders scramble for their Pandoras. Mr. Larson is already slipping into the water, but I grab his arm before he can swim away. "You better show up on shore with your Pandora in tow, Mr. Larson, or my threat of letting AK-7 maul you will actualize."

He scoffs, but the alarm on his face is real enough. He waves V-5 over and smashes his shoulder under the Pandora's head with more force than necessary.

Madox, Monster, and Rose are already in the water, but the remaining Pandoras fumble over themselves to get out before they're wrapped in the deflated rafts. In her craze, EV-0, Olivia's elephant, manages to overturn one of the Pandora rafts.

The water is colder than I remember it being, and my teeth chatter from the temperature and inexorable fear. Madox and Monster swim ahead, but turn back as if egging me to follow. I check behind me to ensure I see all Contenders and Pandoras, and my gaze zeroes in on something beneath the overturned raft.

It's a bag.

It's a *blood* bag.

It was taped to the bottom of the raft, and I have no doubt that it was slowly oozing its contents the entire time we rowed through the ocean. There must be more beneath the other two rafts, covertly attracting man-eaters from miles away. We never noticed the bags as the rafts were being inflated, but why would we have thought to look? A bolt of terror shoots down my spine as I wonder if they still drip, even now.

I swim.

I swim hard and fast, and every other second I swear I sense a shark beneath me, rising up from the depths to disembowel me.

From the distance, I hear the unmistakable sound of a Pandora howling in pain. The noise is followed by a Contender — Braun, I think — crying out.

And then I know. It's exactly as I suspected, exactly as I feared.

There's something in the water.

CHAPTER TWENTY-NINE

A sharp sting explodes against my left shoulder blade, and I yelp. Madox shoots a worried look in my direction, but I urge him onward with my mind.

As pain fires up and down my back, I realize what they've filled the entrance with.

Jellyfish.

I search my memory, attempting to recall all I know on the subject. Jellyfish don't seem as worrisome as sharks. But, wait, didn't I watch five minutes of a documentary about a woman who got stung by a Portuguese man-of-war? She writhed in pain; that much I know. But did she live? It didn't seem like she would live; that's why I turned it off. That and my best friend, Hannah, was texting me about Ryan Gosling and asking whether if I saw him on the street, would I play it cool in hopes that he'd relate to me on a personal level or would I fangirl and call it a day?

Answer: fangirl.

This is good. My husband, Ryan Gosling, is keeping my mind off the searing agony coursing through my body. My Pandoras help, too. Madox takes AK-7's shape, and the two bears attempt to lift me from the water. But I know my weight will slow the animals down, so I push them forward and keep an eye on FDR-1.

Every few minutes, howls rip through the evening air. Pandoras and Contenders alike scream, and up ahead, I see Cotton swiping a tendril from his cheek. He growls and punches at the water.

I startle when Harper's head appears. "I thought it would help to swim beneath them," she says, while catching her breath. "But there are even more down deep."

I keep moving, and Harper swims close by, keeping a steady eye on me at all times as if she's remembered why she's returned to the race. Despite the waves crashing over our heads, despite the stings we suffer on our necks and hands and lips — we make headway. But as the green rafts close in and a plump wave swells above us, shuddering as it anticipates cresting, I glimpse what rides the wave a moment before it smashes into Harper.

The jellyfish's globular head resembles an iridescent, retro football helmet, and its tendrils trail lazily behind. It doesn't look like the others I've seen, not exactly, and when it touches Harper's skin, I know it's the worst we'll encounter.

The tendrils slide around Harper's throat, and she screams as she fights to tear them from her body. She's successful, and the jellyfish rides the next wave and floats away from us.

But Harper's nails still tear at her skin, and her head disappears under the water. Overhead, RX-13 beats her wings and tries repeatedly to dive after her Contender. It's no use. I find Harper easily, and when I jerk her head above water, she cries out and beats against my face with her eyes clenched closed.

"Harper," I yell. "Stop fighting me. We have to get to shore."

"It hurts," she sobs.

Another piece of me dies hearing my strong, brave friend begging for help. The green rafts are closer than ever, and so I wave toward them, pleading for assistance. The Contenders ignore us. They didn't pull our flag, but that's the most they'll do.

But finally, when I accept that it's no use shouting, a woman, who looks more like a man, says, "We'll take one of you."

"Here," I say in an instant, shoving Harper toward their raft.

Harper doesn't fight me. She just takes a boy's hand and flops to the bottom of their boat and out of sight. The woman waves the two Contenders who are paddling forward, and as they pass by, I hear someone mutter above Harper's wailing, "It's from a box jellyfish. Has to be."

I don't know what that means or if Harper's life is in danger. I only know that I have to get to shore. So I put my face into the water, and I stroke toward land with everything I have. I'm almost there, so excruciatingly close, when I hear a Contender's voice I recognize yelling for help.

Though Madox is nosing me to continue, I stop. Willow is a few yards back, flailing in the water. Immediately, I begin swimming toward her, but then I spy Olivia only ten feet from Willow. Olivia hesitates, and then drives toward the younger girl, her elephant following behind. I'm wondering what must have struck Willow when Olivia reaches her. The ten-year-old Contender seems to have a hold on Willow, but then Olivia's head drops from sight.

I see arms flapping near Willow's head, and understanding dawns on me — Olivia is drowning. The elephant beats her trunk toward the water, and I speed toward the two girls. I don't know what I'm headed into, but I can't leave them behind. I cry out for the umpteenth time when I'm stung yet again. When Willow sees me approaching, Olivia pops into view once more. Now Cotton is there, too, coming from beneath the girls with impressive stealth. He grabs hold of Willow and powers toward shore. I confirm Olivia is swimming after them before turning back to the island myself. There's no telling what happened out there, but it's all the more reason to get out of this wretched ocean.

I am stung uncountable times during my remaining trek in, and my pulse never slows. My three Pandoras are stung, too, though they hide their discomfort well. At last, with Braun and Mr. Larson in my sight, my feet touch the ocean floor. Relief showers over my body, cleansing me — for one beautiful instant — of the calamities I've endured. With the last bit of strength I have left, I wade to shore. Then I stumble to my knees and collapse.

Minutes pass, or maybe it's hours. When I lift my head, Madox is whining at me, back in fox form.

I made it.

We made it.

I scan the beachfront and the torches lighting the way to base camp, and then I see them — the group of Contenders from the green rafts. They're hunched over a body, staring down at someone who isn't moving.

It doesn't take me long to grasp who that someone is.

Harper.

THE GLADIATOR

CHAPTER THIRTY

Harper sleeps inside a mud-and-grass shelter for six and a half hours before she wakes. I spend the time alternating between hating the man who won a phone call with his niece and dozing off in the chair beside Harper's bed. When I do doze, I dream of sopapillas with thick honey drizzled over their cinnamon sugar skins. There is a room full of them, and I swim through their deliciousness with snorkel mask in place. Not once do I get stung by jellyfish.

When Harper's eyes flutter open, it's the middle of the night, and a kerosene lamp casts a soft glow about the area. She pulls herself up in bed, and no matter how many times I offer her water or push cornmeal biscuits toward her, she refuses.

"They say it was a box jellyfish," I say, encouraging her to lie down and tucking a blanket around her shoulders. "You could have died."

She works her bottom lip between her teeth, and her green eyes glisten. Harper's silence is jarring. It's like she doesn't care that she lived.

I take her hand in mine and swallow the fear of what I'm about to say. "I'm glad you returned for me, Harper. But maybe it's time you went home to be with your family."

Harper shifts in the bed, and a sad smile parts her mouth. Her mouth opens and closes twice before she finally says what it is she wants to say. "My daughter, she was only two years old, but she had this attitude, you know? If I didn't give her what she wanted, she'd cock a hand on her hip and jut her chest out like a tiny diva."

I grip Harper's hand tighter.

"My parents never even wanted me to have her. They said I was only sixteen, that I wouldn't know how to take care of her, and that her dad would disappear.

"When she got sick, I never expected her to get better. Not once. I suppose I just knew. I wasn't surprised when the men here told me she was dead. On the trip back, I told the two guys dressed as police officers escorting me home that I wanted to return to the race after Lil — after my daughter's funeral. They said it was impossible, but a couple of weeks later, one of them showed up on my doorstep. I recognized him immediately, and I was ready. My mother begged me to stay. She didn't know where I was going, but she knew I wouldn't be coming home again if I left a second time."

Harper meets my gaze. "Mothers know this stuff."

"Harper, prove her wrong. Go home. Please, for me, go back to your parents. You've lost your daughter — but they don't deserve to lose their daughter, too."

She shakes her head. "No. I said I'd return to help you win, Tella, but I'm here for my daughter, too. You know, before those jackasses dropped me off at my parents' house, they told me I couldn't tell anyone about the race. That if I did, it could cause my family undue grief. The way they explained it . . . I knew it was them who made her sick. So when you told me everything else about the race, I wasn't surprised. I'd figured most of it out. The moment I saw RX-13 again, though, that thought sank to the back of my mind. I was so happy they'd kept her that, for a day or so, I could breathe again. Until you reminded me of what they'd done."

Her eyes close, and I think she's done speaking. When she opens her eyes again, though, the look on her face freezes me to my bones.

"I bet that at the end of the race, there will be more employees there," she continues. Her head falls back on the pillow, and she glowers at the ceiling. "Like a whole bunch of them just clapping and smiling and shit. But you know what? I'm going to be there, too. And I'll remember my daughter when I see them."

I want to ask Harper exactly what she means by the threat, but when her eyes slip closed again, I decide to let it lie. Now that Harper is feeling better, I can focus on other things. Like the fact that Guy still hasn't arrived at base camp. Not that any of the other swimmers have, either.

When I leave the small structure, I find RX-13 outside and tell the bird that Harper's awake. The bird pushes through the dried-leather door, and I shake my head. An eagle that understands English. I wish I could go back to kindergarten with a Pandora for show-and-tell and hand Ben Gregory's ass to him, and maybe sic Madox on that empty wasp nest of his that everyone thought was *so* cool.

Outside, Contenders lounge around an open fire. This base camp closely resembles the one in the jungle with the cleared dirt floor and surrounding trees. Only these trees aren't quite as tall or thick, and here it's much easier to take in the expansive night sky.

I spot Willow and move toward her, wishing I'd stolen a blanket from the shelter to combat the cold. It doesn't seem like it should be this chilly on an island in October. But maybe that means we're somewhere in the north. Birds call in the distance, and an animal I'm certain isn't a Pandora trills stridently. The fire crackles, and embers pop and rise with the smoke. I sit down next to Willow, deciding this little girl needs directness.

"What happened out there while we were swimming for shore?" I ask.

She shrugs, keeping her eyes on the white rat in her hands.

A knot forms in my stomach. "Did you try to hurt Olivia, Willow?"

She faces me, her eyes large with shock. "Something had ahold of my leg."

I glance at her exposed calves. She tucks one beneath her, but not before I see that there isn't a wound. Pulling my knees to my chest, I say, "This race can make us do terrible things. Things we never thought we were capable of. You're so young. If you did try to hurt Olivia, and I'm not saying you did, then it would be understandable. But that doesn't make it okay. At the end of the Brimstone Bleed, we'll have to return home, and we'll have to live with the things we've done here. You don't want to carry more regrets than you must. Does that make sense?"

Willow crawls into my lap and lays her head against me. It's the first time she's ever showed me much affection, and I'm not sure how to react. "It's been so scary," the girl says as her Pandora scurries up her arm. "But I feel better when you're around. I feel like . . . like you wouldn't let anything bad happen to me."

When her fingers curl around mine, my chest tightens. This isn't right. The child is too quick to name me her protector, and I'm no one's hero but Cody's. What's more, the people she's latched on to seem to be the ones most likely of having an advantage in this race. It's too calculating. I stand up, and she stumbles backward onto the ground. She catches herself, scowling, as C-90 teleports to the top of her head.

"I'm here for my brother, Willow," I say simply, evenly.

She sits up and glares fiercely into the fire. I'm about to walk away when I hear the girl say, "The only thing I'd ever regret is letting my grandfather die."

I startle at the vehemence in her voice, but it doesn't take me long to recover. We're each surviving the only way we know how, and sometimes sounding strong is a tactic. I can't be sure Willow tried to hurt Olivia in the ocean without asking Olivia, who is asleep. As I near my Pandoras, I notice that Madox and Monster are asleep as well, and though I want to allow them adequate rest, I also haven't had alone time with my Pandoras in days.

Madox is curled between AK-7 and the bull, though the bull appears to be leaving as much room between him and the slight fox as he can. I whisper in my Pandora's ear until he opens his eyes. It doesn't take him long to go from a dead sleep to bounding at my feet, elated to receive attention. The grizzly bear is much harder to wake up, and I've all but resolved to leave him behind when he stumbles to his feet. Before the three of us depart, I scratch behind the black bull's ear. He opens one eye and moans with contentment. "You'll keep an eye on the iguana, won't you?" I say, noting the snoozing green lizard a few feet away.

Y-21 groans and shuts his eye.

Together with my Pandoras, I exit the ring of torches and head toward the beach, fighting the false sense that I've left the security of the camp behind. I locate a good place to sit and run my fingers through the pure, cool sand. The sky is so vast, it seems to lie on top of me, swollen by glittering constellations.

AK-7 plops down on my right, and KD-8 does the same on my left. "I don't know what I'd do without you two," I say to Monster, and then think to Madox.

I wonder where they take the Pandoras they don't use anymore.

I allow myself to imagine that the three of us stay together after the race. That it'd be totally plausible for me to show up for my junior year at some fabulous new high school with Monster and Madox in tow. *Oh, the animals? I have them for medical reasons. Will they kill faculty and students alike? No, you're bananas! They're completely tame. Do you not see their couture collars?*

My wristband catches my eye, and I finger the thick plastic zip-tie. My band is still red, but some of the other Contenders have had their band colors swapped. The men said that because there will only be fifty-four of us continuing, at most, that we needed to be reassigned. But no one misses the fact that the Contenders without wristbands, the ones on the "flesh-colored" team, did not receive medical attention for their jellyfish stings nearly as fast as those of us with bands. In comparison, the two Brimstone Bleed men worked on my shoulder and stings like the devil himself had demanded a perfect rehabilitation.

Over the next few hours, I watch the ocean with Madox's head in my lap and Monster snoring like he's trying to wake a volcano. Two Contenders appear in the time I sit staring into the ocean. When the first one appears, I race to her side, asking what she needs. The woman shoves me away and staggers toward base camp, barely able to keep her eyes open. I have no idea whether she was one of the selected swimmers or if her raft simply deflated, but she's here now.

The next guy arrives, and I make a movement like I'm going to get to my feet, but he rights himself with difficulty and passes by without acknowledging my existence. Eventually, I stop waiting for Contenders. I stop waiting for *him*. I lie back and gaze upon the sky, my hand beneath my head. The moon is suspended directly above me, shining like a promise of heaven at the end of a life well lived.

When I wake again, Olivia is curled against my side, sandwiched between Monster and me. Her elephant is on the other side of Madox, and I notice Guy's lion is at my feet. It takes my mind a moment to adjust to my surroundings, but when I remember where I am, I stroke Olivia's hair. It's still night or perhaps very early morning.

A sound reaches me, and I realize it's the same one that worried me awake. My heart leaps into my throat with pulsing hope, and I climb to my feet, careful not to wake Olivia. I lean down and run my hands through M-4's unruly mane. He lets me do it without complaint.

"Did you hear something, too, lion?" I glance around, searching for the source of the noise.

His ears flick in the gentle island wind, and I wonder if he decided to stroll to the beach to investigate the sound. But, no, he wouldn't have heard it from base camp, would he? I don't believe so, which means he came for another reason.

"You came to sleep next to me, huh?" I whisper. "It's okay to admit you like me."

The lion shows his teeth in a show of mock aggression.

I look toward the sea. "Where is he?"

M-4 produces a low, pained moan.

The noise comes a third time, and this time when I look up, I believe my eyes deceitful. That they're playing a brutal joke and showing me what I want most. But it's not a hoax. I'm not imagining things.

The moon casts an eerie sheen across his wide shoulders. Rivers of inky water race down his bare chest. And like a mighty winter storm, Guy Chambers appears from the ocean.

CHAPTER THIRTY-ONE

I want to rush to him, to take his face in my hands. I want to kick him, and to kiss him. He strides closer, his bare feet leaving footprints in the sand. His wet shoes are gone. The reservation he's worn since we left the desert base camp — gone. He gets within an arm's length of me and drops to his knees. A hoarse sigh escapes his lips, as if he's traveled a thousand miles and somehow missed his destination by a breath.

I close the distance between us and cup his chin. Water slips into my palm, tickling my skin. Guy gazes up at me. He crawls one step forward on his knees, and then lays his head against my stomach. His arms rise to encircle my waist ceremoniously, as if I'm a shrine and he's come to offer prayer.

He breathes deeply, his lungs expanding against my legs. I run my fingers through his wet hair and wait for him to speak. Finally, he does.

"I didn't think I would make it," he says, while trying to catch his breath. "You were right. I was in better physical condition when I trained, and I hadn't anticipated the toll that being without adequate sleep and water had taken. But you had forgotten something, too. I had something else."

"Tell me," I whisper.

"You didn't take into account that I would hold you in my mind. That I would focus so wholly on the feel of your skin against mine, that it was as if my body moved through the water on its own." Guy burrows his head deeper into my stomach, which has been flattened by surviving on raw fish and desert fruit and snake cooked over an open fire. "You say all the wrong things. You're completely untrained and ill prepared when it comes to surviving this race. You care too much for the Contenders and Pandoras when you should focus only on your brother's welfare." He swallows and shakes his head, hesitating. "I may have saved you in that jungle, Tella, and in the desert, too. But out there in the ocean, you saved me."

I drop to my knees.

I'm not accustomed to Guy lowering his guard, and I never expected him to say what he has. There *is* something between us, even if he has been distant recently. There are two sides of my Green Beret: the side that thinks only of winning and the side that aches for companionship like the rest of us.

But I've changed since he told me I couldn't win. It's been a gradual process, but I no longer rely on Guy as I once did. He is still the first person I look to — maybe he always will be as long as we're inside the race — but now there's a voice in my head that whispers guidance. Each hour that I remembered his words at the desert base camp — that voice grew stronger.

Our foreheads touch, and Guy slumps to his side. He takes me with him. We lay there in the sand, Guy's chest still heaving from exertion, my heart racing from his vulnerable admission. That he needed someone besides himself to continue.

I don't respond to what he's said. He's already fast asleep, and M-4 is tucked firmly against Guy's back, purring blissfully. Olivia hasn't heard a word of our exchange, and neither have any of the other Pandoras.

"You know he loves you, right, lion?" I say to Guy's Pandora.

Now that his Contender is here, safe, M-4 closes his eyes and sleeps.

Guy's arms are still wrapped around my body, his head heavy on my chest. I fall asleep this way, entangled in his embrace, entranced by this person I have no future with. It's then, as I drift into oblivion, that I realize — the Brimstone Bleed breaks much more than our spirits.

Strong arms carry me. My head lies limply against a chest made of stone. I am laid onto a bed, and my eyes attempt to open. But it's too difficult. I'm three leaps past exhausted. A cool blanket grazes my exposed skin, and the sensation is luxurious beyond measure. At last, as the person who carried me moves away, I convince my lids to lift a fraction.

Cotton stands in the doorway, silhouetted by darkness.

He stares at me, his hands clenched, his jaw tight. Cotton looks as if he wants me dead. So why, then, did he carry me here?

I can't force myself to think on the question. I swam too far, I was stung too many times, and I worried over my friend's dying and Guy's returning for what felt like months. Madox leaps onto my bed and curls into a ball near my feet.

My Pandora is here, and so I return to sleep.

CHAPTER THIRTY-TWO

The next morning, I wake to find Guy curled on the floor. The room is small, but I count eleven other beds besides the one I occupy. A silky soft blanket bunches near my knees, the same one Cotton used to cover me last night. I kick it to my feet and sit up. Madox stirs, and a few beds down I catch sight of a white wolf pacing. The creature seems to be chasing boredom, so I call the animal over. It doesn't come, but it does wag its tail with interest.

I stifle a laugh when Madox pushes his head under my hand, trying to redirect my attention back to its rightful place.

"You hungry?" I whisper to Madox. His ears perk.

From the ground, I hear Guy pulling himself up. One moment he's fast asleep, the next it's as if he's waited hours for me to rise. He rubs one knuckle into his right eye, making the scar over his brow stretch and whiten. "Can you walk with me?"

I nod, and ask Madox to stay put as Guy and I leave the structure. The sun hasn't been visible long, and the chill in the air is biting. I rub my hands over my arms as Guy leads me to the camp's perimeter. We disappear into the island foliage, but not so far that we can't easily spot the Contenders and Pandoras milling around the quieted fire.

"Do you remember the chip we saw in Braun's Pandora?" Guy asks when we're safe from eavesdropping.

"I do," I respond. "What do you think it is?"

He shakes his head, admitting he doesn't know.

I tell him about the blood bags beneath the rafts, but he doesn't seem surprised. Finally, I say that I plan to include Braun and Olivia in what we know about the race, and that I've already told Harper.

Guy sighs. "I told you that in confidence. You forget I have a plan."

"It's *our* plan now."

"You can't tell them about the race. I can't believe you said anything to Harper without talking to me."

This is the part where I'd usually get upset, but this time I don't. "We will tell them because it's the right thing to do. And because I get a vote in this, too."

Guy looks at me for a long time before nodding his acceptance. "What happened to the girl who followed me in the jungle?" He smiles, but I can tell he's hurt, too. "Will she ever listen to anything I have to say again? Does she not need me anymore?"

I grin, because it seems at last he understands I'm thinking for myself and has accepted it. But I don't want it to be so black-and-white between us. I care about Guy, and what I want more than anything is for us to exist in the gray, where both our opinions are heard and we treat each other as partners and equals. I open my mouth to explain this, but then decide showing him might be better. And more fun.

My hands slide over his chest, and I raise my head to his. I take one step closer, and my breath comes faster. Guy's eyes run over my face, and a mixture of desire and fear softens his features. I rise up onto my toes and lick my lips. Guy does the same.

His hand finds my hip, and he pulls me closer.

We are so close, nothing between us. Guy lowers his head, his lips almost touching mine —

And then he steps back.

"Tella . . ."

His sudden distance is a slap across the face. "You still don't believe in me."

He grabs my arm. "That's not it. I saw you out there in the ocean. I know what you're capable of when you put your mind to it."

"Then what?" I hate the sound of my voice.

He shakes his head.

I don't know when I started relying on Guy so severely, but it ended yesterday. There is still this, though — the desire to touch him, the desire to feel wanted in this cold, heartless race. "You never wanted me."

"That's not true." He reaches for me, but I step back.

"I can't do this hot-and-cold thing with you anymore. Tell me how you feel, or I'm walking away. Tell me how you feel, or you and I are only partners from here on out."

He opens his mouth, and my entire body tenses. But then he closes it. He closes it, and my heart slams shut. Finally, he's stopped demanding I listen to him. He's admitted he thinks I'm more capable than he originally thought. And now he can't do this one little thing. He can't tell me how he feels.

"It doesn't matter," I say, a little more harshly than I intended. "I'm here for my brother. Not for you."

I spin on my heel and storm away, but before I can get too far, Guy overtakes me. His hands are suddenly everywhere: in my hair, clutching my back, stroking the planes of my lips. I fall into him, allowing his touch to overtake my senses. His lips graze my collarbone and work their way up, moving with fervor. My head falls back, allowing him full access to my throat. Each hurried, passionate kiss along my neck is like a flame licking my skin. He lifts me up, draws my body closer. My hands slide into his hair, and I grip those dark locks between my fingers.

His mouth moves from my neck and hovers an inch from my lips.

I remember myself and jerk backward. My feet touch the ground, and I pull away from his grasp. This time when he grabs hold of me, I push him backward. "You won't do that again. Not until you can say what you feel aloud."

I turn and stride toward the huts, my pulse hammering inside my body.

CHAPTER THIRTY-THREE

Two weeks ago, I told Braun and Olivia everything I knew about the race. We decided as a group to keep the information between us, for now. I figured Harper would want to tell Willow, too, but she never broached the issue. No one pushed for Cotton to know, either. And after the night he carried me to bed, I was more than a little conflicted about whether I should trust him.

Mr. Larson's name wasn't even brought up. In fact, Mr. Larson has given us a wide berth ever since we arrived at base camp. I've tried numerous times to approach him, asking if he wants to eat with Harper and me, but he tells me he's relieved to get away from the lot of us.

I don't believe a word he says. He wants companions as much as the next person, but he also knows the other Contenders in our group detest him. At least he hasn't abandoned his Pandora, though each time I finish talking with Mr. Larson, the alligator attempts to follow me back to wherever I came from.

Guy wasn't pleased that I told Braun and Olivia what he confided in me, but of course I knew he wouldn't be. Ever since that day on the ocean camp's perimeter, Guy and I have shared information. If I make a decision about something important, I tell him. He grants me the same favor. I don't tell him about the Cotton issue, or lack thereof. That's my puzzle to mull over.

Guy watches me as if I'm an exotic animal thriving in its natural habitat, perpetually out of reach. He is forever in my head, the feel of his lips lingering in my memory. But even now he is quiet.

"Tell us what's on your mind," I say to him.

The five of us huddle together behind one of the grass-and-mud structures, our backs pressed to the exterior wall, the wind threading through our bodies.

Guy presses a thumb to the center of his chin. "They're building something."

Braun shakes his head. "No, whatever it is they visit at night is preexisting. Maybe it's houses that the island people live in. The people we've seen gliding through camp from time to time? Maybe that's where they go."

"Those island people make a mean snack," Olivia says, munching on a blackberry-and-currant corn cake drizzled with honey.

I nuzzle AK-7's side with my shoe-covered foot and try to think, wishing I could get a pair of legit shoes with, I don't know, some cushion. A modicum of cute. Dare I dream for a bit of sparkle? The two men working the race have left base camp every night and disappeared into the island foliage. They return at sunrise empty-handed. Every once in a while, we hear the sound of chain saws and falling timber, and we know something big is happening. We once tried to follow them, but ran into a line of six island men, their hair in thick, dark dreads, scowls dipping their mouths.

We shouldn't chance a scuffle, I'd said. *We have less than a week until we leave. Let's lie low.*

"I think it has to do with our Pandoras," Harper ventures. "They haven't taken their eyes off them since we arrived."

All five of us — Guy, Braun, Harper, Olivia, and I — regard our Pandoras, our protectors. We silently contemplate what she's suggested. We're still tossing theories around after dinner, when a sharp whistle sounds throughout the camp.

We scramble to our feet, knowing this is it. We've spent days resting and recovering from our injuries. We've discussed the race to death. But mostly, we've watched and waited for the next obstacle. Before we became Contenders, we lived for the future. Now we live in the moment, knowing there won't be a tomorrow if we don't conquer today.

By the time we leave our partially hidden hangout, Contenders and Pandoras are already lined up around the fire pit. The two men stand side by side, and as I suspected, one has a whistle hanging from a green rope around his neck. I have a sudden, intense desire to scream, *Put me in, Coach!*

The man without the whistle holds up a white device. "You'll be receiving a message in a few moments. I want to stress that there will be no questions or carrying on once she's done talking."

My forehead beads with sweat despite the weather. We've heard several messages before that could easily be classified as disturbing. If they think we'll react badly to this one, then whatever's coming won't be good.

FDR-1 wraps her tail over my calf, and a yard away Madox lies on his back, kicking his legs up at Cotton's bull. The bull is not amused. Olivia takes my hand, and my body aches in response to her touch. We've spent many nights weeping for Jaxon, but every time I comfort Olivia, I can't help thinking what it'd be like if he were still here.

Harper is back on the ground, Willow curled in her lap. The rat shimmies under Willow's hair and hides, and RX-13 steps back with obvious repulsion. I tighten my arm around Olivia's shoulders before digging the device from my pocket and slipping it into my ear.

Once we all have our devices in place, we wait. It's a full century before the woman begins speaking, an eternity of silence.

Clicking.

Static.

"I'm pleased to see so many of you at the ocean base camp. As a courtesy, we extended the break between ocean and the final leg of the race to two weeks instead of the typical one."

The woman pauses, and a Contender coughs loudly.

"Sixty-four Contenders entered the ocean portion of the Brimstone Bleed, and today, we have forty-one eligible to continue on to the last leg of the race."

Forty-eight Contenders should be able to move on, but she said forty-one. My stomach lurches when I realize that means seven Contenders died at sea, or at the very least, have yet to appear at base camp.

"In four days, you'll progress to the final part of the Brimstone Bleed. We have something very special we'll be supplying the first five people to reach the final base camp. And of course, one lucky person will ultimately hold the Cure to save their loved one's life."

Guy and I exchange a look. It was he who told me exactly what the first five Contenders would receive. But hearing her imply what he's divulged leads me to trust his information even more.

The woman from the device hesitates for a long time. So long, Olivia tugs on my hand in question. When she begins to speak again, my heart hammers in my chest.

"We've decided to do something special to give Contenders an advantage over one another, an opportunity for you to prove your dedication to your loved one. After this message ends, you will communicate to any Pandoras assisting you in this race that they have a choice. If they elect to participate in a specific challenge, you will be granted a twenty-four-hour head start in the last ecosystem over other Contenders. If they decline, however, you must remain behind during the first day of the final leg."

My pulse pounds, and my eyes fall on Madox, my sweet black fox. What would they have him do? My stomach lurches as I imagine the possibilities.

"If your Pandora chooses to participate, tomorrow morning they will be matched against another creature in what we call the Pandora Wars.

"They will fight to the death."

CHAPTER THIRTY-FOUR

That next morning, I wake to find Madox standing in the doorway of our small hut. He faces outward toward the sea, though I know he can't see it from here. Last night, I told him what the woman from the device said, and then I silently pleaded for him to decline. Because AK-7 belongs to me more than anyone else, he and Madox must both agree to fight or I'll be required to lose a day in the race. I guess this is the downside of collecting Pandoras, even if I already did make a plan for Rose.

After I informed them of their challenge, the iguana fidgeted throughout the evening and night, and Madox gazed toward the ocean, deep in thought. The grizzly bear listened to what I had to say and then flumped onto the floor and slept like the dead.

A whistle blows, and I imagine shoving that same whistle down the skinny, pinheaded man's throat. Madox perks at the sudden noise, and he strides from sight like he's been waiting for that sound for days instead of hours.

Madox, wait. I scramble to my feet. When I get outside, I find that Pandoras are already lining up before the two men working the race. Both men wear light jackets over green collared shirts, and their jackets have serpents embroidered on the left breast. The skinny man is yelling something when Braun appears at my side.

"What's he yelling about?" he asks.

You could find these two dudes, the Brimstone Bleed guys, in any suburban town with their 2.5 children and their maybe, maybe not pregnant wife. They don't look particularly intimidating, and they probably haven't seen the inside of a weight room since that one summer they were going to *show everyone* before their sophomore year of high school. But they work for the race, and so we believe unequivocally that they could withhold the Cure. And that, my friends, is all it takes to behave. Just the bittersweet promise of recovery for someone you care about.

"I think they're getting ready to take them somewhere," I answer.

Braun glances between me and Madox. "Thank you," he says. "I'm still not sure what I'm doing is right."

I look at Rose, who is already in line. Last night I gave her to Braun and said the decision was his. It felt a little like handing over a newborn to a starving, desperate hyena. Braun leaves in silence as if he's ashamed and can't stand to face me any longer than necessary.

Madox stands a few yards from the line, watching the other Pandoras intently.

I scoop him into my arms, and he struggles against me fiercely. I drop him, surprised by his distant demeanor. Madox trots a couple of paces and stops again.

Please don't do this, I beg.

Madox's stance remains firm, his fox eyes trained on his competition.

Heavy plodding comes from behind me, and I turn to find AK-7. He stops at my side and noses the top of my head. I throw my arms around his massive neck and bury my head into his fur chilled from the cold. "Stay with me. That's an order."

The bear lowers his head farther and sniffs my dressed shoulder.

"Don't worry about that. You saved my life."

AK-7 pulls away suddenly and heads toward the line.

My throat burns. "Monster, no."

The grizzly bear sidles toward the end of the line. I lace my fingers over my head and try to breathe. The woman said it was our Pandora's choice, but surely there's something I can do to stop them. If I can get Madox to stay behind, then there will be no reason for the bear to fight, either.

Madox, listen. If you die, I won't make it in the last leg.

I don't care about that right now. I care about *him*. My fox's ear curves in my direction like a satellite.

I can't tell you what the plan involves yet, but you have to trust me. If we're to win this thing, if I'm to save my brother's life, then you have to follow my order. Don't fight. Choose to help me. Choose to stay behind.

One of the two men calls out for any remaining Pandoras to get in line. A handful of Contenders and their Pandoras who have chosen not to enter are behind me, along with several Contenders who no longer have Pandoras. Guy's lion, Willow's rat, Harper's eagle, Cotton's bull, and Olivia's elephant have all made the decision to fight. Mr. Larson and his alligator are among the ones who linger in the back.

KD-8, please.

Madox strides forward without a backward glance. My legs shake beneath me, and Guy appears. His arm sweeps around my waist. I lean on him for a moment before finding my strength and pushing away.

"I don't need coddling." I march toward my fellow Contenders. It isn't Guy I'm angry with, but anger dilutes my fear, so I willingly succumb.

"When do you think they'll do it?" Harper asks when I reach her.

"Tonight." I don't know why I think this, but it seems right.

"Our Pandoras are the best," Olivia says. "And mine is huge. I mean, a baby elephant can do more damage than most full-grown animals."

Olivia's elephant, EV-0, has only ever shown the ability to pull water from the earth. But the girl is trying to convince herself that her Pandora will win, so nobody comments.

Braun comes to find us, his head lowered.

Cotton, who stands beside Harper, raises his hand as if to comfort Braun and then drops it. "It'll be awful to watch this whether it's your original Pandora or not."

Braun meets Cotton's gaze and nods.

Cotton turns his attention to me. "I've envied you, Tella. The way other people's Pandoras are drawn to you? But today, I'm not envious at all."

"Cotton," Harper scolds, pulling Willow closer to her side.

He shrugs. "Didn't mean anything by it."

Braun inspects his nails, which, despite the things we've endured, still manage to look impeccable. "You have two strong Pandoras, Tinker Bell. They'll win their fights."

This conversation does nothing to combat the dizziness threatening to overtake my mind. I have three Pandoras. I'll have to watch three fights, even if one is technically fighting for Braun. It's highly likely that tonight I'll witness the death of one of my beloved creatures.

The two men continue walking into the island foliage. The Pandoras disappear behind layers of tree trunks and liana vines and overgrown spider ferns.

Everything in my body calls out for action: to rush to Madox's side, to save my Pandora from this terrible task. But as we watch our closest companions vanish from sight, I realize something.

Madox — my small black fox hatched in a sticky green slime — has always looked to me for direction. I was his steady compass, his guiding hand.

But today he makes his own decisions.

Today he walks alone.

Just like me.

CHAPTER THIRTY-FIVE

The sun is long gone when one of the Brimstone Bleed men returns to camp. Two women are with him, dressed in long, swinging skirts, dark hair grazing the bottoms of their backs. Both women wear necklaces adorned with wooden spikes stained red and orange, which rattle with the sway of their hips. Above their heads are wicker baskets overflowing with dried cod, plantain bananas, and sticky buns stuffed with dates.

The men tell us to eat, but most of us refuse the offer. We want our Pandoras, and that is all. After they're done torturing us with anticipation, they ask us to follow them.

As we leave the circle of torches and the kerosene fumes they emit, I catch sight of Olivia's face. I grab the back of her shirt and casually tug her toward me. "Walk beside me, okay?"

Her upper lip stiffens. "I don't need anyone to comfort me."

"It's me who needs comforting," I say, though her words resonate. It was only this morning that I pulled away from Guy, thinking I didn't need his solace. I search him out now and wave him over. He drifts toward me as if an invisible string connects us. When he reaches me, I don't take his hand. I don't wrap my arms around him in a quick embrace. I just meet his gaze and hold it. Then I return my eyes to the men leading our pilgrimage.

Harper and Willow walk before me, and Braun and Cotton trudge behind. It's odd beyond explanation to travel without our Pandoras now. There are no animal cries or tongues licking or wings beating. It's only us — the sound of forty-one Contenders of varying ages, ethnicities, and genders trekking down a path that's been worn by feet traveling this same distance time and again.

The island people have most likely used this path too many times to count. But what about past Contenders? Have past races always ended the ocean portions here? And if so, did the Contenders fret over Pandoras whose lives could end that very night? Are we stepping where they once did?

My fingers brush the blue-and-green feather that dangles over my right shoulder. I've had to retie the rawhide string into my curling hair more than once, but I haven't lost it, and I don't intend to.

"There's a light up ahead," Cotton whispers.

He's right. There are torches lit, much like the ones surrounding our base camp. Inside is a massive construction, and as we move closer, I make out the curves and slopes in detail. The structure is circular in nature, crisscrossing often so that you can see through hexagonal openings. The entire thing is made of thin, bendable wood that's tied at intersections with straw-colored twine. Rich, dark soil makes up the floor, covering twenty feet in diameter at best guess. The dome-shaped creation appears twenty feet high as well.

I imagine this is what the two men have been occupied with each night, and I'm absolutely positive that this is the fighting ring our Pandoras will enter.

The smell of salt and sweat is heavy in the air, and the dread of what's to come is palpable. Guy's arm brushes mine, and I nearly jump out of my skin from nerves. One of the Brimstone Bleed men, the skinny one, raises his arm into the air. It seems like he's mimicking the Statue of Liberty, and I'd love to light his hand on fire to see if anyone else notices the resemblance.

"Each Pandora has now been matched against another Pandora, based on input from headquarters. Each round will last until one Pandora has destroyed its competitor. You will not, under any circumstance, interfere with the fights."

I flinch at the word *destroyed.*

"Regardless of whether your Pandora wins, you will be granted a head start above Contenders whose Pandoras have chosen not to partake." His voice is nasally. He's tall and skinny, and he sounds like he just hit puberty. "If you are with your Pandora now, please keep them still as we come around and mark them. It's only spray paint, nothing to worry about. The mark will help us keep track of the Pandoras tonight."

As he speaks, the second, portlier Brimstone Bleed man walks from Pandora to Pandora, marking each of them with a slick red stripe of spray paint. One of the animals, the white wolf I saw two weeks ago, tries to lick it off, but the man pops the animal hard on the nose. The wolf yelps.

"Hey!" I exclaim.

The man's head snaps up, and he glares at me. I glance down, implying it was a mistake. If Guy taught me one thing, it's to keep a low profile and remember the end goal. Speaking out, even if it was a knee-jerk reaction, was a blunder. The man moves to the next animal, but the wolf and the other Pandoras continue to regard me intently.

When the man sprays the alligator, Mr. Larson crosses his arms. He may not think much of his Pandora, but he doesn't like these men any more than I do, and that puts us on the same team.

"Now that that's done," the first man booms, scratching his stomach absently, "the Pandora Wars can begin!"

CHAPTER THIRTY-SIX

Island men enter the clearing, small drums strapped around their necks and cradled to their stomachs. They beat open palms against the leather skins, producing an ominous melodic offering to unseen gods. There are six men in total, and only one doesn't have a drum. That man — the largest of them, dreaded hair to his waist — strides forward on bare feet. Behind him are two Pandoras.

The first is a hippopotamus, the lines of the Pandora's body painted in green war paint. A chill rushes through me when the hippo opens her mighty jaws and generates a strident trumpeting sound. Fear may eat at every nerve ending in her substantial body, but she doesn't show it. This Pandora is ready.

The next creature appears with a quiet air of royalty. His body is similar to that of a reindeer, but he's larger, his horns taller and heftier. The animal is adorned in a dense brown coat and hangs his head close to the ground like a calm, underestimated boxer. Blue paint coats his horns, and a single line of it trails his backbone.

The man unlatches an arched door and waves the Pandoras inside. These are not my Pandoras, but my heart pounds all the same. Everything we've been through, our Pandoras had to endure as well. They've been there for us regardless of how dangerous the circumstances were, and this is how we reward them.

I want to stop this — I *have* to stop this — but I don't know how. Maybe the only way I truly can is by sticking to the plan Guy created — endure the Brimstone Bleed, and then take it down from the inside so that this never happens again. But watching these two Pandoras circle each other — bloodlust in their eyes, the beat of drums working them into a fever — I realize remaining quiet will be harder than I thought.

The drums beat faster.

The man blows his whistle.

And the elk gallops toward the hippo. With a sweep of his head, the elk rams his horns into the other Pandora. A Contender cheers, watching his Pandora make the first strike. But he's the only one. Most onlookers appear disgusted, and it's a far cry from the whoops and hollers I heard at the start of the jungle race.

The hippo staggers a couple of steps and opens her jaws in pain. As she does, the elk slams her again, one of his horns catching the hippo inside the mouth. The hippo falls to one knee, but finds her feet quickly. Tired of being bullied, the hippo charges at the elk full force, three thousand pounds of thick skin and muscle behind her. The elk's legs buckle beneath him upon impact, and the hippo brings her giant incisors down on the elk's torso.

The elk releases a piercing wail before jabbing a horn directly into the hippo's left eye. Badly wounded, she falls back. But now the hippo is furious, and so she charges the elk again. This time, though, the elk is ready. The animal lowers his head to the ground as he did when entering the ring. His branching horns suddenly glow red-hot like the embers from last night's fire.

The hippo stops short in her attack, but it's too late. The elk closes the distance between them and slides a burning horn across the hippo's blue-gray skin. A roar rips through the air as the hippo's Contender clutches the arena's exterior and shakes the bars. The island man shoves him back, and my hands ball at my sides. How much longer can I watch this? How much more can I take?

The elk drags a horn across the hippo's midsection again, and her stomach opens in a gaping wound. The hippo stumbles, nods her head — up and down, up and down — and then opens her powerful jaws. She makes the same trumpeting sound she did as she approached the ring, but this time it builds until the Pandoras behind us shriek in agony. The elk drops to his knees and slams the side of his head into the dirt, trying to escape the sound. To me and to the other Contenders, it seems, the noise is uncomfortable to hear, but that's where it ends. The hippo must be producing a frequency that's excruciatingly painful to Pandora ears.

After several seconds, the hippo closes her jaws, her sides working hard to regain much-needed breath. As she struggles to do so, blood spills from her wound. The hippo staggers. Seeing his opportunity, the elk bolts upright. Hooves beat the dirt as he speeds forward, but the hippo is ready for him. She dips as low as her three-thousand-pound body will allow, and then clamps down on the elk's throat a moment before the elk can attack.

When the elk collapses and his throat is slowly crushed in the hippo's mouth, I look away. Tears burn hot trails down my cheeks when I realize it's over. But then —

The same male Contender cries out. I spin and catch sight of the elk whipping his head sideways. He can't move much, not with the hippo cinching his throat, but it's enough. Enough to drive his horn into her injured eye. Except this time, his horn is burning like a branding rod, and it drives right through the hippo's eye and into the Pandora's skull.

The hippo collapses.

The Contender doesn't make a sound. I don't, either. Tears still drip down my face, but I don't have it in me to scream. Because if I do, I'm afraid I'll never stop. And I have to keep ahold of myself. When it's one of my Pandoras' turns, I have to appear confident so that they aren't afraid.

It's good that I can keep my composure. It's good that I can continue to stand after watching someone's animal companion die.

Because the next two Pandoras are being led to the arena.

CHAPTER THIRTY-SEVEN

I watch twelve more animals compete in the Pandora Wars — peacocks and cobras, owls and otters — and each time one kills the other, my grief deepens. So far, Cotton's bull is the only one of our Pandoras that has battled. The beast won against a kangaroo in under two minutes with his red sleeping smoke and deadly horns.

As each fight begins, I battle conflicting impulses to flee or start a riot. And every time two new Pandoras are led to the ring, I'm blinded by anxiety that this is the moment I'll see Madox, or Monster, or Rose. I feel that sensation now, because the island man is discarding a zebra's carcass, with the help of three other men, and waving in someone I can't see. Though the giraffe who overtook the zebra won, a man still marks the triumphant Pandora with red spray paint. I wonder why some of the victors get painted when others don't.

When yet another island man appears, I barely glance in his direction. It's the Pandoras I care about. But then I see what creature he's leading to the arena, and I have to cover my mouth to keep from crying out.

The first Pandora is Guy's lion, M-4. His mouth hangs open, and he pants in the cool air, pink tongue curled. His back is striped with a long, thick stroke of blue paint, and more decorates his paws. M-4's eyes are steady on the wooden dome, though I know he must want to seek out his Contender desperately. When it comes to our Pandoras' safety, we Contenders don't seem to want to be consoled, so I simply stand close to Guy, ready if he needs me.

The island man swings the arched door open, and the lion springs inside, turns on the man, and roars. The Contenders surrounding the ring startle, and the island man stumbles backward and lands on his rear. Guy barks a laugh. The man brushes himself off and sneers at the lion, but he doesn't challenge the Pandora.

I'm beginning to wonder what animal M-4's competitor will be when I see her. My heart lurches into my throat, and Willow throws her face into Harper's stomach.

Willow's rat scurries toward the arena — a splatter of green war paint on her back — and crawls through one of the octagonal openings. The man slams the door shut and, once again, the drums start beating. Sweat and blood mingle in the air until I can almost taste the metallic, musky scent on my tongue.

"Shh . . ." Harper bends down and wraps her arms around Willow. "C-90 will be okay."

Guy tilts his head toward Harper ever so slightly, and then he turns his attention back to the arena.

A whistle is blown, beginning the match, and the lion lies down on his stomach.

"What's he doing?" I whisper.

Guy shakes his head. He doesn't know.

Willow's rat scurries close and then springs back as if bitten. The lion never moves. As the drums beat faster, demanding action, M-4's idleness begins to feel discombobulating, even if it is a nice change from the instant, aggressive assaults we've seen tonight. Willow's rat stands on her hind legs and vanishes. A moment later, the rat is within inches of the lion's back paw.

The lion lies still.

C-90 vanishes and lands on the other side of the arena. And then, once again, the rat jumps across the space, invisible, getting close to the lion before returning to safety. Watching this dance, I begin to suspect what's going on. M-4's advantage is his size and strength, along with his ability to light fire. But he must instill a false sense of confidence into the rat before he strikes, since his fire doesn't burn far and the rat is quick as a winter day.

At last, the rat lands near M-4's tail and bites down. The lion spins around, and the rat vanishes. Now C-90 is clinging to the arena's roof, and M-4 releases a fireball over his head in irritation. The rat is gone before the flames leave the lion's mouth. This time, the rat lands on the ground, and M-4 springs at her, his patience waning. The rat vanishes before the lion can move halfway across the arena.

Now the rat lands on the lion's back, and it may be my imagination, but C-90's long pink tail seems to lengthen. Before anything can happen, though, M-4 jumps in a circle, dislodging the rodent. C-90 falls to the ground, and before she can vanish, the lion releases a fireball. This time, the rat is almost singed in the flames. Once she dodges the fiery danger, C-90 darts in and out of view on the opposite side of the ring, drawing the lion forward.

I can hardly breathe as M-4 lowers to the ground and stalks, inch by inch, toward C-90. When he's halfway across the ring, he lowers almost to his belly, his tail flicking wildly, tempting the white rat to make a move. The lion's yellow eyes zero in on his prey, and like a punch to the gut, I understand that he has a plan. In a flash, the lion springs after the rat.

The rat vanishes.

The lion stops midspring and turns.

A fireball erupts from his mouth in the opposite direction of where the rat just stood.

When C-90 appears, her fur is blackened and there's a dollop of fire licking the end of her tail. The rat squeals and drops to her side, stunned and hurting. M-4 pounces. The rat is caught between the lion's claws, and I know this is it. It's like a smaller, faster boxer in the ring with a heavyweight; they can dodge all they want, tiring their opponent, but once that heavy hitter swings, it's TKO.

Willow screams.

The lion's jaws snap down.

But suddenly, the white rat — who isn't so white anymore — appears on M-4's thick mane, directly behind his head. The rat scurries backward, half tumbling, and in a movement so quick, my eyes nearly miss it, the rat's tail lengthens and curves over her back. It becomes thinner at the tip, and sharper.

C-90's tail comes down, stinging like a scorpion's. The lion roars and rolls onto his back. When he does, the rat goes with him. M-4 springs to his feet, and the rat lies on her side, pink, clawed feet kicking.

The lion draws his mighty head back and releases a fireball larger than I've ever seen. C-90 is engulfed. Her squeals don't last long, and when the flames die, M-4 lowers his head and sniffs the body. Satisfied the rat is dead, the lion roars long and loud.

Everyone but Guy turns toward Willow.

Her mouth is open in a perfect O, but she promptly regains her composure, anger locking her body tighter than rigor mortis. Harper wraps her arms around the little girl, but Willow pays her no mind; her gaze is set firmly on Guy. She eyes him the way M-4 did the rat, like he is her target.

The girl spins on her heel and makes like she's going to leave the clearing. One of the Brimstone Bleed men calls after her, and before she can get too far, he grabs hold of her arm. I'm not sure how I feel about Willow, but the torment of watching her Pandora die has to cut deep. Right now she needs someone to see her as a human and not a Contender.

I make my way toward her, pushing Contenders out of my way. They hardly say a word as I pass, but their Pandoras crane their necks to follow my movements. I'm almost to Willow when I hear Guy mutter something, his lips close to my ear.

"What?" I ask.

Guy points toward the ring. "They're leading Madox to the arena."

CHAPTER THIRTY-EIGHT

They say when you experience tragedy, time speeds up. But watching my black fox enter the Pandora Wars, knowing he has exactly half a chance of survival, feels tragic, and yet every step he takes is too quick. He is in the round ring before I can utter a word, but my legs power beneath me anyway, carrying my body close enough to the arena to see the matted fur on my Pandora's neck painted green.

I say his name once in my head so he knows I'm here, but commit to staying silent thereafter. I won't be the reason he loses concentration.

Madox keeps his gaze bolted on the arena door, awaiting his opponent. KD-8 doesn't have to wait long. As the drums beat their baleful song, demanding *death, death, death, death*, a second Pandora appears: a panther, as strong and sleek as a marble statue.

The panther strides toward the arena, shoulder blades rising and falling like a black tide. His eyes resemble M-4's — yellow, cunning — and his paint color is blue. The animal's Contender, a woman with a wide mouth pulled into a frown, stands opposite the ring. She calls out to her Pandora, and the creature growls low in his throat at Madox.

My fox doesn't appear afraid. He can mimic any animal, including this one. But he steps back from the panther because he doesn't want this fight. I know my Pandora, and killing any creature, no matter the reason, will be hard for him. Maybe impossible. The Creators may not have intended to instill Pandoras with personalities, with things like compassion and morality, but Madox has both, and it may be his Achilles' heel tonight.

I struggle to keep my legs beneath me, but I can't slow the racing in my heart. Madox has to win. I don't want to wish ill will on the panther, but I can't lose my Pandora. Guy comes to stand behind me. I can feel him there, and for once, I don't move away. As much as I hate to admit it, I need him here. Because if something happens to Madox . . .

The whistle blows.

The panther lunges, and Madox springs out of the animal's path. Changing course, the panther trails the perimeter of the ring. For every step the cat takes, my fox takes two, maintaining a safe distance between them. The panther hunkers down a second time, and as my hand flies to my chest, the cat leaps through the air. This time, he doesn't miss. Madox rolls across the dirt floor, and the panther rolls with him. Together they look like a black tumbleweed zipping across the ring.

Their momentum dies, and Madox bounces to his feet. Then he hastily circles the panther's body and bites down on the cat's back leg. The panther kicks KD-8 in the face with his other leg, and my fox releases his hold.

"He needs to change." I don't have to check to know that Guy is listening and that he agrees. There's no way my Pandora can win against the panther with only his teeth and small claws. So what's he waiting for?

Madox crosses the ring and pushes down on his front paws like a pup that wants to play. The panther shakes his back leg and then puts pressure on it gingerly. It must not bother him too much, because he rushes at Madox, a battle cry ripping through his throat.

Madox dives under his front legs and is almost out of reach when one of the panther's claws hooks into Madox's back thigh. Immediately, fingers of blue crawl up Madox's leg and over the back of his torso.

My Pandora yelps as ice forms over him, hardening until the fox can't move part of his body. Thinking quickly, Madox spins with his upper torso and bites down on the panther's paw. My fox tears his head back and forth viciously, and the panther bats my fox with his other paw to loosen his grip.

My fox flies three feet across the arena, and as soon as the panther's claw is retracted from his skin, the ice melts away. Madox stumbles, and then he's upright, shaking his damp fur. His hackles rise, but I can tell he's frightened. It's written all over his face, dripping from his hurt-filled eyes. With his tail tucked between his legs, Madox limps backward to get away from the panther.

Guy offers his hand.

I take it.

"Something's wrong." Nerves cause my words to quiver. "He either can't change, or he's too afraid to kill."

Guy's words come fast, certain. "He'll find a way."

But I'm not sure that's true. The panther sits back, and then he sails through the air, his paws outstretched as if he intends to hug Madox. The cat collides into my fox, and his claw snags his skin. Ice shoots across my fox's back, and the panther doesn't hesitate. He opens his jaws and brings them down.

Madox slips from his grasp without a second to spare, pulling himself sideways with his unfrozen left legs. As the ice melts, Madox vaults to the panther's side and bites down on the Pandora's belly. Blood splatters the arena's floor, both from my fox's legs and from the panther's stomach.

The panther stumbles to the side, moaning. Madox sees an opening and readies himself to launch another attack, but when he hears the pained sound the panther makes, he stops. It's obvious he doesn't want to hurt the other Pandora, but this may be his only chance. I consider urging him to attack with my mind and reassuring him I won't be upset — though of course I will be — but I remain silent.

The panther's Contender yells something from across the ring, and I seriously consider starting my own fight outside the arena to shut her up. The panther looks to the woman and then sets his gaze on Madox. Bloodlust pools in the panther's eyes, and I can tell that this Pandora is about to bring his worst. Madox will either have to match his desire to live or be killed.

Madox backs up, apprehension stiffening his small body. He knows what I know: that this is the moment he must decide what he's willing to do for survival. I take a step closer, and sweat dampens my scalp. My pulse matches the manic rhythm of the drums, and my entire body feels electric with angst.

The panther lunges through the air, his claws extended. Always on the defense, Madox dodges his attack.

But it isn't enough.

The panther's claw catches Madox in the gut a heartbeat before he can escape. My fox rolls across the ring and comes to a stop inches from where I stand. He doesn't move.

Madox! Oh my God, Madox! Get up. Please get up!

I don't care about interrupting my Pandora's concentration anymore. I'm more concerned about whether he's breathing. When Madox flinches and then slowly climbs to his feet, wobbling, I gasp with relief.

But the panther is stalking toward my fox, teeth bared. He sees that the fox is hurt, and now he's going to make his final strike.

Madox raises his head.

For the first time during this fight, his eyes meet mine.

What I see in them is something that chills me to the bone. Madox isn't a sweet Pandora that needs protecting. He isn't gentle or kind or even merciful — not when it comes to protecting me. My small black fox is deceitful, conniving. He's a Pandora that will pretend to be afraid, will be beaten badly in front of an audience to ensure he makes the kill.

Madox glances at something over my shoulder, and his body shifts. His ears lengthen, and his body expands, and white fur replaces black. The panther falls back, disoriented by this sudden change.

Madox sets his sharp wolf eyes on me once more before he turns.

Then he springs onto the panther and rips his throat out.

The panther is dead before he even comprehends that he's been attacked. When Madox turns again, his white muzzle is smeared in red, and his eyes blaze with triumph.

I thought I knew my Pandora well.

I do not know my Pandora at all.

CHAPTER THIRTY-NINE

Across the ring, the panther's Contender screams. She runs at the arched door to the ring and pulls at it until it flings open. Two island men race inside the ring and grab her forcefully. She only wants to mourn the loss of her Pandora. If it had been Madox, I'd do the same.

My feet carry me toward the arena's entrance, though I'm not entirely sure what I'm doing. It's the bottled-up emotions demanding action. I'm like a red balloon that's been overfilled with worry for these animals, and now I feel myself about to explode in a sudden sonic *boom*.

"Give her a minute," I yell at the men, my voice carrying all the fear I've held inside. "That's her Pandora." The crowd mumbles their agreement, and I lunge at the man who's dragging the woman from the ring. "Let her go!"

Madox is by my side in an instant, back in fox form. As I tug the man's arms, a male Contender appears, who must be friends with the woman. His fist crunches into the man's nose.

The Contenders and Pandoras go wild.

The drums stop.

The Contender who came to help me calls out to his Pandora, and a rooster soars at the second man's face, claws leading his flight.

The first man gets to his feet and grabs the rooster by the neck, throws him to the ground. Then he kicks a penguin Pandora that ventured too close. I throw myself in front of the penguin so it doesn't receive a second blow. The Contender who came to the woman's rescue backs away with her in tow, his courage depleted.

Now it's just me and the island men. I hold up my hands like I don't want to fight, but one of them lunges at me anyway. Madox tears at his ankles, and Mr. Larson appears at my side with Guy and Harper in tow.

Mr. Larson takes an openhanded hit, which was intended for me, and staggers.

He hesitates only a second before pouncing on the man.

Over Mr. Larson's shoulder, I spot one of the Brimstone Bleed men trekking toward us.

"Stop," the man hollers.

No one stops.

The Brimstone Bleed man shoves his hand inside his jacket and retrieves a glittering silver gun. He raises the gun and points it directly at my chest.

When Mr. Larson sees it, I expect him to freeze. I expect him to hold his hands above his head like he's a bandit in an old Western movie.

He does neither.

Instead, he jabs a finger at the gunman and yells something about fighting man-to-man. The guy must not like Mr. Larson's sudden movement, or maybe he just isn't thinking.

The gun goes off.

Mr. Larson slumps to the ground. I crumble with him and take the man's head in my hands. "Oh my God," I moan, as if I'm physically wounded. But, no, there's the bullet, caught neatly in Mr. Larson's enormous belly. It's he who's hurt, not me.

Guy drops to the other side of Mr. Larson and places his hands over the wound. Blood gushes through his fingers, black and persistent.

The shooter's face twists with shock at seeing Mr. Larson's color seep away. He looks at the gun in his hand as if he's surprised to see it there.

Mr. Larson tries to speak, and though I'm choked by tears, I lower my head and ask him what he said. "Christina," he mumbles. "Christina, Christina."

My head drops to my chest, and I'm not sure I'll ever be able to raise it again. If Mr. Larson hadn't yelled at the man, the gun would still have been trained on me. And if I'd kept my mouth shut, none of this would have happened.

The second Brimstone Bleed man yells something, but I barely make it out. Not until Guy is pulling me to my feet.

Mr. Larson isn't moving. Blood still seeps from his wound, but his lips no longer speak Christina's name. Why isn't anyone helping him? I start to shout for assistance when I see what stands between Guy and the Brimstone Bleed man.

Mr. Larson's alligator, V-5, opens his powerful jaws and hisses. The sound is a warning, and I can only imagine what will follow that terrible noise. Mr. Larson may not be the most faithful Contender to his Pandora, but this creature was engineered to have the instinct to protect.

The man points his gun at the alligator and tells the second Brimstone Bleed man, his voice panicked, "I've got to shoot it!"

"No!" I lunge in front of the alligator, barely missing Guy's grab for me. "Listen, I know you didn't mean to shoot that man, right? No one blames you. It was a mistake." My legs quake and my stomach turns, but the man is listening. He's every bit as afraid as I am. "No other Contender or Pandora needs to get hurt tonight. We'll take the injured man back to camp, and he'll be all right. Everything will be fine. Okay?"

The Contenders hold their breath. Not a single Pandora makes a noise. Even the birds and wild creatures that call this island home have quieted.

I take a small step toward the man, attempting to reassure him.

It has the opposite effect.

He raises his gun in my direction. I stay stock-still, my vision blurring, my head spinning. As my heart pounds against my chest, I stare at the barrel of the gun. It feels as if every second is my last. Every breath I take the last to leave my lungs.

How did I get here, with a weapon pointed at my battered body?

The man's eyes widen, and I think, *So this is it.*

But he's looking at something behind me. His eyes enlarge so that he appears almost alien. I don't want to chance startling him, but now his arm is shaking so hard that I'm not sure I could scare him any worse.

Slowly — so slowly, I wonder if I'm moving at all — I crane my neck around.

Two dozen Pandoras stand behind me, teeth bared. Sound comes rushing back, and suddenly I hear their throaty growls, their unmistakable battle cries. They crawl closer, closer, flanking me, taking position like a restless army awaiting orders. Together, they form a shield about my body. I spot Cotton's bull in the mix and Guy's lion. There are Monster and Rose and Harper's eagle and Olivia's baby elephant. There's the white wolf Madox mimicked earlier, and of course, my black fox by its side. Surrounding all of those Pandoras are other creatures, some I have spent time with — offering a bit of my meal or just a quick scratch behind the ears — and some I have not.

Some of the Contenders call out to their Pandoras, ordering them back. But they don't move.

They only eye the man with the gun and close in tighter to my sides.

CHAPTER FORTY

The Brimstone Bleed man's arm shakes so hard now that he can hardly keep control of the gun. Behind him, the other man stays still, his face as red as cranberries. The gunman waves his weapon wildly, aiming at one Pandora, then another. "Tell them to stand down."

I'm not sure what gives me the confidence to challenge him — maybe it's the Pandora Wars I witnessed or the bullet Mr. Larson took or the militia of Pandoras ready to protect me — but I do. "Maybe I don't," I say. "Maybe I tell them to attack. Maybe you kill me before they kill you. But in the end, you still die. And the way you'll go is a lot worse than the way I'll go."

"What about the Cure?" The man stutters his words. "If you kill me, they'll find out. They'll end the contest, and not a one of you will save your people."

Behind me, I hear Contenders mutter. They hate these men. They hate what they've put us through. But the moment he brings up the Cure, the faces of those they love flash through their minds. We're one leg away from saving the people we cherish most in this world, and the men know this.

"What if I decide you're lying?" I square my shoulders. "What if I decide that after all the unspeakably cruel things you've done to us, that there is no Cure? And that tonight is the night I call your bluff?"

The Contenders fall quiet, awaiting the man's response.

It's Guy who stops me from pushing him further. "Tella, think of your brother. Think of what you can do with the Cure *after*."

He's telling me to remember the plan. He's reminding me there's a fight much bigger than this to fight. But it's so hard to back down. Like holding a knife to the neck of someone who killed your best friend and convincing yourself to lower it.

"Tella."

The second time he says my name does the trick. I hold my hands out to the Pandoras and ask them to back down. At first, I'm afraid they'll refuse. Then again, maybe I'm not so afraid of that outcome. The creatures step back — a couple at first, and then more. Madox and Monster stay nearby, and I won't tell them to go.

The man waves his gun, gaining confidence. "The Pandora Wars are over, and the next leg of the race begins immediately. Report back to camp!"

The second he lowers his gun a millimeter, I rush to Mr. Larson. I'm two steps away before Guy pulls me into an embrace and pins me to his chest. I know instantly why he stops me.

"No." I clutch the stretchy material of Guy's shirt. "He can't be gone."

"Let's go!" the man yells.

He wants us to get moving before we change our minds and launch an attack. I don't feel like I can take a single step, not once I see Mr. Larson's face, eyes staring blankly, skin the color of concrete.

Harper grabs on to my elbow. "Walk."

I walk.

We follow the two men as the island people hang back, Guy and Harper supporting and leading me on either side. With every step I take, I think of Mr. Larson. With every breath in between, I recall the look on Madox's face a moment before he slaughtered the panther. Up ahead, I spot Olivia trying to console Willow, but Willow glances at the older girl as if she has the plague.

When we reach base camp, one of the men runs inside their shelter and retrieves the wooden box.

"Two lines!"

There is only one line.

"Sleeves up!"

Our sleeves go up.

It seems that even though there are forty-one separate Contenders, tonight we think as one. We're scared, our teeth are on edge, and we know how close we came to a revolution. But — there's always a *but* — we are so painfully close to the end. In each of our minds, in the end, it's we who hold the Cure. It's we who return home a savior.

The needle slips into my flesh, and I bite my lip to keep from screaming. Just that one prick is too much. I meet the man's eyes. He's not the one who held the gun, but he might as well be. He stays at my side for a moment longer than he does the rest.

"We'll be keeping an eye on you," he snaps. "Don't think we won't remember this."

Then he glances at my wrist, at the red band there, and his mouth quirks upward in a stark contrast to his threat. It's hardly noticeable, the gesture, but I don't miss his change in demeanor. He almost seems pleased with my performance tonight, despite the warning.

As the drug nibbles the corners of my mind, I reach for Braun. He turns toward me. We're supposed to face forward when in line, but they don't correct his protocol breach. Braun and I take each other's hands.

His wrist now sports a blue band, though I'm sure it used to be green. He didn't tell me his color changed. Inspecting Braun's kind face, I think about what happened minutes before, when the Pandoras lined up behind me as if I were their general. Is it so easy to earn their loyalty? If so, is it because their own Contenders treat them poorly?

Or is it because they seek a leader?

I remember sitting in Mrs. Radford's world history class, and as she spoke about insurgencies, I pretended to act interested. There was a hot new guy who'd moved to our school, and he was into history. So by default, I was, too. That day, Mrs. Radford spoke about what it takes to start an uprising. There were many factors, she'd say, but none so important as this: *The people look ahead at their future, and what they see is bleak.*

As Contenders, we have the promise of a Cure. But the Pandoras have no such promise. What does the future hold for them?

My body begins to shake. My consciousness is slipping away. For whatever reason, as I lose control of my will to stand, my mind snaps ahold of this memory about the race:

"It is bigger now than Santiago ever thought it could be," Guy says. "There are people out there ignorant of the details, gambling on what they believe is an illegal horse race."

And then this:

Contender Joseph – 31 – Red

Contender Courtney – 101 – Green

The first thing was something Guy told me at the end of the desert race. The second is what I saw on the woman's chart that night in the desert base camp.

In a moment of clarity, I understand everything. I glance at the red bracelet around my wrist, my vision blurring from the injection.

That woman — the one with impeccable fashion sense — she is an oddsmaker. She estimates how efficiently each Contender will finish the race and reports back to headquarters. Then they send those numbers to bookies, and those bookies collect bets.

Contender Joseph – 31 – Red

Contender Courtney – 101 – Green

Contender Joseph, three-to-one odds that he finishes in the top five. Red bracelet.

Contender Courtney, ten-to-one odds that she finishes in the top five. Green bracelet.

No bracelet means you're a long shot. Big payout, low chance of placing.

People are betting on us like we're horses, just like Guy said.

I'm a horse.

He's a horse.

We're all horses.

But not for long.

THE FROST

CHAPTER FORTY-ONE

I'm numb.

That's what wakes me, the tingling sensation in my body that says I don't actually *have* any sensation. The only part of me that isn't numb is my left cheek, which is on fire. I jerk my face up, and my eyes snap open.

I'm lying in the snow. They dumped us here like dogs, even though we are horses. All around me are Contenders and Pandoras, some knocked out, some on their feet. Guy is still asleep. It makes me feel like a superhero to awaken before he does. Maybe I am. Who knows.

Almost instantly, my heart begins racing. This is the last leg, and every second counts. I search the ground. There are twenty-nine Contenders in total. Looking at them, I wonder where they're holding the remaining twelve. The people running this race must have decided to let everyone whose Pandora even entered the wars, regardless of whether they fought, continue. That was real swell of them. I should send a card.

My fingers flutter next to my hair. Blue-and-green feather — check. At least I have that going for me. Monster is on his side, snoring. His muzzle is buried in the snow, and I wonder how he can even breathe. Madox is curled in a ball, snoozing between the bull and the bear. It's hard for me to look at him. Not because of what he did, but because I'm the one he did it for.

I search for our crew . . . for Mr. Larson. But he's gone because I opened my mouth. The last thing he said before he died was *Christina*. I don't know who she was to him, but I do know I'll say her name again when I kill the man who killed Mac Larson.

Or maybe I'll say Levi's name, the boy who died with a spear in his back. Or Jaxon, my friend who was eaten by sharks lured by their blood bags. Or maybe Harper's daughter, who died while her mother fought for her life. I used to be the girl who cataloged sandwich shops by which had the best oatmeal cookies. Now I'm the girl who catalogs death and the girl who vows revenge. The same girl who won't hesitate to lead the Pandoras, should the need arise again.

I find Rose in the snow and nudge her awake. She wraps her tail around me happily, and I try on a smile.

"Let's go wake the others, lizard. We can't waste time."

I head toward Harper with the iguana following me and stop when I spot V-5. The alligator has a red spray-paint stripe on his back that matches Rose's, but otherwise he looks to be okay. They sent him here. Why? Did they think he was mine? Instead of questioning it further, I take it as a stroke of luck.

"Hey, there." I run my gloved hand over his back until he wakes. "It's okay. I'm going to watch after you. You're safe, alligator." I pause, debating. "You're safe, *Oz*."

The alligator turns his reptilian head toward my hand.

As more Contenders pull themselves up, I inspect our new landscape. Snow infects everything. It clings to the aspens and firs, making their boughs droop with the added weight. It piles in great heaps over boulders and dusts even the sunniest bits of the ground. I can't find a single place that isn't touched by snow, and even though I know it'll be a source of profound frustration over the next several days, I have to admit it's stunning.

There's something perfect about the mountain's being the last leg of the race. It's a physical analogy of how far we've come. The peak offers a promise, a reward of sorts. In our eagerness to win, we all believe we can reach it first. I can almost see my brother standing at the top, his boots planted firmly in the snow. Maybe he'll be wearing his lopsided grin when I get there. Maybe he'll give me one of his rare hugs where he lifts me off the ground and groans about the weight. Or maybe he'll cry and call me Telly and say he already feels better knowing how hard I've fought to save him.

Three paths cut away from where we were dropped and climb into the mountains. As it is now, we stand on an incline, but it isn't terribly steep. Snow falls softly to the ground, but it's the cotton-candy kind that will melt as the sun burns down. From inspecting the sky, I guess it to be early evening, and it worries me that it'll get colder as the day expires. Because the cold — it is all encompassing. Already, it clouds my thoughts and has me anxious to search for cover.

I can't believe I thought it was cold in the ocean. That was nothing. That was a stroll down Rodeo Drive on a warm spring day. This is the epitome of freezing. What skin I can see on the other Contenders is tinged blue; my own teeth chatter; and my entire body shakes from lack of warmth. The more awake I become, the more aware I am, and the worse it becomes.

I evaluate my clothing: long underwear on top and bottom, turtleneck, stocking cap, wool socks, and insulated jacket, pants, boots, and climbing gloves. I feel stiff in all these layers, but I'm thankful for their protection from the elements.

"They left us in the snow." Harper stares at me like I'm supposed to offer an explanation for this. I try to give her one.

"They don't care if we die at this point."

Cotton paces over. His eyes linger on Harper for a moment longer than is natural. Of course, he looks at me the same way. I still don't know what his deal is, but right now all I care about is finding a way out of this cold.

I scan the area until I find Olivia and then pull her to her feet. I do the same for Guy and Braun and even Willow, because I remember Guy once saying something about keeping worrisome people in sight.

There are packs on the ground, as there were in the desert, and we each pull one on. A man twice my age grabs three packs and races out of view. He's not waiting for the woman from the device for permission to get started. I don't blame him for that, but I do despise him for stealing other Contenders' resources. I want to make like the guy and run straightaway, but there's racing quickly and racing smart, and I intend to do both.

It isn't long before Guy, Harper, Cotton, Braun, Olivia, and I are all in cahoots. Willow hovers close, but not too close. I'm not sure whether she'll travel with us, and I'm not sure I care, though I do hate that she'd be trekking through the mountains without a Pandora, and it still makes me sick remembering how her white rat died.

As if M-4 reads my mind, he noses my left hand. It's the first time the animal has ever approached me, and I don't take the gesture lightly. Bending over, I lay my head against his cold fur and run all ten fingers through his mane. When I've got him purring up a storm, I raise my head. Guy is watching me, a goofy half smile on his face.

I step back from M-4. "What?"

His smile vanishes, and he shakes his head. I've caught the Green Beret looking happy, and to him, nothing could be so embarrassing. "We should get going. Now."

Harper and Cotton discuss which path may be best, but I interrupt them both.

"No, we wait until the message comes over the device. Then we decide what course of action to take." I meet Guy's gaze, daring him to challenge me. Snow drifts lightly over his strong shoulders, his dark hair. In his navy jacket, with the fur-lined hood, and his heavy, black snow boots, he looks like a Russian soldier. Guy's eyes have always been a cold, hard blue. But right now, against the wintry backdrop, they appear almost lethal.

I want him to touch me so badly, I can practically feel his skin on mine.

I want to touch him so badly, I could scream.

Guy tugs at his gloves. "Okay, we wait."

It doesn't take long, but by the time the device starts blinking, half the Contenders have gone and electricity is coursing through my veins.

As I listen to the static, followed by the familiar clicking, I can't help remembering the first time I put this white device in my ear. I stood in my room, empty blue box in my hand, and listened as a voice I didn't recognize told me I was invited to join the Brimstone Bleed. *"All Contenders must report within forty-eight hours to select their Pandora companions. . . . The Pandora Selection Process will take place at the Old Red Museum,"* she'd said. I arrived in time, but it was Guy who showed me where the last egg lay hidden with a subtle flick of his eyes. Even then he was my protector.

I don't need him the way I once did. But it's hard not to *want* him when it was he who gave me my small black fox.

The message begins, and my mind returns to the present.

"If you're hearing this message, you have officially reached the final leg of the Brimstone Bleed. We want to congratulate each and every one of you for making it this far. One hundred and twenty-two people joined the race, and today, forty-one continue. Some of you have been granted a twenty-four-hour head start. Please use this to your advantage, and remember that this time, there is no deadline for reaching base camp. One person will win the Cure to save their loved one's life, and the rest of you will be located and returned home."

I trace the serpent outline embroidered on my jacket and listen to the woman spill her lies.

"The flags will be your most loyal friends during this leg of the race,

pointing you toward safety and success. All you have to do is follow them quickly, and the prize is yours."

I can hear the woman lick her lips. I imagine they look like two pink slugs.

"For the last and final time, Contenders of the Brimstone Bleed —

"Go!"

CHAPTER FORTY-TWO

Contenders tuck their devices away and race up one of the three paths. As for me, I pull my gray-and-orange pack higher on my back and stay rooted in place. Our group needs to discuss how long we'll travel together and what everyone's ultimate goal is, but that's a conversation we can have once we find shelter. "We shouldn't follow the paths."

Olivia grabs hold of her elephant's ear for balance in the snow. "I agree. It's too obvious."

"The woman said the flags will be our friends. Not that we can trust everything they say, but so far that, at least, has been true. If the flags are the only thing we should rely on, then we can assume the paths are a diversion." I turn away from the paths, toward virgin snow and uneven terrain. "Let's head this way."

Guy lifts his legs high and calls for M-4 to keep up. I'm so happy he's following my direction, I could hug him. And kiss him. And maybe have a full-on fantasy that involves chocolate-covered strawberries and Guy in swim trunks.

The image of Mr. Larson lying on his back, lifeless, rushes into my mind, and I want to berate myself for feeling any joy at all. Not when he's gone. And not when Jaxon isn't here to hit on Harper and crack jokes.

Olivia tries walking next to Harper, but Harper falls back like she doesn't want to be anywhere near the girl. Their silent exchange reminds me — I spin around and spot Willow standing alone, her bottom lip trembling. She's trying hard to pretend she doesn't care that we're leaving her, but for once her emotions show through that facade. Willow splits herself between being a fierce competitor and pretending to be weak to garner help. But right now she looks like what she is — an agonizingly young girl who doesn't want to be left behind.

I stop and throw my arms up as if I'm frustrated, though I'm anything but. "Willow, get your ass moving. I want you at my side with your eyes on the perimeter."

When she doesn't move, I yell once more.

"I said, *Let's go!*"

She jogs forward, stumbling once in the foot-deep snow. When she catches up, Harper stops the girl in her tracks and hugs her quickly. I'm not sure why Harper wasn't the one to ensure she came along. Maybe she saw the way Willow looked at Guy last night, or maybe she's also wondered what happened in the ocean between her and Olivia after I told her about it.

Once Harper releases Willow, she shoves her toward me.

I point toward the alligator. "V-5 is your responsibility. I expect you to take good care of him. You can call him Oz if you want."

Willow's brow furrows. "I don't need you to feel sorry for me."

"Well, good," I say. "I don't."

Braun laughs under his breath, and I have to hide my own smile.

We move quickly and quietly, the promise of the Cure driving us forward faster than we've ever traveled before.

CHAPTER FORTY-THREE

During our brisk march, Madox shifts shapes to mimic Monster. Then he changes his mind and pulls on the bull's appearance. My fox, dressed as a bull, sidles up to Y-21, and when the real bull sees his mirror image, he tosses his head in surprise.

We get a kick out of this.

I pat Cotton's Pandora on the back. "It's a compliment, Y."

We pace for another two hours after that, before Harper has the idea to send her eagle searching for a flag. She explains what she wants, and the bird takes flight. Snow scrunches under our boots as we continue toward the closest sloping cliff face, where the trees thicken. My hope is to find a densely foliaged area where we can light a fire and explore the contents of our packs; let the trees catch the majority of the swirling wet flurries and hide our presence. Earlier, when I explained my plan to Guy, he pressed his lips together in thought. Since he continued our march toward the cliff, I knew he believed it was as good a plan as any.

We reach the cliff at nightfall, the brush becoming thicker with every step, and Harper's eagle returns. She isn't clutching a blue flag, but she does soar a few feet up the mountain and land somewhere out of sight.

"Where'd she go?" Olivia asks.

I gaze toward where I last saw the eagle, and my heart leaps in triumph when I spot what she's found. "It's a cave. RX-13 found a cave!"

Braun wraps his arms around himself, which is an impressive feat. "Can we make it up there?"

"We can," Guy responds.

Cotton eyes his bull. "What about our Pandoras?"

"They can, too." I'm bursting with relief and gratefulness for

Harper's eagle. I've experienced cold like this before in Boston and Montana both, but I'm not sure I've ever spent so many hours in it without a break. My lips are chapped, and my fingers burn, and pain nips at my entire body. It's only been three hours, and already this ecosystem has been the hardest. Of course, maybe I'm forgetting how bloody hot it was in the desert.

We ascend the mountain by marching back and forth along its belly like thread being pulled from a sweater. Before the last of the night crumbles away, we are standing outside the cave. It's deep and high and large enough so that we are all accommodated. There's a tiny part of me that says I don't do caves. That I need a vanilla soy latte and my leopard-print slippers, and where are my cute earmuffs? But that was Jungle Tella. Maybe Desert Tella.

And today I'm Mountain Tella.

So I go inside, and after gathering some branches outside the entrance, I have M-4 light a fire. The iguana glows, providing the lion light until he can get the wet sticks to catch. Finally, we settle along the ground and inspect our surroundings. The inside of the cave isn't black like I expected. It's more a medley of grays and browns and jutting, angular rock organs. The ground is uncomfortable, and the entire thing smells like wet dog. It is . . . spectacular. I decide Mountain Tella is pretty cool. She sleeps in caves, which is fierce and totally something I could blog about one day. Or maybe vlog if I'm feeling saucy.

The fire crackles to life, and we push toward one another like pieces of a stinky, weather-beaten puzzle. I squish in between Guy and Harper, my two people. Monster plops down behind me, and I lean against his girth, running my fingers through his coat. Madox climbs into my lap and lays his head on my knee. I hesitate only a moment before pulling him closer. Guy's lion and Cotton's bull lean against each other with obvious distaste but for warmth's sake, and Willow lies back on Oz's alligator tail, with

Rose snuggled nearby. The eagle perches on the elephant's back, and for once, the elephant doesn't knock the bird off with her trunk as she has in the past.

We are all accounted for. Except that we're not.

As the fire warms our weary bones, Harper retrieves her pack and drags it into her lap. She unzips it, and we all stare to see what she discovers. Because of the cold and our late start, we opted to wait until dark before exploring our packs. We knew more than anything that we needed to keep our bodies moving and to find cover before the sun set. But now the packs have our full attention.

Harper digs her hand inside and produces a handful of brown crumpled paper.

Olivia cocks her head and bites her bottom lip. "Oh, I know. For lighting fires."

When Harper unfolds the papers and doesn't find anything written on them, we decide Olivia is right. For many Contenders, this will be a godsend. We have a lion that can light wet wood, but if we didn't, this dry paper could be the difference between life and death.

Braun elbows Harper. "Keep going, Barbie."

Harper grimaces and then reaches in a second time. She discovers more brown paper and tosses it to the floor with the rest. The third time she pulls out brown paper, my stomach sinks.

Harper pulls the paper out faster and faster, fistfuls of the stuff flying out until she's growling with rage. Finally, she gets to the bottom. I scarcely breathe, wondering what might lie there. Harper ducks her head in and stares as blood throbs inside my ears. When her head falls back and her eyes squeeze closed, I know what she's found isn't good. "They stuffed the bags with paper and rocks."

The rest of us grab our packs at once. We unzip them and shove our arms inside. When we find the same things Harper did, Cotton gets to his feet and races toward the cave entrance.

Then he drops the bag midstride and punts it like this is the freaking NFL. He stands panting at the mouth of the cave, his hands clenched.

When he turns back around, Guy says simply, "Nice kick."

Olivia's face turns almost purple with excitement. "Hey, are you a Vikings fan? Blair Walsh kicks like he doesn't have a hip bone, right? Dude's amazing!"

I giggle, and Cotton points at me as if this is my fault. "This isn't a joke."

"Everything's a joke," Harper says, exasperated.

"How can you guys do this?" Cotton paces back and forth. "How can you act like everything is okay when these people are doing everything they can to break us? Haven't you noticed things have gotten worse since the ocean race started? Every single day, worse! Sometimes I don't even know if they want us to survive at all."

Braun stands up, walks over to Cotton, and puts a hand on his shoulder. "It's okay," he says. "I understand. You're from Minnesota. I'd be angry, too, if my team hadn't gone to the Super Bowl since the seventies."

Cotton jerks back but smiles despite himself. "I'm from Pittsburgh, dick."

"Jesus H. Christ," Guy pipes in. "The Steelers are the worst."

"You want to say that to my face?" Cotton says.

Guy cracks his knuckles absently. "Think I just did."

The guys are having a good time, and I want them to — we desperately need it — but the way he said . . .

I stand up. "Cotton? What about the jungle?"

He shrugs. "What about it?"

"What about how hard it was there?"

He doesn't reply.

"How about the desert, then? What do you think was the worst part about the desert?"

"The heat."

"But what about the flags? Don't you think it's odd that they changed color for the desert portion only? They were trying to rattle us then, too."

"What's your problem, Tella?" Cotton strides toward me, and Guy stands up.

"Answer the question," I say.

"Yeah, it was odd. Who cares? We're here now, aren't we? Why the hell are you in my face?"

"Enough." Guy steps between us, but it's not me he glares at. "Go blow off some steam, Cotton."

"But I'm not —"

"Go. Now."

Cotton storms past our group and disappears down the guts of the cave until he's completely out of sight. With Cotton gone, Guy turns on the rest of us. "Not a word. Discuss something else. We don't need to be at each other's throats. Not now. Not when we're so close."

I hear what he's saying, but his face holds a different message. He understands what happened, what Cotton just admitted. He doesn't want Willow finding out something we don't want her to know.

The desert flags were blue as all the others have been, but Cotton agreed with my lie. Harper's stiff spine tells me she picked up on everything, and Olivia is glancing back and forth at all of us, confused but not opening her mouth. But we all know this:

Cotton never competed in the first half of the race.

CHAPTER FORTY-FOUR

When I wake in the middle of the night, Cotton still hasn't returned and Guy is keeping watch. My eyelids feel weighted, but I've opened them far enough to see that Guy is sitting beside me, his body curved toward mine like a human shield. He's staring into the dying fire and chewing on the inside of his cheek.

The hood of his jacket is pulled up around his head, and the fire casts shadows over his angular features. Everything about his face — his harsh, deep-set eyes, his strong jaw, the scar cutting through a dark eyebrow — they come together like an artist's capturing of crude, raw masculinity.

He sees me watching. He bends to kiss my forehead. His lips linger there, and the warmth of them is so delicious, I forget to breathe. He smells like nice, safe things: campfire smoke and snow-covered cedars. But his body looks fatal.

His lips leave my skin, and his voice is rough when he speaks. "Go back to sleep."

And so I do.

CHAPTER FORTY-FIVE

We send RX-13 and Madox dressed as an eagle out the next morning to hunt for food. They return later with game to eat, which is exciting enough, but in their clutches is something even better: a flag. I consider asking them to return it so other Contenders don't lose their way and die in the cold. But this is the last leg of the race, and I have to remember that my brother's life is at stake.

Later, as we eat our breakfast in a rush — three chipmunks and two squirrels skinned and smoked over a fire — Cotton turns the flag over in his hands. "I don't remember much of the first two legs of the race," he says suddenly. "I didn't want anyone to know."

Guy wipes his mouth with the back of his hand. "Why?"

"Why didn't I want anyone to know?"

"Why don't you remember?"

Cotton stares down at the flag. He shakes his head.

"You don't remember anything?" Harper pulls her knees to her chest as she asks this, and even I can hear the doubt in her voice.

"I remember the heat, and I remember the boxes they put us in before we started the race." Cotton lifts his pointer finger as if something else has occurred to him. "And I remember the sounds in the jungle."

"They never stopped," Olivia offers.

A corner of Cotton's mouth tugs into a smile as he touches a hand to the back of his black hair. "I found a lump. I think I may have hit my head."

I get to my feet and walk to where he sits. "May I?"

He lowers his head, and I part his hair. When I find a bump at the base of his scalp, I know he's telling the truth, but that doesn't prove he was present for the first half of the race or that he had memory loss. Even the things he said he does remember — the heat, the boxes, the unending sounds in the jungle — he could have overheard us talking about them. Didn't we mention as much on the sailboat?

I decide to let it go for now. Once we find a pattern to the flags, we'll have every reason to part ways. For now I don't want a potential enemy on our tail. "I believe you."

He glances up, his brown eyes heavy with longing. "You should."

Olivia gathers snow from outside the cave and throws fistfuls of it over the embers as if the conversation is settled. Taking a cue from the girl, Guy stands and straps his empty pack onto his back. I sigh and reach my hand out to Cotton. He takes it and pulls himself up.

As I start to turn away, he says, "It would weird me out, too. If one of you said you didn't remember, I would think it was weird."

For some reason, his stating the obvious makes me feel better, but I decide it's still best to remain on guard. Harper crosses the distance between us, and Cotton watches every move she makes. "When should we leave?" she asks.

With our bodies no longer huddled together, I shiver. Last night, I slept like the dead, but this morning, I'm colder than I ever imagined possible. My body hurts from head to foot. I cringe as I gaze into the colorless purgatory outside the cave, even as I hear myself, Mountain Tella, say, "We're heading out now."

CHAPTER FORTY-SIX

Harper's eagle leads the way, and the rest of us follow along at a fast pace. I keep a close eye on Rose, since she's the smallest and slowest of the Pandoras, but I'm not nearly as protective as Guy is with his lion. I guess like the rest of us, he's afraid of losing his edge so close to the finish line.

Plowing through the snow, Guy looks like a man made of steel. He seems to have regained his stamina and some weight while at the ocean base camp. That's how quickly he recuperates. His body is like a kudzu vine; cut him down, and he comes back faster, stronger.

I blush, remembering the kiss he laid on my forehead last night.

Guy wouldn't ever read sonnets to me or suggest we take a picnic at Crane Beach, but he does other things, *better* things. He makes me feel beautiful with cropped hair and dirt smudged across my skin. He stands close when I'm afraid, and leaves me be when I can stand on my own. He believes I'm strong, even if it took some time for him to respect that. And he allows me to lead when I know he could do a better job himself.

Guy is strong, courageous, unbreakable.

But even he experiences fear. I saw it in the jungle when I jumped into the river to save Caroline, and I saw it in the desert when he saved me from Titus. I saw it when he told me about his plan to destroy the race, and I saw it on the beach when he knelt before me in the sand.

I saw that fear when I told him I was here for my brother and not him.

And I saw it last night when he lowered his lips to my skin, his head bending quickly so as to avoid rejection.

I am afraid of everything — of the chimps in the jungle, of the Triggers who stalked me in the desert, of the little boy who turned out to be a Pandora, of the sharks that took Jaxon from me in the ocean, and of the wretched cold that endangers my spirit with every step. I'm afraid of losing the Brimstone Bleed, of killing my brother because I've failed, of what's at the top of this mountain, of the cackling sound in the towering trees.

But Guy Chambers is afraid, too.

He's afraid of me.

Harper's eagle roller coasters in the sky, her excitement growing as we march nearer to the place where she spotted the flag. RX-13 hasn't found a single flag during this entire race until now, and I think it's disappointed Harper. It may have disappointed me, too. If I had a bald eagle Pandora — and I guess I do, in a way, because of Madox's ability — I'd expect it to spot every flag within a hundred-mile radius. But I suppose an eagle's vision relies on sudden movements, and so far the flags have been heavy, limp things that don't scurry like prey would. This time, she's found it, though, and she's all too eager to please her Contender.

Willow and Olivia walk directly ahead of me because they have the youngest eyes and can spot pitfalls before they become a problem.

Because they're the youngest, and I want to ensure they're safe.

Monster plods by my side, delighted to have my full attention. Madox and Y-21 stride ahead of us all, and once again, Madox has pulled on the bull's appearance. The real bull doesn't knock the fox-bull aside as he sometimes does, and I may be wrong, but it seems like Y is enjoying his traveling companion. Or maybe *tolerating* is a better word.

The grizzly bear keeps watch over my fox the same way I do. Sometimes I think of Monster as a gentle, quiet father figure to

Madox. Monster is Madox's safe place, the Pandora he most often curls up next to when the sun is MIA. But Y-21 is new and shiny, and the older brother Madox strives to emulate. I wish Madox were more entranced by M-4, a Pandora whose Contender I feel comfortable with, but I guess you can't pick your Pandora's playmates.

Harper comes to walk by my side. "We're almost there."

"Yeah, you'd think it's mating season from her performance up there."

Harper laughs, and as she does, the snow falls faster, as if she somehow beckoned it by smiling. The sky looks bloated, and I curse myself for not paying attention to my surroundings. Of course, it's hard to do anything besides put one foot in front of the other in this weather.

Now that I'm paying attention, I realize I no longer hear birds' raucous calls or the sound of nails scuttling across bark. The world has fallen still, and I've learned that nothing good happens in silence. Not when you're a Contender in the Brimstone Bleed.

I turn to Guy. "It's too quiet."

He stops and listens as if he was lost in his own head, too. His brow furrows, and he opens his hands, palms up. When he glances at the sky and then back at me, his face tells me my suspicions aren't unfounded.

Braun grabs his right ankle and bends his leg behind his body in a stretch. "What's going on? Why are we stopping?"

"There's a storm coming," Guy says simply, since a storm is no bother to a man made of steel.

"Should we go back to the cave?" Cotton asks.

"There may not be enough time."

A shiver trickles down my spine as I hear his response. At the same time, I inspect our surroundings. Yes, the snow is falling faster, and, yes, the sky is darker, but we're too close to stop now.

"Let's push onward," I say. "We need to pinpoint the flag's location."

Guy straightens, his posture defiant. "No, we have to seek shelter immediately."

"You said there may not be enough time to return to the cave. Besides, we have as much chance of finding shelter ahead as we do by turning back."

"We should spread out," Guy says.

"We're staying together," I retort.

Harper touches my elbow. "Maybe we should do what he says."

I glare at her. "Maybe *you* should do what he says. I'm following RX-13. I'll use Madox if I have to."

Harper grabs the back of my neck and pushes our foreheads together. "Don't snap at me, bitch. I'm here to make sure you win, remember?"

I can't help smiling, not when our faces are so close that her two eyes merge into one, making her look like a Cyclops. "I'm really cold."

"My nipples are frozen," she whispers.

I pull back and bark with laughter. Guy, Braun, and Cotton eye us as if we're nuts, and Olivia and Willow stand staring. I point at the two young girls. "You guys look like Smurfs. You're almost blue."

Harper actually slaps her knee and laughs even harder.

"The weather is making you two mean," Braun says.

Cotton shakes his head. "My sister was like that. Nice one moment, banshee crazy the next. I think it's hormones."

I stop laughing when I notice Madox's back is nearly white from snow. Regardless of what decision we make, we're wasting time. "Let's go. We keep heading toward the flag. I want everyone looking for shelter as we travel."

"Shall we bow to you as we walk, Queen Tinker Bell?" Braun mocks me, but I detect the relief in his voice. It used to be me teasing Guy over his militaristic orders and ultra-seriousness. When we were creating a raft to float down the jungle river, we all mocked Guy's soberness and Harper even shook her butt at him. But deep down, we were thankful that he had answers. We knew he may not be right every time, but he made concrete decisions, and that enabled the rest of us to relax.

Now I'm the one allowing others that same relief. The question is *Should they trust me?* My eyes slide upward toward the mountaintop. Though there are dozens of hills and valleys, the tallest mountain looms over us like a giant from a fairy tale, jagged teeth set in a permanent under bite. I have no doubt it's where every Contender is headed.

I forge ahead, and when I glance over my shoulder, I notice the Contenders and Pandoras following. Guy's lion trails behind, stumbling over his feet. It isn't like him. Every couple of steps, EV-0 raises her trunk and taps the lion's rear to keep him moving.

I turn back to the mountain, tug my jacket tighter, and push onward. When the snow starts to fall even harder, whipping across my field of vision with disorienting fury, I begin to wonder if I've made a terrible mistake.

CHAPTER FORTY-SEVEN

The wind howls, and the snow falls in such abundance that I can barely see twenty feet ahead, which makes searching for shelter difficult. RX-13 takes to the ground and walks with open wings, occasionally hopping along to keep pace. She wants us to make it to her prize every bit as much as I do, and for that I'm thankful.

Each step I take sinks through a foot of snow, whereas before it was half as much. I can't understand how it's deepened so fast . . . but remembering the river rising from the rain in the jungle, maybe I can.

Even though my hands are wrapped in insulated gloves, I can still feel the cold eating away at my flesh like a brown recluse spider bite. My hood does little to block the frost clinging to my ears and lips and nose, and even our Pandoras moan with distress.

I move faster, urging the eagle to pick up her speed.

And then I see the flagstaff.

It stands out among the tall, spindly trees like a Persian cat among a pack of thieves. The pole is roughly ten feet in height, made of smooth, unpolished wood, and there's something on it that shouldn't be there — another flag.

The flag is attached at the very top, stiff and blue, tip pointing directly to the right. The eagle must have accidentally stumbled along a second flagstaff. But, no, RX-13 is flapping her wings and screeching with pride. Harper pats her Pandora on the head, and as the snow rushes down thicker and faster, I contemplate why there were two flags on this pole.

I wave Guy over and yell above the whistling wind. "Maybe it's pointing to the next flag location."

He shakes his head, not convinced.

I don't know what else to do. So I spin in a circle and memorize the area. I spot a tree that doesn't look like the rest. It's covered in something that resembles black tar, and will serve as a landmark so that I can ensure we're in the same place should we return. I motion for the others to survey their surroundings, too. Then I glance at the flag once more.

This is the only ecosystem in which all remaining Contenders could easily die within forty-eight hours. Every race leg has had its own challenges, but even in the desert, the night brought relief. Here, the night brings only colder temperatures and probably predatory animals. They wouldn't bring us all this way to let us die like this. It's not nearly climactic enough.

There were two flags on this pole. One to tell us we're headed in the right direction, and a second . . .

The flags will be your most loyal friends during this leg of the race, pointing you toward safety and success.

And a second to lead us to safety. I have no idea if what I'm doing is right, but I have no time to second-guess my decision. Not when the snow is suffocating, and not when I'm confusing which direction we even came from.

I mimic the flag and point east, farther up the mountain. "We go that way." Without waiting for a response, I tap Madox on his bull back and cock my chin forward. He strides forward with renewed vigor.

Within minutes after leaving the staff, I believe with all my heart that we're going to die. My pulse doesn't race. In fact, I can hardly sense the dull beat inside my chest. My body threatens to collapse at any minute, and my field of vision has been reduced to ten feet. The snow rises to my knees, and I wonder how much longer it'll be until we're drowning in the freezing powder.

It seems the mountain itself is made of snow. There are no trees, no ground, no animals that call this mountain home. It's only snow and more snow and a promise of death. One day, our bodies will disintegrate, and we'll become snow, too. Maybe that's all this mountain is: one great, big pile of Contenders who never made it.

I shake the morbid thought from my mind and stride forward. Deciding I must do something, I call for M-4 to lead the way. He trots ahead immediately and blows rounds of fire toward the ground as we walk. The snow melts a marginal amount for the rest of us to trudge through. I align EV-0 directly behind the lion so that her girth cuts a path. Then come Madox and Monster, with their sturdy bodies, then the alligator, eagle, and iguana, and then us. We take hands under my instruction so we don't lose anyone in our quest to find refuge.

"Stop," Harper calls out. "Willow fell."

Braun, who is directly behind me, releases my hand.

"No, don't let go of each other," I holler.

Immediately, I feel Braun's baseball glove of a hand grab mine.

I can't see far enough back to know what's happened, but after a few seconds, I hear Harper's voice ring out again. "Okay, keep going!"

The fear in her voice drives me onward, and I bring my knees up high as I walk like Guy taught me to do in the jungle. Except this time, it isn't to avoid being heard so much as it is to avoid being swallowed by the snow.

M-4 releases a ball of fire, and even though fatigue makes it much smaller than his previous ones, it's enough to spot what's ahead. A dark, solid shadow looms above our heads like an alien ship touching down. But it isn't a ship.

It's a house.

Okay, it's a tiny, one-story cabin that looks like it was built by the League of Unextraordinary Senior Citizens. There are no windows and no peaks, just a mud-and-lumber hut with a tin roof and single door. Still, it's shelter.

We rush toward it as if there's a sharpshooter aiming for our hungry, bony asses. I push open the door, and the Pandoras become a living bulldozer. Guy jerks me out of the way before I'm pulverized by the Pandora stampede, and then we follow them inside.

"Real nice," Olivia says to her elephant, which more or less destroyed the doorframe. "Way to leave us in the cold. I see how it is."

I'd laugh, but I'm afraid my lips are frozen together.

The inside has no furniture to speak of, only wooden floors and stale air. Cotton walks into the cabin's interior, leaves down a short hallway to a single bedroom in the back, returns. "How will we get warm?"

"It's not like we were warm in the cave," Harper says.

Willow clings to Harper, who I think carried her after she fell. "Warmer than this. How cold does it have to be to get frostbite?"

Olivia stares at the two girls with obvious jealousy before turning her face away. "They don't want us to be warm. I'm not even sure they want us to live."

"They do want us to live," I say suddenly. "At least, someone out there does."

I have their attention.

"What do you mean?" Guy asks.

I hesitate. He hasn't wanted to share his insights into the race, his plans. But as he works with Braun to push the door back into place and Willow pulls Harper to the floor beside her, I decide we're in this together. At this point, I'm not sure who wouldn't suspect that the people running this race are doing much more than simply providing a Cure.

So I tell everyone what Guy told me — Cotton and Willow, too, this time — and I also add something fresh to the mix. I tell them our plan to infiltrate headquarters and destroy the race forever. To his credit, Guy never interrupts or even looks at me with disapproval, and the Contenders seem eager when I discuss what we'll do at the close of the Brimstone Bleed. When I'm done telling the full story, I end with my newest discovery.

After I explain my theory, everyone gazes at their wristbands.

"What does green mean?" Harper asks, alarm coloring her voice.

"Screw that." Braun stands up. "Why did they change my color from green to blue? Did they think I was doing better or worse?"

"You lost your Pandora," Cotton offers.

Braun runs his hands over his head. "So . . . worse. I'm now in the worst category."

"Hey, watch it!" Olivia points to her own blue wristband.

"You don't know blue is the worst," Harper says. "Maybe orange is the bottom."

Olivia laughs. "So that means they're betting on people like Guy and Cotton losing? Yeah, freaking right."

"Mine is orange, too," Willow declares, her tone defensive.

Guy stares at my red wristband. It isn't long before the others follow his gaze.

Cotton states the obvious. "Yours is the only one that's red, Tella."

"What color was Mr. Larson's?" Willow interrupts.

No one answers her, but I understand what she's implying.

"Wasn't it orange, too?" Braun asks. We avoid looking at him, though I can still see his face fall when he remembers. "No, it was blue, huh?"

"I don't know why you're acting so offended." Olivia pushes her face into her elephant's side. When she speaks again, her words are muffled. "I was blue from the very beginning."

It's quiet for a long time before Cotton suddenly asks, "Is that why they let Harper come back? So they didn't lose a Contender they had bets on?"

No one speaks for the next few minutes. I'm not sure we have an answer.

Or perhaps we do, but it's too awful to think about.

CHAPTER FORTY-EIGHT

Through the cracks around the door, we can tell that the sun has fallen. Either that or the snow is deep enough that it's blocked out the light. It's a horrible thought, and I find my throat constricting, thinking about being trapped underground. The only way we can see anything at all is courtesy of Rose, who glows like a lightning bug on a hot summer night.

Harper rubs her gloved hands over her arms. "We're going to freeze to death. We need a fire."

"There's nothing to burn," Cotton replies.

Harper narrows her gaze. "Was I talking to you?"

Cotton grins and inspects his hands.

"What's so funny?"

He shakes his head, a smile still dangling from his lips.

"He's right," Guy interjects. "There's nothing to burn, and we can't go outside. Not in this weather. We should have kept the paper in the backpacks."

We turn this over in our minds until I have a thought. "Remember in the desert, when we asked our Pandoras for help? We might never have realized that Olivia's elephant could pull water from the ground if Olivia hadn't made it known that she needed help surviving."

"Shouldn't they know to help?" Cotton asks. "I mean, sometimes they help without us asking."

"They're animals," Braun offers. "Maybe they only know to help when it's obvious something is very wrong, like when Caroline fell into the river and Dink dove in to save her."

Olivia shivers. "Please don't mention Dink."

"Who's Dink?" Willow asks.

Olivia glares at the younger girl.

"Everyone, ask your Pandora for help," I say. "Tell them you're too cold and that you're afraid you'll die without their help."

All the Contenders do exactly as I instructed, myself included. In response to my plea, Monster moves closer and collapses next to my body. He then immediately returns to sleep. Madox mimics Monster's bear form and lies on the other side of my body. Most of the other Pandoras do the same thing, squeezing next to their Contenders to provide body heat. Guy's lion breathes fire a few times, but everyone agrees it's too dangerous. We're not sure the cabin could catch fire in this weather, but if it did, we'd die.

I glance around. We're huddled together as tightly as we can, but it's not enough. I spot the alligator lying a few feet away from the circle. He's hardly moving, and I know that even with his thick reptilian skin he must be freezing.

"Oz, get closer to the group." My teeth chatter so hard, I can barely speak.

"Leave him over there," Willow says, as if she's bored. "He holds up the group when we walk, and he has no abilities. We don't need him."

The disappointment in her voice is bottomless. I wonder how many times she's whispered for him to unveil his abilities over the last thirty-six hours and been frustrated when he didn't respond.

I climb to my feet, and I swear I hear my bones crackle the same way ice would in a warm glass of water. "Just because a Pandora doesn't display abilities doesn't mean they're dispensable. Do you understand me, Willow?"

She rolls her eyes.

"Answer me."

Willow bites down and diverts her gaze.

Harper stares at the girl with an unreadable look on her face. "Answer her."

"Fine, I understand!"

I stride toward the alligator and sit on the floor next to him. The Pandora doesn't move. "Why don't you come lie in the circle with us?" I tell him. The alligator bends at the side and turns his front half away. As the memory of Mr. Larson dying presents itself, grief unfolds inside my body, battling the cold to deliver the most pain. "Do you miss your Contender?"

I can't fathom how misplaced I'd feel if Madox or Monster died. Even though Mr. Larson wasn't exactly a nurturing Contender, it must be dreadful for the alligator to lose his reason for existing inside this race.

Running my hand over the red spray-painted stripe along V-5's back, I say, "I think I'll lie with you for a while."

"Tella, you need to get back over here," Harper says.

Guy shifts near the circle of Contenders and Pandoras. "She's right. Come back."

I ignore their appeals and lie down next to V-5, wrapping my arm around his midsection and laying my head atop his back. I throw my right leg over his body and cuddle closer and realize, under no uncertain terms, that I'm spooning an alligator.

The reptile's body is bitterly cold and is leaching what little warmth I have left. But I won't leave him. I go to ask Cotton and Guy if maybe we can drag the Pandora toward our group, but when I turn my head, I spot Madox and Monster plodding toward me. They lie down, one on my side and one on the alligator's opposite side. Seconds later, Rose sashays over, her lengthy tail sliding across the wooden floor.

I smile to myself and thank God once again for these magnificent beasts. Then I tell the alligator, my voice a whisper, "Don't be afraid. I won't leave you."

"This is ridiculous." Olivia gets to her feet and marches toward our smaller huddle. She drops down beside Monster, and her Pandora follows after her, elephant back brushing the ceiling. I'm not sure who gets up next, but before I know it, we're all piled together, mere feet from where we once were. Except now we're sandwiched around one green alligator.

Ten minutes pass without anyone speaking a word. Finally, Willow says, "I never thought I could be so cold."

"I never knew cold could *hurt* this much," Braun adds.

I'm not sure what causes me to become so morose, but I sigh heavily and mutter, "I don't think I can live through this. Not unless I get warm."

V-5 shifts beneath me, and everyone groans at having to reposition themselves. I cling tighter to the alligator, and as I do, a strange sensation creeps across my skin. It feels like needles are being jabbed into every inch of my body. Or maybe it feels like a thousand yellow jackets stinging me at once. Take your pick. Either way, it's murderous. But then, suddenly, it's candy-apple sunshine. It's grape-flavored rain and clouds made of laughter, and I think . . . I think I feel warm!

Is this what happens before you croak? You get the warm fuzzies, and then you see the light at the end of the tunnel? If it is, I may not fight too hard on my way out.

I open one eyeball and slip off a glove.

"Put that back on," Guy says, ever protective, ever watchful.

Stalker.

I lay my hand against V-5 and feel him pressing back against my palm. In the last few minutes, the creature has nuzzled firmly against my body, and now I'm absolutely sure of the reason why.

The alligator is giving off heat.

"I'll admit it's warmer when we're all together like this," Cotton says. "But it's awkward as hell."

"No, it's not us." I grin until my cheeks twitch. "Oz is producing heat."

Harper scoffs, "Yeah, so are the rest of us."

Guy yanks off his glove and stretches over Olivia to touch the alligator's skin. He smiles, and fireworks burst in my chest. "He feels like a furnace."

Four more hands shoot across the space to see for themselves, and after they discover the same thing I have, the Contenders pat the alligator on the back and call him ol' buddy and ol' pal and rejoice that we're going to make it through the cold. Except for Willow, who pouts that she wasn't the one who made the discovery.

As my Contender friends celebrate our newfound luck, I lower my mouth to the alligator and whisper softly, "You saved me, Oz. Thank you."

The alligator sucks in a deep breath, his entire body filling with pride.

I lay my head on his and drape my arm over his wide neck. And as we fall asleep together, human and reptile, I find I'm brilliantly, wonderfully happy.

CHAPTER FORTY-NINE

When I wake, no one is keeping watch. I bolt upright, my body as hot as the desert sand. My eyes search the cabin and land on nothing in particular. Until I see him. He's sitting a short distance away, legs pulled up, thick forearms resting upon his knees. I can barely see him, save for the soft glow the iguana emits.

His fingers are clasped, and his head is heavy against his chest. When I get to my feet, his head pops up.

"I fell asleep," he whispers in apology.

I wave my hand. "We never assigned watch."

"It goes without saying."

I shake my head. "No, it doesn't. Why were you watching over us?"

"I wasn't." He stands, as if expecting something.

I swallow and stare at him in the dark, my entire body itching to feel his touch. When I see the anticipation in his stance, the way he looks at me as if I'm both infuriating and appealing — it makes me feel powerful. But when he takes a step in my direction, that power plummets to some place untouchable. Now I'm a seventeen-year-old girl again, standing in the shadows with someone who feels like he's lived three lives to my one.

"Come with me," he orders.

There's no room for refusal, and I don't want there to be. He takes my hand to help me step over sleeping bodies, both human and Pandora. When I stumble, he leans over and sweeps himself beneath my knees and arms. I'm brought into his arms with the same ease I may use to curl a rabbit to my chest. But I'm not such an innocent, silent creature.

I've got spirit and fire in spades. Though, right now, as he carries me to the single back bedroom, I have neither. I'm somebody else now. I'm Tella Holloway, Boston girl turned Montana transplant, sitting on the edge of her queen-size bed, awaiting her very first date with the boy who makes her parents uneasy. A boy who doesn't speak nearly enough, but when he does, this girl stops and listens. In my mind's eye, I'm wearing the silver-sequined dress that's hibernated in my closet far too long. I feel beautiful and confident, and who cares if he said we're going to the lake at night? I want to glimpse the look on his face when he sees me. I envision how his entire face will light up as if it's lit from within. How his full lips will part slightly and his cold blue eyes will soften.

Guy sets me on my feet, and I gaze up at him.

Oh yes. Right there. That's the look I imagined.

There's no door to this room. No bed, no nightstand, no sequined dress. But he's here. Guy raises his hand to my feather. His fingers brush over the blue and green bristles with tenderness. He inspects it closely, eyeing the muddied, stiff ornament that was once lovely. Now the string it hangs from is in tatters, and the feather itself appears almost blackened with rain and sand, salt and snow. It's horribly ugly, and quite frankly, it smells.

But somehow, it's even better than it was before.

He drops the feather to my shoulder, and his arms come to rest by his sides. When he doesn't say anything, I ask, "Why did you bring me back here?"

He shrugs one shoulder.

I turn away from him, hurt by this sudden detachment.

"You always had it in you to win," he says quietly. "I just forgot."

"You believe that?"

He circles around me and takes my chin in his hand. It takes him a long time to vocalize what he has on his mind. It's always hard for him to put into words what he's thinking. But finally, he says, "I thought you would win this race the moment I first saw you. I watched, you know? When you fought that girl on the ground for the last Pandora egg? When you cut your hair off in the front seat of that car? I watched you." He raises his face to the ceiling, and his throat works. "I saw this blinding life in you, Tella. I knew then that you'd battle fiercely to win. But I also knew that you were kind and that you'd care too much about the other Contenders." Guy shakes his head. "You shouldn't open yourself up so much."

"It's okay to care about other people," I say.

He shakes his head. "Not here."

"Anywhere."

"The Pandoras were prepared to fight for you at base camp." He shakes his head, befuddled. "You've changed everything. You're not the only one who's divided. Many enter the race conflicted. One side of them says to remember their humanity, the other side says to become an animal, to live and breathe only to win the Cure. I thought you'd go one way or the other, just like the rest." Guy looks down at me. "But you're still fighting like a soldier and trying to protect everyone along the way, too. Don't you understand that you can't do both? You can't keep worrying about other Contenders. And you certainly can't keep worrying about the Pandoras."

"Yes, I can."

He grabs his mangled left earlobe, and his brow furrows.

"You know, it's okay to do things differently than the way you first set out to do them," I say. "And it *is* okay to care about people during this race, Guy. It's okay to be afraid of losing those people, too." I take a small step toward him. "It's even okay to stay up at night, watching over them, just to ensure they're safe."

His jaw tightens. "I only care about getting inside this race. That's *all* I can do."

I place a hand on his chest, and he stares down at the place where I touch him. "You don't have to be the thing your father taught you to be."

His eyes snap to mine.

"It's okay to admit you've fallen from the narrow, vengeful path you started down." I wet my lips and bring my voice to just above a whisper. "It's okay to admit you've fallen."

His hands grasp my face.

His lips crash over mine.

He lifts me up, and now I'm the one falling, falling.

My feet touch the ground softly. His hands grasp my back hard. He bends over me, and I bend with him. My concerns slip away every time he whispers my name against his lips, every time I feel the urgency of his embrace pulling me closer. Too close, maybe. Close enough so that he can lose himself in this moment.

I don't care.

I'm losing myself, too.

I don't want to be me anymore. I want to be me with him. I want to hand my heart to the guy who showed me the last Pandora egg, who didn't walk too quickly in the jungle so that the girl with the feather could follow him. The guy who kissed me at the jungle base camp, who held me when I got a letter from Cody and told me his cousin loved the smell of lemon. The person who saved me from Titus, who put salve on my skin where a leech had bitten me, who appeared from the ocean like a ghost and fell to his knees, who told me his secrets and believed I was strong, and who is too afraid to say the words you can't take back because his father tried to make him into a machine.

Our lips break apart, and we gasp for breath. My mind spins, and my body aches to be closer to him still.

"Tell me," I whisper. "Say it."

He turns his face to the side. I turn it back.

"You don't have to go this race alone, Guy Chambers. You opened up to me before. Do it again. Admit you care. Say how you feel. Say it outright."

He clenches his eyes shut, and his entire face pulls together as if pained.

"Tell me," I say again, even softer.

He releases me, and the hurt I feel is unique in its own right. It could stand against any obstacle I've withstood inside the Brimstone Bleed.

"If you don't tell me how you feel," I say, my voice shaking, "then I won't know. It's that simple." I consider telling him what's in my heart, but I pull the words back down my throat. He doesn't want to hear it.

I turn and walk away.

"Tella," he says, but he's not saying my name to stop me, only to will me to understand.

I keep walking.

When I get into the main room, I find something that causes my steps to falter. Cotton is sleeping behind Harper, one hand beneath her head, the other stroking her blond hair. He glances up at me, and his skin flushes.

"Get away from her."

"I'm only trying to keep her warm. She was shivering and —"

"I said, get away from her."

He slowly pulls his arm out from beneath her and backs away along the floor. Harper's eagle watches the exchange between us with interest. After Cotton is a safe distance away, I sit on the ground and pull my knees to my chest, trying to regain some of the warmth I lost in the other room.

M-4 raises his head from his paws and glances toward the back, searching for his Contender. I scoot toward the lion and pet his mane as best I can through gloves. The Pandora moans and closes his eyes as if he was battling to keep them open. He feels hot like Oz, but that can't be right.

Harper begins to shiver, and I chew the inside of my cheek, wondering if I made a mistake scolding Cotton. When one of her hands reaches back, feeling for something, or rather, for *someone*, I know I have.

I grind my teeth. "Well, go back over there, then."

Cotton is by her side in a flash, curling himself around her. She relaxes and allows herself to be swallowed by his sculpted body. Harper is half asleep, but I know she realizes who it is who's holding her so tightly.

"I was only trying to keep her warm," Cotton repeats in a hushed tone.

"What is it with you guys and your lies? Why can't you say what's on your mind?"

A shadow passes over Cotton's face, and his demeanor darkens. "Maybe we have to be asked the right questions."

I'm about to ask what he means when Guy appears in the short hallway. Our eyes meet for a moment. Then I get up and return to my place next to V-5. We don't speak to each other again that night, but my lips burn from the memory of his mouth on mine.

CHAPTER FIFTY

For the next two days, we travel with an even greater sense of urgency. In order to keep from sinking into the deep snow, we create crisscrossed grids made of twigs and branches, and attach them to the bottoms of our boots with our laces. This has made walking more than a little complicated, but it seems we've remembered how close we are to the finish line, and so it doesn't slow us down much.

Before we left the first cabin, we made a pact: We'd travel together until we found five flags. Then we'd make a choice to either travel the rest of the way on our own or to stick with the group. I don't know how we'd ever elect who would be *first* to enter base camp and receive the Cure, but maybe when it comes down to it, we won't have to. Not if each Contender decides to travel on their own anyway.

A part of me hopes we stay together until the end. That each of us decides to do our part to help take this race down, whether that's to support the others or to be chosen to go inside headquarters. Then again, staying together will make it even harder to say good-bye.

The sun shines bright. It softens the snow, and somewhere in the distance, I hear the sound of rushing water. We've located three flags so far, which means we have two more until it's decision time. We've deduced that the flags are farther up the mountain each time, that they are hidden by a thick cluster of trees, and that they stand in a zigzag pattern.

Since the first and third flags were on the right side of the mountain, and the second one was farther on the left, that's the direction we head now. Madox is in fox shape today because his lighter body makes it easier for him to travel atop the packed snow. RX-13 is in flight overhead, keeping her eagle eyes trained on the ground in search of a flag. She hasn't found one since the first day when the wind blew, keeping the flag in motion and triggering her hunting instincts, but we hold out hope that she will again.

Guy's lion trails toward the back, panting. It's obvious he's not a fan of this weather. The rest of the Pandoras march beside their Contenders, and I do my best to lead the group and shout encouragements. Every once in a while, though, because he's more resilient, I lean on Guy to take charge.

Today, I have no problem walking up front. At each flag location, we've discovered a small cabin in the direction the flag is pointing, and we're hoping for the same today. It's never easy finding the flags, regardless of the ecosystem, and this mountain is no exception. We've walked in circles, squares, and octagons, searching for flags. But somehow, we end up finding them. Of course, I suppose that means other Contenders do as well.

"When are we going to take a break?" Willow whines.

Harper rubs the girl's back. "Not much longer, I'm sure."

"My legs hurt."

"Mine do, too," Harper admits.

Olivia jogs over to Harper, her stout body swaying as she moves. "I could carry your pack for you."

"I shouldn't even be carrying a pack." Harper shoots a pointed look at Guy. "Not like we're going to find anything out here we need."

"They wouldn't have given them to us if they were useless," he argues.

Cotton chokes on a laugh. "Yeah, they'd never supply empty packs just to screw with us."

"Exactly," Harper says. "At least we have one intelligent person in this group."

Braun holds out his arms. "What the hell?"

But Harper and Cotton are having a moment in which Cotton is smiling at her and she's not exactly looking away.

"Really, I don't mind carrying the pack. It's empty anyway, right?" Olivia reaches for the pack, but Harper turns to the side so she can't reach it. The young girl tries again. "It's okay. I want to help. You said your legs hurt, so I can —"

"Olivia, just shut your fat mouth. Jesus!"

We all stop.

Olivia's face reddens, and tears fill her eyes.

"Harper," I say, barely containing my anger. "I can't believe you —"

"No," Olivia says, wiping her eyes and breathing through flared nostrils. "It's fine. I don't care. We're tired, that's all."

I want to continue scolding Harper, but I'm worried it will embarrass the girl further. And I certainly don't want Willow piping in and making matters worse with that smug smile she's wearing. So I don't say anything else. For now.

"Olivia," Guy says. "Why don't you walk with me?"

"Go to hell," she snaps.

Guy laughs.

I don't think it's funny, though, because Olivia is obviously hurt. But, lo and behold, the girl smiles, too.

"You going to flip me off?" Guy asks her, his voice devoid of emotion. "With your gimpy hand? Because that hand doesn't really have a middle finger now, does it?"

Olivia's bites her lip to keep from laughing, and when Guy waves for me to keep walking, I do. When I glance back later, Olivia is walking next to Guy, staring up at him with affection.

CHAPTER FIFTY-ONE

I keep driving forward, pushing the conversation between Harper and Olivia from my mind so I can concentrate on finding shelter. Usually, we travel through thick crops of skinny trees that kiss the sky, but we've tried those areas without luck, so now we walk out in the open. We're on a slight incline, snow blanketing every last molecule on the mountain, and beside us Oz keeps his internal heater blazing. With each step he takes, he melts the snow beneath him. It's rather amusing to watch.

When we get thirsty, M-4 melts a spot of snow with his fire and EV-0 forces her elephant trunk into the frozen earth and produces clean, cold water. It's more refreshing than eating snow. The eagle and Madox catch us meals when we get hungry, and M-4 cooks them. The bull helps cut a path with his strength, and manages *not* to smoke us out with his red nose funk no matter how many times Braun says he will.

And today — for the first time since that day in the ocean when the iguana tail-whipped her — RX-13 pulls on her invisibility. Harper whoops, and the iguana almost seems relieved when she gets dive-bombed by an invisible eagle. After that one retribution, though, RX-13 keeps her distance.

Today isn't a bad day. We have warmth. We have one another. Our Pandoras are healthy. And we agree we've made great time finding flags. So when I spot a lone tree in the distance that stands like an orphan child among the white, I begin to think our luck has come to a head.

"Is that what I think it is?" I ask.

Braun comes to stand by my side. "No way. We've never found one this early."

Willow's stomach rumbles. "We could actually find the cabin before nightfall. Relax for a few hours."

Even though we're in the final stretch of the Brimstone Bleed and my mind is screaming at me to keep moving, to keep my eye on the prize, I find myself nodding. "It'd give us a chance to strategize. Maybe if we have longer to rest today, we can find two flags tomorrow."

Because the flags are in a zigzag pattern, I'd been wondering whether to just drive a straight line up the mountain using one side. It'd allow us to skip this back-and-forth we've been doing and save time. I'd wanted to ensure there was a clear zigzag pattern before saying anything, but with the introduction of this fourth flag, I'm gaining confidence, maybe enough to discuss cutting a new path tomorrow morning.

I call out to Y-21 to push onward, and the bull lowers his head and does just that. Before long, I'm certain it's a flag. What's more, I can make out the direction the upper flag is facing, and when I turn in that direction, I nearly weep when I spot the faint blur of what must be the cabin.

I show everyone what I see, and we practically run through the snow, elated by the possibility of true warmth sooner than we'd expected. While Oz does his best to keep us insulated while we walk, it's nothing compared to the heat he can radiate when we're crammed between four walls.

"We should go straight to the cabin," Harper says. "Why waste time taking the flag?"

"Because we don't take shortcuts," Guy responds.

"Why would we not take shortcuts? That's the whole point. Get there as quickly as possible."

Guy glances at me as if I should weigh in.

"It's a long ways to what we think is the cabin," I say. "Let's get to the flag and ensure we're headed in the right direction."

Harper sighs, but I don't care. Not after what she said to Olivia.

It is only about a thirty-minute walk before we reach the pole, and as expected, there are two flags. The lower one is reachable, the higher one pointing stiffly toward what we now know is a cabin. In fact, I can make out the sloping tin roof and doorway.

Braun reaches up to take the lower flag, but I stop him. "No, we should be leaving them."

"We took the others," Cotton points out.

"We shouldn't have." Now that I voice the thought, I feel like an idiot for not thinking of this sooner. "I think we've made it before the other Contenders, or the second flag would be missing. If we keep taking the lower one, they'll always know we're ahead."

"Fine, so we leave it," Harper agrees. "Make them think they're winning so they don't push themselves too hard."

Guy poses a question that makes my pulse quicken. "What if someone else has been doing the same thing? Passing them by without taking anything?"

"Ugh," Olivia groans. "Why do you have to be all negative?"

I run my hand over the smooth pole, my fingers itching to snatch the limp blue cloth to satisfy some competitive instinct. "He's right. If the snow covers our footprints, it's covering theirs, too. This flag doesn't necessarily mean we're in the lead, but we should still leave it."

"What about the other one?" Willow asks.

I gaze upward. "What about it?" No sooner do I say this than I spot something I hadn't before. A long, thin rope is looped around the top of the pole, attaching the flag in place. The rope is tan and easily blends in with the flagstaff, but I'm positive there wasn't a rope on the other three we've discovered. "Guy, there's a rope up there."

As soon as he spies what I'm referencing, his posture changes. In an instant, he withdraws into his head, carefully calculating what it could mean, if anything.

Harper pulls the pack off her back and unzips it. "We should take it with us."

"Can your Pandora get to it?" I ask.

In response, Harper places her two pointer fingers into her mouth and whistles. RX-13 swoops down from the cloudless sky and lands on top of the pole, cocking her eagle head at her Contender. "RX-13," Harper says. "I need you to get that rope from the staff."

"It may be nothing," Guy mutters.

"You may be right," I agree. "But we should take it anyway."

He steps back as if giving the eagle room to work. It's not needed, though, because it takes only two swipes from RX-13's back hallux talon to remove the flag. She reaches her beak down and takes the rope into it.

I clap once, satisfied that the task is done. But as the eagle flies into the air, and the tail end of the rope jerks away from the pole, I hear a faint snapping noise.

It sounds like a trigger being released.

CHAPTER FIFTY-TWO

"What was that?" I ask when I hear a soft cracking sound. Guy turns toward me, a question in his gaze.

"Yeah," Harper says. "I hear it, too."

Everyone stops.

When the second crackling, crunching sound emanates from above us, the features in Guy's face turn from confusion to alarm.

The world pulls in a long, beautiful breath.

Holds it.

And then an explosion rocks the ground beneath our feet. It's so loud that it almost seems like the absence of sound. Like every last creature that calls this mountain home vanished in a heartbeat and left only hollowness.

Then the sound is everywhere, eating me up, rattling my skull, grinding my bones.

A tidal wave of snow falls toward us. We can't outrun it. It's not possible. But the others, they try anyway. Guy is yelling something. *Run to the side,* he must be saying. He's pointing in that direction anyway, fear stretched across a face that knows no fear.

I'm not sure why I don't run. I'm not sure why I'm frozen in place. There go my Pandoras. There go my friends. There goes the guy who holds my heart. I should have told him how I felt. Why did I feel like he had to say it first?

I'm running now.

I don't know how I found my legs, but there they are. I scream as I trudge through the snow, the weight distributors on my boots breaking away.

No one turns and glances over their shoulder. There isn't time. Like a sloth trying to outrun the rain, we keep moving. Keep hoping for a miracle. I'm at the very back. I stopped and watched the thing that will kill us all, and now I'll be the first to be swallowed.

Racing sideways across the mountain, I realize something. We'll all get buried, but the others will get slammed by the edge of the avalanche. There may not be enough snow to bury them indefinitely. With enough effort, they could crawl out. But me? That's not how I'm going.

So with a sob breaking in my chest, I stop. I turn back to the avalanche again and face it like a warrior. When it kills me, when it squeezes the last breath from my lungs, I want it to believe I wasn't afraid. If the people running this race are watching — somehow, somewhere — I want them to see my face.

I've only stopped in place for a second when a body slams into mine. He shoves me forward so that I'm stumbling down the mountain toward the cabin. Before I can regain my balance, he shoves me again and again so that I'm rolling end over end.

Sky.

Snow.

Cabin.

Sky.

Snow.

Cabin.

Sky —

Strong arms lift me up, and I hear the crack of a door being kicked in. I tumble inside a cabin that stands directly in the avalanche's path. I have only a moment to savor this last second of life before snow buries us beneath its greedy, ravenous belly.

With my legs shaking, my body broken and bruised, I turn and face the person who granted me an extra moment of life.

My eyes land on Cotton.

CHAPTER FIFTY-THREE

The avalanche rushes toward the cabin. It sounds like a 747 crashing into the mountainside. The force of the oncoming tidal wave causes the floor to shake beneath my feet. Cotton flies across the room and dives on top of my body like he's a defensive all-star and I'm a running back three yards from the end zone.

I groan from the weight of him, but in truth I'm glad he's here. If I'm to die, at least I won't be alone. Then a thought occurs to me a second before the snow delivers its final punch.

I shouldn't be happy he's here. It only means two will die instead of one.

The avalanche slams into the cabin.

The two of us are thrown like tiny, plastic chess pieces across the floor, tumbling into the far wall. The entire cabin shakes and groans as if it's a living, breathing thing saying good-bye to this bittersweet life. One side of the cabin collapses. The ceiling crashes to the floor as if it was never meant to be there to begin with. Snow rushes in, and we scramble across the ground to the opposite end of the cabin.

I'm being buried alive. I'm a miner under a mile of collapsed bedrock, a body being lowered six feet beneath freshly turned soil. I can't breathe. I can't hear. I can't feel anything besides Cotton's short nails digging into my forearm.

The entire cabin lifts from its shoddy foundation, and I scream.

Cotton squeezes his arms around my body and palms my head against his chest.

And then, at once, the cabin slams back into place. The walls give one last mournful wail. The rushing sound moves away from us, and even though my ears still ring from the noise, I can tell the worst has passed. The worst has passed, and I'm alive.

I'm alive!

I want to celebrate, but I'm too terrified to move. We could be ten feet under snow. Twenty. The smallest motion could cause the remainder of the ceiling to fall. Shaking, I crane my neck toward Cotton. His head is between his knees. Slowly, he straightens until we're eye to eye.

"It's over," he says.

I can't find my voice. I can't fathom what happened and how my heart is still beating.

He glances at the ceiling. He's thinking the same thing I am. That this could still end badly. We could be trapped down here. We could be crushed. We could freeze to death without Oz.

"There can't be that much above us." Cotton gets to his feet, and I notice he's shaking, too. It makes it worse that he's scared, because I've always thought of him as I have Guy. The two have always seemed incapable of experiencing true fear. But when I remember the look on Guy's face after the explosion sounded, I know that's not true.

"Ma-maybe we shouldn't . . . move," I force out.

Cotton is already inspecting the ceiling, laying his hand against the three walls he can reach, analyzing the snow that covers a third of the space. "We'll have to eventually. Why not now?"

Watching him work, I feel as if he's decided that it wouldn't be so bad to die. I don't understand it one bit, but he does have a point. We have to find a way out. There's no telling how long we have until the ceiling comes down.

I climb to my feet but nearly collapse when my ankle rolls. Cotton makes a movement as if he's going to help me right myself but then stops. Darkness crosses his face, and he turns away. I don't dwell on what I saw in his features. Instead, I propose a plan.

"We could pull the snow into the cabin. Maybe if we do it little by little, it will open a hole above us."

Cotton considers this. "But if it doesn't, we'll get colder faster and run out of air even quicker."

The thought is enough to send a tremor through me once again. After all this, I could still go down suffocating at the bottom of an avalanche. "We could wait. Maybe the others saw where we went. They'll come to dig us out."

Cotton continues studying the snow and sighs. He doesn't believe the others made it out alive. I hate him for this, even if he did save my life. Guy's face flashes in my mind, but I push it away. I can't hold a memorial for him already. He's alive. He has to be. Guy Chambers is invincible. And the other Contenders? My Pandoras and theirs? They have to be okay, too.

Madox, are you out there? I'm here. I'm in the cabin. I need you.

"We have two choices. We can try and dig our way out now, or we can wait to see if the snow begins to melt." Cotton points to the snow that oozes into the cabin. "If it starts to melt or more slides in, that'll be a good sign, I think."

"How do you know?" I ask.

He rubs the back of his neck. "I don't."

My pulse still beats inside my ears as if my heart is trying to climb out of my body, but I've at least calmed down enough to think. As I do, a new, disquieting question dawns. Cotton inspects the cabin — taking in the tight space, the lack of windows or alternative doors, the logs laid one on top of the other as a true pioneer cabin might have — and I inspect him. His dark hair falls to his shoulders, tousled as a surfer's, and his insulated navy jacket and pants do little to hide his thickly muscled build. Fine lines crease his face, and though he's probably seven or eight years older than I am, the lines seem born more from stress than age.

Cotton pushes the snow toward the far wall so that there's more room for us to move around. As he works, my eyes never stray from his strong body. He's built like an engine. Or perhaps a weapon. I should help him work. I should do something. But I can't. Because every second that passes is another second my mind wraps itself around one single question I desperately want to ask.

Finally, after I can't stand to remain silent on the subject any longer, I open my mouth to speak.

"Cotton," I say in a whisper, "why did you save me?"

He stops working. He stands.

When he turns and faces me — his full lips pressed into a thin line, his brown eyes burning with some deeply suppressed emotion — I know I shouldn't have asked.

I shouldn't have asked, but I did, and I can't take it back.

Cotton moves toward me like a hunter.

CHAPTER FIFTY-FOUR

Cotton continues advancing toward me, and I back up until I can back up no longer, my question hanging in the air.

"I may not have saved you." His voice is low and soothing. He speaks as if I'm a startled fawn that may bolt, but there's nowhere to go. There is only him. "Why do you look so afraid?"

"We're buried under snow," I explain. "The ceiling could collapse."

He rubs his jaw. "That's not the only reason, now is it?"

"I don't know what you mean."

He laughs. The sound wriggles inside of me like a worm in sodden earth. Cotton taps his temple and leans his face in close. "You're a smart one, Tella." Though he's acting aggressive, it isn't quite convincing. It's like someone's told him to take me out, and he isn't sure he can finish the job.

I step past him like I've remembered something important. "We have to get out of here, Cotton. Here, I'll help you move the snow. Give us room to think."

Cotton grabs my arm and slams me into place. When my back hits the wall, the ceiling groans. I flinch, both from the threat of being crushed and from the grip Cotton maintains on my bicep.

"Tell me why you look afraid," Cotton says.

"I told you."

Cotton touches his chest. "I like to think I'm a guy people can be honest with. So, please, humor me."

"Have *you* been honest?" I ask, no longer able to hide my suspicion. I've survived innumerable near-death encounters, and now I'm going to cower before a Contender in the last few minutes of my life? No.

I step toward him until our chests brush. He falls back a fraction.

"Did you really hit your head?" I ask. "Did you really forget the first two legs of the Brimstone Bleed? Did your Pandora really toss Braun's Pandora overboard on accident? Did you really sleep next to Harper only to keep her warm?"

I eye his dark hair and remember the black ink I saw running down his neck aboard the ship. Then I look at his scalp, and when I do, my heart clenches so hard, I'm sure it'll rupture. There's a difference between questioning the things someone has said and wondering if there's more to them than meets the eye, and actually having the truth slap you in the face.

Cotton says he's been in the race for two and a half months. Enough time to cover the jungle, desert, and ocean, and arrive safely at base camp. But then why, when I inspect his dyed black hair, don't I see blond roots that reflect that same story? It's something I've thought before but never really dwelled on.

I swallow, clench my fists, and prepare for a fight if need be. "When did you dye your hair, Cotton?"

His brow furrows at this sudden change in questioning.

"Did you do it before you left for the race?" I ask. He pushes toward me again, but I stop him with a hand to his chest. "And if you did, why does your hair look in every way like a dye job done four weeks ago?"

He shoves himself toward me, and I throw both hands into his chest and push with everything I have.

"No!" I scream, no longer caring about the fragile ceiling. "Who are you? Why are you here?!"

Cotton snatches my wrists and shoves them to my sides as easily as if I were a bothersome moth. Then he grabs the back of my neck and jerks my face forward. His lips touch my ear, and the hair on my arms rises.

"You want to know who I am, Contender? You want me to tell you my secret? Okay, here goes. Six weeks ago, you stood on a cliff and watched as a Contender fell to his death." He pulls his face back so that our eyes meet. "That Contender? His name was Titus Hoffman. And he was my brother."

CHAPTER FIFTY-FIVE

He releases me, and I charge past him. I stumble and fall in the snow, wetness coating my left side. I scramble backward on it, trying in vain to put distance between me and Cotton. He is Titus's brother. The sociopath who drowned one of his own guys in quicksand, who forced his tongue inside my mouth, who tried to kill me when I wouldn't become his partner — that guy shares DNA with Cotton.

Cotton scratches his head. "We don't look that much alike, not really, but I figured I should dye my hair anyway. I think the people running this race loved that. Thought it would make for a good curveball. You know, it was them who suggested I could be a good Contender in Titus's place. 'Course I didn't really know what they were talking about until I accepted."

"I didn't want to kill him," I whisper.

Cotton cocks his head. "Oh, I'm sure you didn't. I'm sure you felt awful about shoving my little brother to his death."

I fight to stop my hands from shaking. "You're not like him. He did bad things in this race, Cotton."

His face softens. He wants to keep this aggressive front up, but I can also tell he's curious about how his brother fared in his final weeks. "He did what he had to do to save our father."

I shake my head. "No. No, Titus did far more than that. He abused his Pandora. He created a team of guys called the Triggers, and they bullied other Contenders for amusement. He drowned a Contender in quicksand just because that Contender touched me. He kidnapped me, Cotton. He took me away from my friends and he tried to make me —"

"Stop."

Slowly, I climb to my feet. "The Contenders, they become

different inside this place. Some of us turn into animals, and it's understandable."

"And you?" Cotton sneers. "Did you turn into an animal?"

I turn my face away. "I don't pretend to be any better than the rest. We've all made mistakes here, and I'm no different."

His arms tighten at his sides, and he drops his head. "You know what I don't understand? How you can be this girl who wants to protect everyone — the Pandoras and the Contenders, too — and be the same person who took him away."

Even though Cotton's eyes are lowered, I spot the torment in them. On one hand, he wants revenge for his brother's death, but on the other, I'm not the monster he expected me to be. "You don't have to do what they expect you to do," I venture. "You can be different. You can help us take this race down forever. I know you miss your brother, but —"

His gaze flicks up, ablaze with fury.

I pull in a deep breath and continue. "I know you care for Harper, too. I see the way you look at her. She's lost someone, too. You could be the one to help her."

Cotton storms across the room. I fall back on the snow, and he drops on top of me. His hands wrap around my throat, and he squeezes. "You killed him!" he growls. "You act like a saint while everyone's looking, but up on that cliff you were a murderer. No matter what you say my brother did, at least he wasn't two-faced. But you? You're the one with secrets. You're the one who will kill us in the end!"

His fingers tighten, cutting off my air. I rip at his hands and tear at his face. Adrenaline floods my nervous system until I feel as if I'll explode like the mountain did. "I didn't . . . push him."

Cotton roars with frustration and anger. "Yes, you did! They saw you. Two people fighting, one falling. It was you!"

Stars dance in my peripheral vision, and warmth seeps into my skin. But that can't be right, because I'm lying in snow. "His Pandora pushed him," I choke out. "AK-7 was his Pandora. He . . . shoved him off."

Cotton's hold lessens. "You're lying."

I do my best to shake my head, but I can hardly move my neck. "The bear was his. Titus told me to kill him, and I wouldn't."

He falls back, and I roll to my side, coughing and gasping for air. It's a long time before I'm able to sit up, and even when I do, I can hardly swallow. Pain shoots daggers through my neck, and I can almost sense where each of his fingers dug into my flesh.

Cotton has backed against the opposite wall. He's sitting on the floor, and his legs are pulled close to his chest. "I thought maybe they were lying," he says, his voice breaking. "I thought maybe he was still alive."

There's so much I want to say to him, or maybe there's nothing I want to say. He came here to kill me, but he also saved me during the avalanche. How am I supposed to feel toward someone like that? I open my mouth to speak, but then snap it back shut and crane my head to the side, listening. A creaking noise rips my attention from Cotton, and I bolt upright. When I glance back at him, his eyes become as round as shiny quarters.

"Is it the ceiling?" he whispers.

I don't respond, because he already knows the answer. My gaze flies across the room, considering our options. There's only one I believe could work. I walk slowly on hands and knees toward the mound of snow. Cotton seems to understand what I'm doing and follows along.

We move like feral cats trailing a finch. *Slow now. Not too quick. Not even a tail flick, lest we lose our prize.* The ceiling wails and whimpers as a child would during a temper tantrum. Every step I take I believe is my last and that this is the position some future robot will find me in. "Human expired while walking like dog. *Bleep, blurp, bleep.* Shall I gather the bones? *Bleep.*"

When we reach the snow, we can't stop ourselves any longer. We throw our bodies on top of it and pray that when the roof falls, it won't hurt us since it's already collapsed on this side.

The ceiling gives one final groan, and then more or less farts. I think to myself, *Yeah, that's about right.*

It crashes to the floor.

We scramble backward, and then the snow is everywhere. It spills from the ceiling like a waterfall and races toward our legs like high tide on a beach. I used to think the snow wanted to swallow me, but now I know better. It wants inside of my body. It rushes into my ears and rams up my nose and presses at my clenched lips. I pull in one final breath before breathing is impossible.

I'm suspended in white like a fly in a Jell-O mold. My lids are closed, but I feel the snow pushed against them, begging for a taste of my mother's eyes. I thought dying inside the Brimstone Bleed would be chaotic, all bared teeth and intense pain. But this is a surprise. Turns out I'll die quietly inside a cotton-ball tomb. Who knew?

The snow clogs my ears and makes me think I'm hearing things. It whispers the sound of Guy calling my name, of Madox barking, mad. What a cruel thing to do. I'd made peace with suffocating, had embraced the slowing *thud-thud* of my heart, and now this? I mean, really, if you're going to kill me, at least have the decency to do it without mockery.

Guy's voice grows louder, Madox's barks more insistent.

Good-bye, Madox. You were a good Pandora and my best friend.

A hand grabs my shoulder. Two hands. My body is wrenched from the snow, and a face I feared I'd never see again hovers overhead. I understand at once who brought the ceiling down, even if it was an accident.

CHAPTER FIFTY-SIX

"Tella? Tella!" Guy yells. Why is he yelling? I'm doing the best I can here. Maybe I should keep my eyes open. No, too difficult. Sleep sounds amazing. Those same hands shake me until my brain rattles inside my skull. "Open your eyes. Don't go to sleep. Damn it, Tella, listen to me!"

My eyes snap open, and all the oxygen in the entire universe rushes out of Guy's lungs. I cough, and snow bursts from my mouth in a watery display. I look like a fountain.

"That's good," Guy says. "Keep coughing if you need to. Eyes open."

I turn my head and see Cotton on the ground next to me. Braun and Harper are braced over his figure.

Something warm touches my face, and when I see it's Madox's tongue, I offer my first smile. That really gets Guy going. He waves something over, and Oz moves in tighter, radiating heat as if he's trying to warm the Dallas Cowboys' stadium. Monster, M-4, Rose, RX-13, and EV-0 all hover nearby, along with Olivia and Willow. They're all trying to peek at the girl dumb enough to hesitate when an avalanche said hello. Only Y-21 is out of view, but when I turn my head again, I see the bull is knelt down next to his Contender, long neck laid across Cotton's stomach.

I go to sit up, but Guy says it's too soon. I push his hand away, because it's not like lying in the snow is therapeutic. Madox climbs into my lap as soon as I'm upright, and I bend my head to cuddle him close. This time, he lets me get as near as I want, tough fox reputation be damned.

Did you hear me calling for you?

Madox barks.

Guy moves in closer and guides my face up. "I thought I lost you. I thought . . . what you said about if I didn't say it, you'd never know." He closes his eyes and opens his mouth as if he's going to say something profound.

"No, don't," I say. "Not when I'm spitting up snow." He laughs, and I tell him how terribly rude it is to laugh while I'm hypothermic. He laughs harder.

"Can you get up?" He stands and offers his hand.

When I climb to my feet, I find I have more strength than I thought I would. I guess becoming a human icicle is invigorating. Screw seaweed body wraps and triple-shot lattes. Avalanches are so *in*.

Cotton is already on his feet. Nerves shoot through me as I remember what he was doing to me seconds before the team found us.

Guy's hand sails to my throat. "What happened here?"

My face must give me away, because the next thing I know, Guy is in front of Cotton, hands balling the front of his jacket.

"What did you do to her?" Guy bellows. Gone is the quiet Contender we've grown to know. In his place is a wild banshee defending his banshee girl. "Did you do that to her? Did you?!"

Y-21 gallops toward Guy, his head lowered, bull horns poised to strike. Before he can get close enough, M-4 lunges across the open space and lands on the bull's back. The two Pandoras fall to their sides and battle for dominance.

The other Pandoras watch on like kids at a playground. I like to think they're placing bets on who will win this fist-and-knuckles scuffle.

I rush over and pull on Guy's back. "Stop, it's not what you think."

Not exactly anyway.

Guy clocks Cotton. The hit is hard enough to trigger another avalanche. Cotton falls into the snow, and his Pandora goes wild with rage.

"Here he goes," Braun says.

Red smoke shoots from Y-21's flared nostrils, and the lion drops like a stone.

Cotton scrambles upright. "I wasn't going to kill her."

Guy tilts his head, and his mouth hangs agape. "I'm sorry? Did you just admit to strangling her?" He lunges again, but this time Braun intervenes, and though Guy is all muscle, Braun is an island of flesh. Guy bounces off him and tries to go around, but Braun, and now Harper and I, manages to hold him back.

Cotton turns his gaze from Guy to Harper and lowers his voice. "I'm sorry. I only did it because —"

"Don't talk to me," Harper snarls. "Don't say one damn word to me."

Cotton throws up his hands. "I'm out of here."

"Damn straight you are," Guy growls.

"Guy, stop," I interject. "You don't know the full story."

"Don't," Cotton pleads. "I'm already going."

But I'm done with keeping secrets from those who support me. "He's Titus's brother," I say in a rush. "I had a hand in Titus's death, and the people running this race thought it'd be amusing to bring his older brother in to take his place and see if he'd seek revenge."

No one speaks. Cotton presses his fingertips to his temples as Y-21 noses his Contender's side.

"Is it true?" Harper asks.

Cotton's arms drop. "It's true. I changed my mind about the revenge part. After I met Tella, I knew I couldn't hurt her. I just wanted to win for my father."

"And that's why you strangled her?" Guy's voice is void of sympathy.

Cotton ignores Guy and looks to Braun, who's holding our only pack. "I want half the rope before I go."

Guy laughs. It's a cold, dry sound. "You really are something."

I put a hand to Guy's chest and say to Cotton, "What will you do if you reach base camp first?"

"I'll send the Cure home to my father," he replies without hesitation. A fire builds in Cotton's stance, shadowy tendrils dancing over his face. "Then I'm going to accept their invitation to work for headquarters. I'm going to slink inside like a virus and infect their minds with unimaginable horrors. I'm going to burn the walls that surround them and watch as the skin melts from their bones. I'm going to stand over their leader's bed as they sleep and open their neck with a rusty, serrated knife. And as the blood gushes from their wound, and they drown inside their own body, I'll whisper my brother's name. That's what I'll do if I win."

"Jeez," Braun says. "Did you rehearse that?"

I consider what Cotton said and then say over my shoulder, "Give me half the rope."

No one contests my decision.

RX-13 uses her talon to cut the rope in two, and we hand it to Cotton. I'm not sure what we may need these tools for besides climbing, but he's traveled with us this far. He had an opportunity to kill me, to have his revenge, and he didn't follow through. In the end, maybe I give him the rope because of what he said. I don't like the thought of inflicting such pain on people I've never met.

But then again, I do.

Cotton turns his attention to me. "I'm sorry," he says, and then he spins and walks away.

As Cotton marches away, Guy grabs my head like it's a bowling ball and smashes it against his chest. "I said I'd never let anything happen to you again."

I wrap my arms around his waist. "Why are you such a filthy liar?"

Watching Cotton disappear from view, I can't help feeling conflicted. After what he did to me, I want him gone. But I also don't want everyone to view him as they did his brother. "He wasn't like Titus," I say to no one in particular, eyeing the collapsed cabin Cotton shoved me inside of. "He saved my life."

But even to me, the words ring hollow.

CHAPTER FIFTY-SEVEN

After three days at a fast march, we're feeling confident. We've found two more flags for a total of six. Braun carries the pack now, and inside we harbor a long length of rope, a pickax, and a harness, all of which we found at the flagpoles. Bonus: This time, nothing bad happened when we retrieved the equipment. The things we've collected are essentially climbing gear, and we certainly need it with how far we've ascended. Every once in a while, we find ourselves on a steep ledge, and I can't help but look down, though I order the others to resist the temptation.

This time, like all the others, my stomach drops to my feet and Eskimo-kisses my frostbitten toes. It's not the depth of the fall that scares me most, but rather the cone-shaped spikes that line the valleys. I don't want to be impaled. I mean, I don't want to fall, either, but impalement is something I really want no part of.

Somehow, the snow is thinner the higher we rise, so we no longer need the crisscrossed weight distributors. Not that we have laces to attach them with even if we did. Now our boots open to the sky, tongues hanging out like heathens. One upside to not feeling your extremities is that you don't sense the blisters forming on your heel. The rule is not to look. *Never* look.

Olivia always looks.

The first night we spent in the snow was the worst, wolves' howls ringing in our ears and frostbite nipping at our fingers and toes. Since then we had one additional night in a cabin. Last night we never found shelter, and I'm beginning to think we won't find it today, either. Call it a hunch.

We don't discuss the avalanche, more than to say we agree it wasn't an accident. And we've pretty much adjusted to a new group dynamic sans Cotton. Guy's lion does moan in his sleep, which can't be great, but then the nights are never good for person or Pandora.

As we walk, though, we try and keep our spirits high. It's the only thing we can do to combat the knowledge that soon we'll near base camp, and in that moment difficult decisions will need to be made.

"Do you think I look good as a Contender?" Braun asks. "I mean, comparatively speaking, I feel like I'm less ragged than the rest of you."

"It's because we had a long way to fall." Olivia touches a hand to her hair, which retains its frizzy quality despite there being zilch humidity. "If we had before and after shots, the difference would be staggering. You, on the other hand . . ."

Braun scoffs, and Harper laughs.

"You think it's funny, Barbie?" Braun says. "You haven't just fallen; you've nose-dived."

Harper shoots him a look. "Please."

"She looks pretty to me," Willow says, taking Harper's hand.

"Yeah, whatever," Harper says, shaking her head. "I could go for a hot shower. That'd help."

"You know what I want?" I say from the front. "A steak. I've never counted myself a steak girl before now, but I want a steak as big as —" I open my arms wide.

Guy speaks up, surprising everyone. "Hot chocolate."

"Lame," Olivia chirps. "Everyone wants hot chocolate."

"With chili powder and jumbo-sized marshmallows," Guy continues.

We continue like this for a while, alternating between food fantasies and ripping on one another, until we come to a crossing. There's a short bridge that isn't quite a bridge connecting one side of the mountain to the other. A crevasse separates the two, and one glance down is enough to make my head spin. Like all the other valleys, it brims with ice spikes reaching upward like ravenous witch's fingers in some gruesome fairy tale. The fissure runs too far to the left and right to make out an end point, so I motion for Braun to remove the pack.

"We'll have to cross," I say, hoping no one hears the angst in my voice.

Guy reaches for Braun's backpack and withdraws the rope, harness, and pickax. "I'll go first and secure a line to the opposite side. The rest of you can follow the rope across."

Harper snatches the rope from him. "Not that I don't appreciate your constant state of martyrdom, but sometimes the rest of us have to take the lead."

Guy glances in my direction. I raise my eyebrows, because Harper's speech is the same one I've given him. "Fine. Turn around."

When she does, he straps the black harness around her body and then attaches the metal ring to the length of rope. He hands her the pickax. "Steady across," he says. "If you fall, we'll have you."

Guy takes the opposite end of the rope and gives it to EV-0. The elephant wraps her trunk around it instinctually and steps back until the rope is taut. Harper pats me on the back once, and our eyes meet.

"Don't be a hero out there," I say.

She laughs, because there's nothing to be a hero about, and moves toward the icy bridge without so much as a backward glance. The bridge is wide enough, ten feet across and fifty feet in length, but it's the height that has me worried. As she places her first foot down onto the crossing, my fingers itch to pull her back. I should have demanded to go in her place, but then I'd be as bad as Guy, always believing I can do things more effectively than the others. So I draw in a deep breath and allow Harper to do what she came here to do, which is to ensure that I prevail in this race.

She takes five sure-footed steps onto the bridge while the rest of us hold the other end of the rope. I even have Monster — and Madox dressed as Monster — step on the end to be sure we've got her, should the worst happen. RX-13 hops along behind Harper on the bridge as if she's providing moral support.

After Harper's made it halfway, she calls back, "Piece of cake."

I wait for her to fall. If this were a movie, this is where she'd eat it. But she continues her passage across the stretch of ice, and makes it to the other side composed. Swinging the pickax above her head, the muscles along her back and biceps flex. She drives the axe into the snow four feet from the edge and secures the rope around the base.

I step forward as the obvious choice of who will go second, but both Guy and Braun stop me in my tracks.

"I should go next," Braun says.

Guy waves to the bridge. "As long as it's not her."

"What the hell, Guy?" I complain. "Are we back here again?"

"I want to go before you, and I don't want to discuss my reasoning," he says.

"Ugh. You're such a freaking caveman."

Guy grabs my shoulders and lowers his head until our foreheads almost touch. "I pulled you from the snow, Tella. You couldn't even keep your eyes open."

I roll my eyes to show him how well they work now.

When I glance back at the bridge, I'm stunned at what I see. Willow is halfway across the bridge, sliding one foot after the other, using the rope as a railing.

"Damn it, Willow," Harper barks. "You should have waited until I could send the harness with RX."

But Willow is already on the other side, hands on her hips, a satisfied smile on her face. Harper squeezes the girl close and releases her just as quickly. Then she hands the harness to her eagle, and RX-13 soars across the space. The bird hesitates overhead, and when she spots Olivia jumping up and down in earnest, she drops the harness. Olivia has herself strapped in before any of us can voice a complaint.

"How is this happening?" I ask.

Olivia rushes toward the bridge as if she's actually excited to cross. "You snooze, you lose." She turns back once before stepping away from safety, and the smile on her face steals the breath from my lungs. She's too happy, too eager to gain Harper's approval. The last thing she needs while balancing over an eighty-foot drop is a competitive desire to beat Willow's time.

Guy bumps me with his elbow. "She'll be fine. We've all got her."

I clench my fists around the rope until the fibers dig into my palms. I wish Guy hadn't said that, about her being fine. It feels as if he sealed an omen with his optimism. Olivia is a third of the way across, and I still can't slow my racing pulse. She has nine fingers. Will that make a difference in the hold she has on the rope? I should have gone with her.

I don't know why I'm panicking about Olivia's being out alone on that ledge, which, now that I think about it, is probably more like seven feet wide. My gut just supplies the anxiety, and I go with the reaction, because that's what I've learned to do in the Brimstone Bleed. Trust your instincts. If they say something bad is about to happen, then ready the cavalry.

"What if she falls?" I ask Guy.

"She's not going to fall. If she does, we'll haul her up."

"Which one is it? She's going to fall, or she isn't?"

He tightens his hold on the rope. "The second one."

It's at that exact moment, as if the mountain has a sense of humor and isn't this a hoot, that Olivia slips. She got too cocky, wanted to be swift and light on her feet like little Willow.

And now she's sliding toward the edge.

CHAPTER FIFTY-EIGHT

Olivia's legs V in a perfect split, and she glides to the right like an ice skater who's missed a crucial jump. Her nine fingers seek purchase along the ice, and her elephant trumpets loudly.

"Don't let go of the rope!" I scream. "Steady."

Braun's giant hand on my shoulder pulls me back down to earth, and I gulp in a breath, willing myself calm so that Olivia can be calm.

Olivia's body stops short of the edge, and I almost lose control again. She's a hair from recovering and a hair from falling. The harness could snap. The rope could be too weak to hold her weight.

"Pull yourself up," I yell to Olivia as if I'm bored and we need to keep this moving. Does she hear the emotion camouflaged by my words? Does she know how I've grown to love her?

When Olivia doesn't move, Guy steps forward. "Olivia, you know how Rose moves side to side like a snake? That's what I want you to do, okay? Be a snake."

I expect Olivia to start crying, but she doesn't. She takes Guy's advice, and carefully, *very* carefully, she slithers back and forth, one millimeter at a time. At first, it doesn't seem that she's getting any farther from the edge, but when I see that she is, my eyes burn with emotion. "You're doing well, Olivia," I holler. "A little more and you can stand up."

Olivia scoots a few more inches and then pulls her knees beneath her. From there, she stands tall and grabs on to the rope again. "Piece of cake," she says, panting.

I laugh too hard. So does everyone else.

It's only when she's on the other side do I calm down and admit I overreacted. We had her, of course we did. EV-0 would never have let go of that rope. Not if it took the elephant over the side of the cliff. Behind me, the elephant stamps the ground with frustration. She wants to coddle her Contender and wrap her trunk around the girl's waist.

When RX-13 drops the harness in my hands, Guy opens his mouth to complain.

"Bite me," I say. Then I kiss him hard on the mouth and run toward the bridge like a schoolgirl.

I'm almost to the bridge, a smile swept across my chapped lips, when I see Harper standing over the pickax. She sees that I'm coming, and she doesn't want to take any chances. Her right boot lifts into the air, and she stomps down onto the axe to drive it farther into the ground. Satisfied it's in deep, she gives me a thumbs-up.

That's what I'll remember about this moment years from now. Her thumb held into the air, just a smidge above her head.

You're good!

What a preposterous thing to see before the ground splits open.

Olivia and Willow stand near the ledge, waiting for me to cross. Olivia has a smile on her face that destroys me, the curls around her face a brunette halo of innocence. She's so happy in this moment. Happier than maybe I've ever seen her. Her chest is still swollen with pride when the ground beneath her feet gives way.

I choke with horror.

Olivia and Willow fall like baby sparrows on uncertain wings.

The screams that rip from their throats create a perfect harmony, and in that moment they are the same, twins who could have been the best of friends.

Harper lunges toward them, but she only has time to save one.

A thousand memories of Harper interacting with the girls flash before my mind, and a sob escapes my throat.

She slides toward the falling ice like a batter going for a home run, bases loaded.

She doesn't even flinch. Not for a moment. Her aim is true, and I know then there was never a decision to be made.

Her hand locks on Olivia's wrist.

And Willow tumbles to her death.

Her scream tears a hole through the world.

CHAPTER FIFTY-NINE

That night, we huddle around Oz as the alligator warms our hands. No one speaks. Trees tower over our heads like bars of a jail cell, and a full moon dangles in the sky. RX-13 nudges Harper's arm with her beak, but Harper doesn't even flinch. Ever since Willow fell, she's been comatose. Olivia hasn't tried to approach her, and I think it's for the best. Even I haven't been able to break through her barrier of guilt, and so we remain silent.

M-4 lies on his side near Guy, moaning as his Contender pets his golden coat. The lion has been tiring quicker each day that we travel, though I suppose that goes for the rest of us, too. Madox sleeps near the elephant tonight, snuggled in a ball near the animal's side, so I give Monster most of my attention, and even ensure that I pat the alligator on occasion.

Harper gets to her feet suddenly. "I'm going for a walk."

"I'll go with you," I say, pushing myself up.

She shoots me a glare cold enough to stop my heart. Slowly, I sit back down. Harper glances around before striding directly ahead. I hear her feet crunching in the snow, and then I don't.

"We have to do something to help her," Braun mumbles.

Guy leans back on his hands but doesn't speak.

Braun is right; we need to figure out a way to lessen the war waging in Harper's head, the one that tells her she shouldn't have stomped that pickax into the ground a second time. The one that says maybe she could have saved them both. She has to understand it was an accident, and that it's a wonder she was able to pull Olivia up at all.

We need to console Harper somehow, but it's impossible when I can't get the sound of Willow's screaming out of my head.

Olivia erupts into tears, and not for the first time tonight.

"Come here," I tell her.

She shoots to her feet instead. "I have to go and talk to her."

"No!" we yell at once.

Her brown eyes sweep across us, and we fall silent. EV-0 rises and marches to where her Contender stands, implying she'd like to come along. Olivia tugs on her elephant's ear lightly. "Stay here. I'll be back."

Olivia trails away from the group, and for the next few minutes, Braun and Guy talk in hushed tones while I fidget. When I can't stand it any longer, I get up and brush the snow from my bottom.

"Not you, too," Braun says.

"Me, too."

I turn and follow Harper's and Olivia's tracks in the snow. I tell myself I want only to ensure they're not killing each other, but I know it's more than that. I'm afraid of what Harper may say to Olivia out of frustration. The last thing that little girl needs is to feel as if Harper regrets her decision.

When I spot two shadows seated along the ground, I stop. The two are shoulder to shoulder on an incline, tall trees bowing toward them. Their backs are to me, and when I notice that Olivia doesn't seem to be upset, I turn to head back. Olivia's laughter catches me off guard, and I freeze.

The young girl's voice chimes up the mountainside like bells on Christmas morning. "So it was you?" Olivia asks Harper.

"Yeah, though I never told anyone that before now."

Olivia's head bobs.

"How about you? I told *you* a secret."

"I'm too young to have secrets."

Harper turns to her. "Nonsense. You make the best secrets when you're young."

"Um, okay. I got one," Olivia says. "About a year ago, my sister bought these boy-short underwear that had some kind of bunny on them. Mom hated them, said they were too racy, but my sister was superexcited to wear them for her first day of high school. I can't remember why, but I took those panties and soaked them in water the night before, then I stuck them in the freezer. To this day, my sister thinks it was my mom who did it."

"Nice," Harper says with a laugh.

There's a long silence before either of them speaks again. Finally, Olivia looks down. "Harper, can I ask you something?" Her voice is softer, more cautious, and I know she's about to bring up what happened today. I ready myself to intervene if need be.

"Shoot."

"Did Willow . . . did she remind you of your daughter?"

Harper sighs as if everyone's burdens just became her own. "My daughter's name was Lillian, and she took after my grandmother in every way. My mom used to joke that Lil was Cleopatra reincarnated, or maybe Madonna. She had this prima donna attitude that was just . . ." Harper shakes her head. "She had the kind of confidence that could fill an entire room. If you were on the opposite side of the house, she'd scream your name as if it were outrageous that you'd left her side for a moment, because, really, what could be more interesting than her?"

Harper leans over her knees, and her shoulders slump. "Willow didn't remind me of my daughter," she says. "But you do."

Olivia raises her face to look at Harper, and when Harper wraps her arm around the girl, my throat tightens with emotion.

"Her father . . ." Olivia says, pressed to Harper's side. "Do you still love him?"

"Who says I loved him?" Harper lowers her voice. "Who says I ever wanted to be with him at all?"

I turn away at her last words, knowing I'm intruding. Part of me wishes I could forget what she may have just admitted, but it explains so much about her tough facade and her reluctance to bond with Olivia. My boots create their own tracks as I make my way back to camp. As I walk, I hold Harper's story in my heart, praying to whoever might be listening for my friend to get a happy ending.

CHAPTER SIXTY

The next morning, we feel separated. Willow is gone, and though we've experienced three deaths in our tribe, each person we lose is fresh and torturous in a unique fashion. Then I remember losing Levi in the jungle and how terrible it was to see his twin brother covered in his blood, and I tick off another mark.

Four.

Today, all I can think of is Willow's grandfather. I'm sure, though I've never met the man, that he'd rather have his granddaughter on his lap for his last few months, happy and healthy in her youth, than to live for another two decades.

We travel for hours on end, stopping only to eat what RX-13 catches and to drink the water EV-0 pulls from the ground. When purples seep into the sky, I begin to worry. We should have found the flag by now. The farther we ascend up on the mountain, the less zigzagging there is to be done. If we don't find our next target soon, we'll have to spend another night in the snow before trying again tomorrow.

"Is that what I think it is?" Braun asks.

A cabin sits like a weary boulder in the snow, and my entire body weakens at the sight. For the last two nights, I've slept with my head on Monster, leaves crushed beneath my limbs, though they do little to block the seeping chill from the snow. This cabin could be the last luxury we experience before reaching base camp, and I'm almost afraid it's a mirage.

Guy's face flushes when I glance in his direction. He pretends my kiss means nothing to him, that he's impervious to such things, but I've seen him looking at me when he thinks I'm not paying attention. So I know he thinks about it.

"Let's go, then," I say, glancing at Harper, unable to stop the smile that blossoms on my face.

She offers a half grin that never reaches her eyes, and motions toward the cabin.

We've only made it a few yards when I stop. Braun bumps into me, and I almost go flying, but Monster is quick to balance me with his girth. As I watch, the cabin door swings open and a man in his midforties steps outside. He wears the same thing we do, matching navy jacket and pants, but when he lifts his leg and scratches at his ankle, my eyes zero in on his boots. Even from this distance, I can see that they're different from the pairs we wear. They're brown, whereas ours are black, and there are silver spikes along the soles.

The man calls out, and as I motion for the others to crouch down, I spot a Bengal tiger trot into sight, a red stripe of paint on its back. The man moves to the side, and the tiger goes inside. A woman steps into view and speaks to him, her mouth moving quickly. She has loud blond hair to his dark, and her fingers twitch at her sides as if playing an invisible instrument. She's younger than him, maybe early thirties, and together they look like a blissfully married couple, and tiger makes three.

Meeting Guy's gaze, I point farther up the mountain. We stoop low and skirt upward and out of sight.

All this time, we arrogantly believed we were in first place. No way could someone have passed us. I saw the boots he wore, and when I think that maybe he got them at a flagstaff, nervous energy courses through my veins. How many items have others picked up that we missed? What advantages do they have?

"Faster," I growl.

The Contenders need no further encouragement. They pick up their heels, they lower their heads to tramp through the snow, and they plunge forward like a closed fist.

CHAPTER SIXTY-ONE

Harper wakes me in the dead of night. It's my turn to keep watch. We covered more ground after nightfall than we ever have, and we've paid the price. In the jungle and desert, we knew night meant rest. In the ocean, we could take shifts rowing through the evening hours. Now, after spotting other Contenders, we're reminded of how much we have to lose by allowing anyone, *anyone*, to beat our time.

Dark circles frame Harper's eyes, her bright green irises floating in a sea of black. "Can you stay awake?" she asks.

I'm not sure.

"Of course," I respond. Madox stirs at the sound of my voice.

Once Harper is asleep, I stretch my legs out and pretend I'm alone in my room in Montana. Usually, when I play this game, I'm in Boston. Tonight, I don't go so far back. I pretend Cody is in the next room over, and though I can hear the rattle in his chest, I'm consoled by it all the same. He's here, he's alive, and I am, too. Tomorrow, Mom will make scrambled eggs with a tablespoon of cottage cheese mixed in, and Dad will complain that cottage cheese shouldn't exist. I'll take my place at the breakfast table and casually mention it's been a while since I got new jeans to see if either takes the bait. Maybe I even call for Cody to get out of bed and stop being so lazy in order to hear him laugh. For now, though, I'm tucked under my blanket, bedside lamp on, *Vogue* across my lap, September edition.

When Madox climbs over my legs and interrupts my daydream, I don't fault him. It's dangerous losing sight of the present. Basking in Oz's heat, I pet my small black fox and hum a song he knows well. It's the sicky song, the same song Mom hums to me when I don't feel well and the one I sang to Madox when he was still inside his egg.

He pushes his nose under my thigh and closes his eyes. After he's asleep, I allow my mind to drift back to my brother.

I'm so close, Cody. You'd be amazed at how far I've come.

I squeeze my eyes shut and imagine his face. Not the ashen, pained one I've grown to know, but the one I remember from before he was sick. I see his lopsided smile, the shaggy chestnut hair hanging over his eyes, the slight acne on his cheeks he tried so hard to hide. I see the droop over his eyelids that turns girls into idiots because *he has puppy dog eyes*. I see his happiness. I see his joy.

My eyes stay closed for too long. That's all it takes before I'm asleep.

When I wake again, Madox is gone from my lap. I glance around, searching for him and cursing myself for falling asleep. Every other Contender and Pandora is accounted for, so I'm not sure where he could have gone. I brush myself off, guilt weighing my limbs. It doesn't feel as if I've been asleep very long, maybe only a few minutes. Since it's not time for Guy to keep watch, I decide to go and find Madox before waking him.

I wipe the snow from my pants and rub my aching neck, wondering how I ever learned to sleep upright. Add it to the list of useful things I've learned from this race.

Madox, I call out with my mind. *Madox, where are you?*

When he doesn't appear immediately, I decide he must be relieving himself. But after I've called for him several more times, I start to worry. An animal could have taken him, or even another Contender. Everyone knows what he's capable of by now, and maybe they want him for themselves. Not that he'd ever help another Contender. Or at least, I don't think he would.

When I silently speak his name for the tenth time, I hear a faint whine. My heart clenches. Racing through the snow, I barrel toward where I heard the sound. The trees press together, and I dodge between them as if I'm running an obstacle course. A green glow stops me in my tracks, and a chill shoots through my limbs when I see what's before me.

A pack of wolves surrounds Madox, hackles raised, noses sniffing the ground. Madox's tail curls between his legs, and the whimper he releases causes my entire body to charge with electric fear. His eyes are glowing green.

A wolf at the front of the pack, the largest, raises its head. It takes a quick step toward Madox, and when my fox stumbles backward, the pack leader takes it as a safe sign to attack. I cry out and rush forward, my arms flailing. I have just one chance to frighten the wolves away, but I make it only three steps before Madox begins to change. I hesitate, watching him. The brown fur abounding from his back tells me he's taking Monster's image.

He never makes a full transition.

The lead wolf slams into my fox, and the two roll to the side. Three different wolves stalk toward me, teeth snapping, warm air billowing from their jaws. That's not what has me worried, though; it's Madox beneath the largest wolf. It's Madox with his throat exposed. Just days before, he gave us a lead in this race by taking the form of a wolf to kill the panther Pandora. Now here we are in the mountains, being attacked by real wolves.

Maybe they're offended. Maybe they don't like being imitated.

The wolf growls as Madox kicks at its face. I try to move toward my Pandora, but the other wolves step between me and my fox, uncertain as to whether I'm a threat. The largest wolf falls back, only to regain its balance. It rears back as if it's going to lunge again, but when I see the blood dripping from Madox's body and into the virgin snow, I lose my mind with rage.

I run forward, screaming.

The wolf flies through the air toward Madox.

And at the exact same time, a new Pandora storms into view.

The wolf halts its advance and takes in the thick black neck, the fifteen hundred pounds of hostility, the deadly horns steadily aimed. Y-21 is poised before my small, injured Pandora like an assassin. His dark eyes flash as if the wolf is a blanket of red he's itching to tear through.

As the bull backs up, creating a shield with his crushing body, he sends a message as lethal as lightning splitting the sky.

If you want the fox, you'll have to go through me first.

Growling, the wolf takes one step back, but it keeps its legs bent in aggression, deciding whether to attack or retreat. I'm not sure what it's protecting, a den of pups somewhere or maybe its pride, but it doesn't seem to be backing down. My head snaps back and forth between the bull and wolf, hardly believing Y-21 is here. Wondering if his Contender is nearby, too.

Y-21 lifts his left hoof and kicks at the ground once, twice. The other wolves abandon their interest in me and instead focus on the bull. They yip and jump and growl, antsy to see what their leader will do.

The largest wolf eyes my fox behind the bull. It seems to decide that if the bull is protecting him, he must be a worthy prey. The wolf growls deep in its throat, and Y-21 lowers his head. In all fairness, the Pandora provided a warning, a chance for the wolves to flee unscathed, and now he'll show them what it means to piss off a Spanish bull.

Y-21 kicks the dirt once more — and when the wolf dashes to the bull's side, eager to steal Madox away — he charges. The ground thunders, and the stars shudder, and the wolf realizes its mistake too late. Y-21 drives his right horn into the wolf's sternum, and the animal is hoisted into the air. A howl of pain rips through the night, and the remaining gray wolves scatter around the bull like spiders along a web.

Y-21 slams his horns against the ground until the wolf is dislodged in a gray, bloodied heap. It's then that I realize I haven't moved an inch. I'm frozen solid, from fear and the cold combined. I race for my fox, who is pulling himself up on wobbly legs.

I grab him and pull his snow-laden body against my chest.

Are you okay? Madox, tell me you're okay!

I turn in time to see the other wolves spring toward Y-21 at once. They have to fight as a pack, and now that their leader is dead, they're wild with fear and hunger and adrenaline. The wolves are still in the air, poised to fall upon the bull, when Y-21 tightens within himself. His eyes close, his body locks, he takes a deep, concentrated breath.

I'm not sure what he's doing when —

A red blast detonates from the bull's body like a bomb.

The wolves are thrown back.

I am thrown, too.

When I uncover my face, the wolves are scattering into the night. The leader lies dead against a giant tree, but Madox and I are okay. My Pandora licks my face, and the gesture brings tears to my eyes. I hold him with one arm and use my free arm to push myself up off the ground. Then I wrap myself around Y-21.

"Thank you," I breathe. "That was incredible." But already the bull is peeling away from me and trotting toward the shadows cast by the woods. I'm torn as to what to do, when Guy rushes into view.

"What's going on?" he asks. And then, seeing Y-21 flee, he says, "Is Cotton here? Did he do something?"

Olivia and Harper are right behind him.

"Is he okay?" Harper asks, nodding toward Madox.

I fight the guilt metastasizing in my gut. "He'll be all right, I think. And, no, Cotton wasn't here. Only his Pandora."

Guy sees the dead wolf and races to my side. "Are *you* okay?"

"I'm fine."

"Why are you out here?" he asks.

I won't lie. I already put us into jeopardy by falling asleep, and I won't add insult to injury. "I nodded off during my watch. When I woke up, Madox was gone. I came to look for him, and he was surrounded by wolves. Y-21 came to our rescue." I curl my thumbs into my palms and squeeze. "I'm sorry I fell asleep. This is my fault."

"Don't worry about it, Tella," Braun says, appearing with the other Pandoras. "It happens to the best of us."

Guy glances again at the perimeter, where Y-21 has already disappeared. "You think he's following us?"

He means Cotton. We all know he means Cotton.

Harper takes two steps forward and peers into the darkness. "It could be that his Pandora is alone and followed because he didn't know what else to do."

We read into what Harper is saying. That Cotton has gone the way of Willow, in some fashion or another. It doesn't seem likely, but strength and agility can only get you so far in the Brimstone Bleed. Sometimes, luck is just as important.

"Should we follow his Pandora?" Olivia poses.

No one responds because we don't know what the right answer is. When Guy turns and heads back to where we were sleeping, one hand on my back, we follow his lead, silent in our retreat.

Madox lets me hold him the entire way.

CHAPTER SIXTY-TWO

We locate the seventh flag early the next morning and an eighth one that night. The following day, we find the ninth. But that's not all we find. A light dances in the distance, and when I see it for the first time, my stomach threatens to turn my breakfast out on its rear.

Guy, Harper, Braun, Olivia, and I stand shoulder to shoulder. Behind us are our Pandoras: a lion, an eagle, an elephant, a fox, a bear, an iguana, and an alligator. This is what remains of our crew. We've battled through jungle, desert, ocean, and mountain to arrive at this destination. We've survived raging rivers, men with spears, dehydration, the Triggers, oceanic storms, jellyfish stings, Pandora Wars, hypothermia, avalanches. We've come out the other side alive and bitter.

We want the Cure.

And we want revenge.

Now that we are so close to both, we're rendered speechless. Finally, after a long moment of reflection, Olivia breaks our silence. "It's base camp, huh? The final one?"

"It could be another Contender lighting a fire," Braun offers.

Harper shakes her head. "No, it's base camp. There isn't much more of the mountain to climb."

"There are five of us," Guy says. "We just have to hope we're the first to make it there."

I pick Madox up off the ground to give my hands something to do. Staring at the light, I feel my pulse pound. I can hardly stand still, and if we don't start running soon, I'll explode from anticipation. "Is everyone sure they want to do this? We've seen what they did to us in the race. Who's to say it won't be worse on the inside?"

“I’m in.” Braun gazes at his blue wristband. “I have too many questions.”

“I’m with you all the way,” Harper says.

Olivia stands tall. “Me, too.”

Guy pats the backpack, which now holds a knife and a second pickax, and the hint of a smile haunts the corner of his mouth.

I put Madox down. “That’s that, then. We race to the finish line, overcome whatever obstacles may lie ahead. First one who reaches the finish line wins the Cure, but we all accept their invitation to work should they offer it.” I say this last part almost in a question, because we never really discussed who would win the Cure if we reached base camp at the same time.

The Contenders nod their assent, and we’re off, no longer able to hold ourselves back. We stride through the snow, practically running, and as the sun falls on our backs, my anxiety slips away. I realize that as soon as I reach base camp, there will be food and warmth and maybe showers. It will be over. The Brimstone Bleed will be over. Regardless of the outcome, there will be no more jungle or desert or ocean or mountain.

My legs power up and up and up, my lungs fighting for the limited oxygen supply. We travel a half mile beside a large crevasse before spotting a big white tent like you’d see at a circus. It’s situated precariously on the edge of the mountain and is surrounded by lit torches. Rows of jagged rocks sit below it like broken teeth, and I suddenly understand exactly what obstacle the climbing equipment was intended for. I don’t see how anyone could ever make it up those cliff faces without tools, but when my eye catches movement along the rocks, I realize it must be possible.

“There are other Contenders on the cliff,” I exclaim.

Olivia starts running, her short legs carrying her faster than I thought possible. “Let’s go, let’s go!”

We don't need any more prompting. We run. All five of us and our Pandoras, too — we race toward the rocks. My hands splice the air, and my legs burn beneath me, and I step inside my body. It's easy in life — especially in the Brimstone Bleed — to live detached. To always have one foot inside your head and another elsewhere, in a memory or in a dream of what's to come. But right now I'm so incredibly *present*. My only thought is Cody. My only ambition to hold that Cure in my hands.

For the last three months, the Contenders and I have grown to be a family. Not anymore. Now we run forward as if we can somehow glimpse our *real* families standing in the distance.

I'm coming, Cody!

I'm going to win for you!

As soon as the thought crosses my mind, I can't dismiss it. I must win. I must save my brother. All this time, I've tried to envision the end, but it felt slippery in my mind, like a ghostly fog the morning after a heavy rain. The same thing happens when I picture what the afterlife might entail.

But this is real. I'm here, and I'm running and counting how many Contenders I spot on the rocks — four. But they have an unfathomable distance to climb without equipment. Will they fight us for the things we've found? How did they even pass us?

They didn't worry about the flags, I think. They decided at the start of the race that speed was the only way they'd win, and they bet on base camp's being at the top of the mountain. But now those same flags will save us. They've provided the tools we need to bypass the other Contenders and make it to the top.

A thought slows my steps. There aren't enough tools to get us all to the top. And what about our Pandoras? My eyes scan the expanse at the base of the vertical cliffs, and I spot animals pacing. Some cry out to their Contenders, who are already several feet above their heads, while others huddle quietly against the driving snow.

"Wait," I yell to the others, but they don't stop.

Madox jumps in place before me, and Monster shoves me from behind. They're operating on instinct now, and those instincts are telling them to keep me moving. But there's no room for mistakes anymore. This is it. So I yell for my Contenders again, and this time Guy turns and looks back. When he sees I'm standing still, he yells for the others. They don't stop until he hollers that he has the climbing equipment.

"What are you doing?" Harper looks as if I've launched a personal attack by *not* running. "Tella, let's go! I can help you climb when we get —"

"What is it?" Guy asks, breathing heavily.

"It's just . . ." It's just what? I've wasted crucial seconds, and I have no idea why. But that's not entirely true. My gut is speaking again, whispering uncertainty to the rest of my body. I look at Guy. "Do you remember in the desert, at the start of the race? All the other Contenders plunged forward, but you rooted us in place. We strategized. We explored our supplies and decided how we would proceed."

"I remember." He's listening so intently, his features so entirely focused, that I want to kiss him. Not like I did when we stood before that icy bridge. I want to kiss him as if time has loosened its dictatorial control, as if we're lying in the grass outside our college dorms and it's the first real day of spring. I want to kiss him so that he understands my feelings for him run to the center of the earth.

My eyes slide over the landscape, searching for the quickest way to the cliff, perhaps hoping there are more supplies we're overlooking.

"There's a light," Harper observes.

Braun is bent over, catching his breath. "We established that."

"No," Harper says. "Not the ones around base camp. It's coming from the crevasse."

We turn toward the jagged break in the land that we've been traveling beside. I see the light, too. It's faint, but something is definitely flickering. Braun starts marching toward the glimmer, and Olivia calls out to him.

"Where're you going?"

"To check it out. Evaluate our options. Like in the desert, right?"

We jog after him, and when we get to the edge and glance down, a clap of thunder sounds through my body. Along the lip of the fault — a few feet down and running in both directions — are lit torches. If I look below them, even farther down the wall, I can see more torches. There's something else, too. Flags. A half dozen of them, at least.

"Holy crap," I hear myself say. "They're leading down."

We crane our heads back up, and I watch the Contenders climbing up the cliff face in the distance. If we linger much longer, we may not reach the tent at the top of the mountain even with our equipment. But . . .

"What if it's a distraction?" Harper asks.

"No way," Olivia responds. "That tent is the distraction."

I think back to the beginning of the mountain race, to what the woman said.

The flags will be your most loyal friends during this leg of the race, pointing you toward safety and success. All you have to do is follow them quickly, and the prize is yours.

"They wanted us to collect the equipment. They wanted us to stay on their path." I reach for Guy's pack. He gives it to me. "We were never meant to use it for climbing. We were meant to use it for descent.

"The way to the final base camp is down."

CHAPTER SIXTY-THREE

Braun picks me up and spins me in a circle. It feels a bit like being hugged by Monster. "You figured it out, Tinker Bell."

"Let's hope," I mumble when he sets me down.

Olivia's Pandora senses we're excited about something and blows through her nose. In response, RX-13 flies onto her back.

Guy pulls the rope, the blade, the harness, and the two pickaxes that protrude from the top of the pack. He hands one end of the rope to RX-13 and asks the eagle to fly to the bottom to see if we have enough slack. The Pandora doesn't move a muscle until Harper gives the same command. Guy holds on to one end as RX-13 disappears, and when she reappears moments later, Guy seems satisfied.

"How are you sure it reaches the bottom?" Braun asks.

"Because I would have felt the rope tighten otherwise," Guy answers. "Let's send V-5 down first." His words rush over one another. "We'll secure the rope around his middle and lower him down. Then we'll lower the elephant and M-4. We can go down last, and if KD-8 mimics the bear, we'll have well over a thousand pounds to manage our weight."

"And then the two bears will descend on their own," I finish for Guy.

"That's right."

"Can we really lower my elephant down?" Olivia asks. "What if she falls?"

"It's a risk we'll all take." Harper brushes Olivia's shoulder. The aggression she once showed the girl has vanished, but the emptiness Harper carries for her own daughter, and for Willow and Jaxon, too, is still real enough to touch.

Guy secures the rope around the alligator's middle, and I murmur in the Pandora's ear, imploring him to stay still. As I watch

Guy work, I see it's obvious the training his father gave him and his three brothers included tying knots. I've never seen such things — works of art, really. Maybe I should still be afraid of Guy. Throw in some duct tape, and you've got yourself a prize-winning kidnapper.

"That'll do him." Guy yanks once on the rope. "He's about six hundred pounds at best guess. But we've got five people and six Pandoras to help lower him down."

I ask Madox to change shape, and we all secure the rope in some fashion. After stepping away from my place, I bend down and hug the alligator, and after much coaxing, the Pandora steps off the side of the ledge. We jolt with the sudden weight. But we've got him. We do. And so, foot by foot, we lower him.

When the rope goes slack, Harper asks RX-13 to fly down and undo the knots. I doubt it's possible that anyone can untie those things, much less a bird, but I've seen RX-13 cut incisions on Harper's stomach to mark our progress in the jungle with expert precision, so maybe I should give the eagle more credit.

Several seconds pass, and the eagle appears with the other end of the rope. We laugh and slap one another on the backs that our plan has worked.

Guy glances behind us, anxious that we're not moving fast enough. I'm anxious, too. My legs itch to continue running toward a visible destination. "Let's do the elephant next," Guy says. "She and M-4 are both about four hundred pounds, I'd say." He looks at Olivia pointedly. "We're lucky your Pandora isn't a full-grown elephant."

Olivia grins as if she had a hand in this.

The baby elephant descends easily enough, but the lion takes more effort with only the Contenders and the bears to help. Finally, we send the iguana and then descend ourselves. I go second to last, right before Guy, and it isn't nearly as terrifying as I thought it would be. The trip takes about two minutes. The worst part is the way my body sits inside the rope and harness. When my feet touch the stone bottom, Harper helps me remove my bindings.

There's a smile on her face that I don't understand until I see what she's referencing. There are lit torches leading along the floor and into a tunnel. "You were right," she says. "This is the way."

"Do you think we're first?" Olivia bounces on the balls of her feet, eager to get going.

I shrug. I want to believe we are, but something stops me. "I don't know. Forty-one people ran in the final leg. It's not like it was hard to see the fire coming from the crevasse once we looked in that direction. For all we know, this could still be a diversion."

"But there were no flags leading to the tented area," Braun says. "And there are here."

I rub the spots where the rope burned my skin. "It's true."

Guy touches down a few seconds later, and AK-7 and KD-8 descend down the frozen rock, using their retractable claws as leverage.

He unties himself and says, "We should get moving. We're lucky another Contender didn't pass by up there."

I take all our equipment — the things we used and the things we didn't — and divide it between us. Harper and I take pickaxes, Braun takes the knife, Olivia gets the rope, and Guy takes the harness.

"Seriously, the harness?" Guy says.

"Yeah, Mr. Green Beret," Harper says through a laugh. "That's what you get for being all capable."

I check on my Pandoras, and our group sets off down the tunnel, running as fast as we can in our deteriorated condition. Rose glows to keep the path visible, and Oz emits heat so we're warm. The pair of Pandoras look like rejects at a retail store with the red stripes decorating their backs. Up ahead, Monster and Madox take the lead, and the elephant and lion take our rear. We don't know what to expect at the other end of this tunnel, but we have friends, we have Pandoras, and we have weapons, so we continue our exploration with heads held high.

Every few yards, another torch burns, telling us we're on the right track. The breath is loud leaving my lungs, and I find it hard to slow my heart. I don't like being underground. Not after being buried under that avalanche.

The tunnel is widening up ahead, and Olivia slips her hand into mine as we race. I hold it in my own as if it's a lifeline to safety and sanity. Somewhere in my head, I question whether we should be slowing. If this is the last stretch, and up ahead is the true base camp, we should keep running at top speed. But our steps quiet as we reach the tunnel's end, and not one person strides quicker than the other.

"It's down to us," Olivia whispers.

"Yeah," Braun says. "The Rambos."

Harper smiles. "I'm proud to call myself a Rambo."

Guy and I nod. We're proud, too.

Madox pads between Olivia and me, his footfalls silent along the stone floor. A musky scent hangs in the air, and somewhere in the distance I hear a slight trickling of water. The walls are moist, and the ceiling stretches ten feet above our heads. It isn't high enough.

As we reach the other side of the tunnel, Guy squeezes in closer to my side, and Harper glances at me every couple of seconds.

This is it, she says with her eyes. *This is what I came back for. Be ready.*

We step outside the tunnel, and my jaw drops when I see what lies before us.

CHAPTER SIXTY-FOUR

When I was in middle school, I ran track. My favorite was the hundred-yard dash — just me, a straight stretch of asphalt, and bright yellow lines separating me from my competitor. Oh, and a middle-aged woman with ghastly elastic gym shorts and a stop-watch. But never mind her.

I'm familiar with a track, but the lanes ahead of us are different. They're separated by glass inserts so that if you ran straight ahead, you could see your running mates nearby but you wouldn't be able to touch them. The room spreads out in a great, yawning cavern, and stalactites spike from the ceiling like a blowfish that's feeling particularly ornery. It's the most divine thing I've ever seen, save for the track.

At the end of each lane is a white door crudely built into stone, and there's little question as to what we're supposed to do next. But Braun retrieves the device from his pocket to check, and my heart pitter-pats when I see the red light is blinking. This is the last message we'll ever receive. I know this the same way I know my own name. The same way I know I'll crumble if I don't win the Cure for Cody.

We fit our white devices into our ears, and my mind rushes through all the challenges I've overcome to arrive here and all the people and Pandoras I've watched die. A question forms in my mind like an iridescent pearl inside the belly of an oyster.

If I could go back to the moment when I drove toward the Old Red Museum, would I still have gone? Would I have stayed quiet as my mom came to my room and tied the blue-and-green feather in my hair? Would I have risked my life so that my brother could meet a girl and fall in love and live a perfectly ordinary life?

Yes. Over and over again, yes.

Clicking.

Static.

The woman's voice comes through my earbud so clearly, it's as if she's standing before me, a sly smile on her intolerable face.

"Contender, if you're hearing this message, you have reached the end of the Brimstone Bleed. Congratulations. We, at headquarters, are proud of your many accomplishments, and impressed with the agility and speed at which you overcame obstacles. If you'll please dispose of any equipment found along your journey, we can move on to what lies next."

The woman pauses, and Guy motions that we should oblige. So we set our things on the ground. Guy disposes of his harness last, which is a real blow, I'm sure. Madox rears up and stretches toward my waist. I pet him with my free hand as my pulse tap-dances.

"We have three final challenges for you to tackle. The first will test your decision making, the second will test your limitations, and the final challenge will test your dedication to procuring the Cure. At this time, we'll ask that you send your Pandora down your chosen lane. Each Contender must complete this last portion of the Brimstone Bleed with a Pandora, so if you do not have one, we'll ask that you first acquire a Pandora and then return."

As the other Contenders pet their Pandoras and whisper instructions, I send my fox a message using my mind.

Madox, we have to complete three final tests before we're finished. I point to the white door at the end of the closest lane. *They want you to go through that door. I'll be right behind —*

He's already gone, tearing down the track like a black bullet. The door slides into the ceiling, and he vanishes from view. Madox is already somewhere I can't touch him. The thought sends the first solid bolt of fear through my body. I was afraid before, but this kind of anxiety I can feel in my teeth. Madox has been waiting for this moment, I realize. He was built to ensure I win. But it's more than that. My Pandora loves me as I do him. We are best friends, he and I.

And he's not about to let me down.

I give Monster and Oz the same instructions, and they take off after Madox, albeit a bit slower. Everyone else's Pandoras do the same, and Braun sends Rose down with a silent look of acknowledgment in my direction.

I'm the farthest Contender on the left. To my right, I see Guy, Harper, Olivia, and then Braun.

Harper steps backward and meets my gaze. She nods once, and understanding passes between us. She won a portion of the Cure before and passed it along to Caroline. Now she's going to win the real thing and pass it along to me. I can tell from the tension in her body that this is better than she envisioned the end would be. Now she doesn't have to help me win or get in anyone's way. *She* just has to win. From the fierce look in her eyes, she's prepared to do anything to make that happen.

Harper steps back to the track, and Guy and I share a look. A million unsaid words hang in the air. Things we wish we could take back. Things we never admitted. Then again, maybe some things don't need to be spoken out loud. Not when we've spent three months overcoming impossible odds. Not when we've carved out stolen moments and made each other stronger, and softer. Not when we've exchanged gentle embraces and fierce kisses.

Guy Chambers raises his pointer and middle fingers. He places them beneath his eyes and points forward. It's the same thing he did to me at the start of the jungle race. This time, it makes me smile. He does, too.

"Are you ready for the final tests, Contender?" the woman says inside my ear.

Beat.

Beat.

Beat.

"Go!"

CHAPTER SIXTY-FIVE

I run, slicing down the track like a bird in flight. Steps before I reach the door, it slides open. I dart through it and land inside a blindingly white room. The space is the size of a large living room, and the walls are constructed from cinder blocks. Across from me is an eight-foot-long table, and upon it, an infinite number of keys. Dirt squishes under my boots as I cross the space. I stare down at the keys with confusion until I spot a door on either side of the room, both different from the one I entered through. I pick up one of the keys and move to the closest door and insert it into the keyhole.

As soon as the key touches the lock, a wall of glass slides down from the ceiling, separating me from the other half of the room. With my heart hammering, I drop the key to the ground and go to inspect the glass. It's completely transparent, and in the center is a door with a keyhole, much like the one on my side of the room.

The far door grumbles open, and Madox walks into the room.

Immediately, my palms begin to sweat. I tap the glass, and he sees me on the other side. My Pandora trots toward me, his eyes sad with worry. I look at the door he came through, expecting to see Monster and V-5 follow him in, but the door closes.

Madox, can you hear me? I think.

He barks.

A click comes from the ceiling, and Madox and I both look up, searching for the source of the noise. Fear grips me when I see green smoke wafting from an air vent on Madox's side of the room. I pound on the glass, knowing whatever is slowly filling his space can't be good. Remembering the table, I rush toward the keys. I tear off my down jacket and scoop as many of the silver antique keys into the bottom of my long-sleeved shirt as I can. Back at the door, I try one key after another, my hands shaking when I see the green mist sinking toward the floor.

Madox barks and lowers to his belly, all too aware that the green gas may be dangerous.

Don't worry, I'll get you out.

My Pandora whines as I try another key. When it doesn't unlock the glass door that separates us, I toss the reject to the ground and reach for another. There are easily fifty keys in my shirt and hundreds more on the table. If the green gas is deadly, I'll never reach him in time. When my eye catches sight of the two other doors in this room, I scream with frustration. One is the door I entered through, and it doesn't have a keyhole, but the other one does. What if that's the secret? What if *that* door leads to Madox and not this one?

I can't be sure unless I try all the options. Two doors, hundreds of keys. My stomach plummets when I notice the green smoke curling around Madox's body, licking his black coat. My Pandora shifts into eagle form and flies toward the vent. He tries to close the slats with his talons, but they don't budge. Next, he shifts to mimic Y-21 and slams into his door with mighty bull horns, but the material doesn't give.

As Madox continues to try different options, I shove keys into the glass door, searching for the solution. Madox falls to the floor, back in fox form, a shrill sound emanating from his throat. Tears blur my vision, and I drop several keys in a panic and cry out in frustration.

Hold on, Madox. Just hold on!

I glance back at the table. There are countless remaining, and another door to try after this one. Still, I push onward. I pluck a key from the pile in my outstretched shirt that's much too big to fit, so I toss it to the ground. Dirt plumes around the discarded key, and the sight gives me an idea.

I drop to a crouch, careful to keep the keys from falling, and dig my hands into the dirt. It's loose and easy to pull away. As Madox howls, kicking at nothing, eyes clenched shut, I drop the rest of the keys to the floor.

We have three final challenges for you to tackle. The first will test your decision making. . . .

I'm not sure if what I'm thinking will work, but the keys never will, not with how quickly the fluorescent fog is filling his side. Not with how much pain my Pandora is already experiencing.

Madox! You have to dig your way out. Take Monster's form and dig!

When he doesn't move, I scream and beat on the glass with open palms. I sound like an animal, as if I've finally waved goodbye to my humanity.

Get up! You have to get up. KD-8, get up, for me!

My fox pulls himself up, stumbles, and tries again. He arches his back, barely able to summon the strength to shift shapes. His nails extend, and he staggers to the glass wall. The fox, dressed as a bear, begins to dig. He's able to dig a few inches before he hits something hard.

Try another spot! Quick!

My fox tries two more places without success until I instruct him to dig beneath the door he came in through. This time, nothing stops his tunneling. As the green gas completely fills the room, Madox shifts into iguana form and slides beneath the door. As his green tail disappears from view, I whoop with triumph.

The glass wall separating me from the toxic fog lifts, rumbling into the ceiling. I back away, tripping over my own feet, the smile on my face dying. As the gas leaks into my side of the room, I begin to panic once again. I won't be able to dig my way out. Not as he did. I look back to the keys, wondering if I made a mistake by not pursuing that option.

As the fog touches the tips of my boots — and I manically decide whether to try and wriggle my way through the tunnel Madox created or resume trying the keys — the door behind me opens.

CHAPTER SIXTY-SIX

The next room I enter is the same as before, white on white. On the left side is an underground pool filled with syrupy green water. On the right is a rectangular black mat, and suspended above it is an iron box the size of a mattress. I marvel at how similar this area looks to the indoor pool room we had at Ridgeline High in Boston, minus the creepy swamp water.

There's no scent of chlorine in the air, but I do smell something that resembles gasoline. It's so strong, I can almost feel it inside my mouth, on my tongue. I hear water lapping against the side of the pool gently, and I think to myself that it shouldn't be moving at all. Unless something is beneath the surface.

"Step onto the performance pad," a woman's voice booms from a mounted speaker. "We'd like to test your endurance."

I search the area for Madox. When I don't see him anywhere, I clear my throat and say, "Where is my Pandora?"

The room echoes my words.

"Get on the performance pad," she replies.

On the far side of the room, I spot a white door. I'm assuming the door behind me won't open again, which means the door ahead is the only way out.

The first will test your decision making, the second will test your limitations. . . .

After sleeping in the snow and hiking until I retched with fatigue, I have to show them I am strong. I raise my chin and stride toward the right side of the room. Guy Chambers believes I am strong, and you know what? I am.

I take off my boots and climb onto what must be the performance pad.

"It is of the utmost importance that you do not leave the pad. Above you hangs a vat of oil, approximately three hundred degrees Fahrenheit. If you leave the treadmill, weight sensors inside the track will decompress and the oil will be discharged. Do you understand?"

My head begins to pound, and I shift my body to prepare. When I do, the iron box creaks with excitement. I freeze.

"Do you understand?" the woman repeats.

Blackness seeps in at the edges of my vision, but I nod my head and shout a confident, "I understand. Let's go."

The black pad is built into the ground, and when it starts moving, it rolls from front to back like a treadmill. I pick up the pace and tell myself to not look up, to keep my eyes straight ahead. I'm a good runner. Even if I'm exhausted, I'm light on my feet and agile. I can run for days. That's what I tell myself anyway. That's what I repeat like a mantra as the belt races faster.

My socked feet hit the ground. *Thump-thump-thump-thump*, and I run. I never ran long-distance in track, but I decide to think of it as a new hobby. The sun has risen above the trees in Montana, and it's a glorious day. I have new running shoes, Nikes with purple swooshes. And I've got a running partner, too: my best friend from Boston, Hannah.

In school, everyone called us powder puff girls. But we've pinkie-promised that we won't be powder puff any longer. Today is our first run, and I'm not about to let her down.

This is good, the daydreaming. I'm doing well.

Until I'm not. Until sweat is racing down my chest, and I recall that I was parched before I descended into the crevasse. Where is this perspiration coming from? And at what cost? My legs burn beneath me, but I pay them no mind. They're not attached to my body any longer. They're doing their own thing down there, and apparently they love them some running.

My head is another matter. Pressure builds behind my eyelids, and my ears ring. It feels as if my brain has swollen, and there's not enough room in my skull to contain the gray, multiplying mass.

I stumble and catch myself a moment before I fall. The iron trap above reminds me it's there, waiting. When the performance pad increases in speed once again, I scream and match it stride for stride.

I'm sweaty, I'm nauseated, and the room is spinning. Mostly, though, I'm furious. After all we've been through, this is our reward? I flatten my hands, check my form, control my breathing.

"Is that all you've got?" I holler. "Come on! Faster! Faster!"

A siren screams from the speaker.

Bleeeeeeeeeeeep!

It sounds like a timer at a basketball game. The moment the noise stops, the pad does the same.

"We've accurately recorded your physical limitations," the woman says. "You may now step off the performance pad. Don't be afraid."

But I am afraid. I glance at the iron cage above my head. Then I lunge off the belt and slide across the floor. Nothing happens. I'm cool. I feel as if someone came at my head with a baseball bat, but I'm cool.

"You will now go into the pool and tread until you hear the timer. If you touch the edge or your head dips below the surface, South American piranhas will be released into the water. Do you understand?"

Do I understand? I understand she just said *piranhas*, and all I'm thinking is, *Are South American piranhas worse than the North American version?* Is *there a North American version?* God, I hope not.

I eye the pool, and something inside me fragments. After spending so much time in the ocean, I hoped to never approach another body of water again, even a pool, and the thought of a fish gouging chunks out of my skin produces terrible memories of Jaxon's death. I tear off my long-sleeved shirt and pants, and step toward the edge. I may regret the decision to strip should they release the fish, but I'm betting on my ability to do this, and clothing will only inhibit my movements.

"Do you under —"

"Yes!" I holler. "I understand. Stop asking me that."

I dip one foot into the water. It's ice-cold, just as I had anticipated. After all, we are beneath a mountain, and here winter is in full effect. The green liquid feels thick as I wade into it, using concrete steps near the corner. I'm halfway in — goose bumps rising across every inch of my skin, my body shaking from the cold — when I spot cages built into the sides of the pool.

Small fish swarm around one another like fog in a blender. Glass separates me from them, but I wonder how fast that glass can slide away. Knowing the people running this race are watching, I swim to the middle of the pool. I won't give them the satisfaction of seeing me afraid.

I tread for several minutes, and even though I know I shouldn't, I find myself glancing at the sides of the pool to ensure the fish haven't been released. I can't see the bottom. It's either too deep or the water is too murky. It reminds me of swimming in a pond that's overfilled with algae and general repulsiveness.

As I tread, my body warms, and I begin to think I'll endure this without problem. I don't see anything else in the room they could test me with, so this has to be the end of the second round. One more after this. One more and I could hold the Cure for Cody.

The overhead lights flip off.

I'm treading water in complete darkness. Terror shoots from the top of my head and down through my feet. I can't see anything. Not the room and not what's beneath the water. I jolt with shock when loud, crashing music comes through the speakers. It sounds like the heavy metal Cody listened to during his grunge phase. The pounding in my head returns with a vengeance, and with the music so loud, I suddenly can't be sure I'm breathing.

Water splashes into my mouth, and I choke. A moment later, something brushes my leg.

"No!" I scream.

I swim toward the ledge, positive I'm about to be consumed. My hand is almost on the steps when I remember what the woman said. I yank my arm back, and, thinking of my brother, I swim back to the middle of the pool. My head hasn't dipped below the surface. I haven't touched the perimeter of the pool. There's nothing in the water besides my overactive imagination.

I breathe.

As I tread — body demolished by exhaustion, music blasting vehemently — I hold Madox in my mind. The sooner I'm done with these tests, the sooner my Pandoras and I will be reunited. Or at least I hope. I also think about my brother, about the time his three-year-old rear broke out of our house while Mom was in the shower, and ran stark naked down the street. A neighbor we didn't know spotted him, put him in their car, and drove slowly by each house asking, "Is that your house? Is *that* your house? How about that one?"

Mom was mortified, and it later became my absolute favorite story to tell every female who passed through our humble abode.

Oh, you're here for my brother? Want to hear a story involving nudity?

I think about other times, too. Like when I was a freshman in high school and all the seniors were handpicking frosh and making them walk across the stage before throwing away their lunch trays. It wasn't a big deal, really, but it was the *first* day of school. And it was the stage, where everyone could gawk and holler at you for a full thirty seconds. When a senior chick told me it was my turn, I was mortified. But my brother, who was a junior at the time, yelled across the cafeteria for me to wait up. He walked across that stage with me, his middle finger waving toward the room like a great American flag. Cody was popular, and from then on out, I was, too. Never mind that he got detention for flipping off half the student body.

Later that night, after Mom and Dad had left the table, I thanked him for what he'd done. He told me to stop talking with my mouth full and that I was disgusting.

I opened my mouth wider.

He laughed.

I won.

At this point, my entire neck is beneath the water. I have to turn my face upward to keep from going completely under. My body burns like vengeance and then prickles from the cold. My lungs tighten, and my heart hardens as if Medusa stepped out in front of me and I looked those snakes dead in the eye. When I reach the point of no return, when I know I have nothing left to give and I'm gasping for air and calling Guy's name, the buzzer sounds.

My body slides beneath the surface.

I can't help it. I have no fight left in my muscles. For a few seconds, I float weightless in the water, not caring if the piranhas have been released. Not caring if they tear me into a billion bite-sized, candy-coated pieces.

When I emerge, the lights are back on and the music has changed to a soothing lullaby. I swim toward the steps, climb them, and collapse onto the ground. The lights dim to a comfortable level, the music lulls me to sleep, and my eyes slip closed. I battle the impulse to sleep. I can't lose consciousness now. I can't!

It's no use.

Tella out.

Minutes later, a buzzer sounds for the third time. I sit up quickly, panting. I'm dead. I must be. I've never felt so awful in my life. If I was depleted of energy before I climbed down the crevasse and into this living nightmare, now I'm completely spent. That five-minute power nap has worsened everything. Now my head feels foggy, and my body screams for more sleep. As it is, I have to literally hold my lids open to keep them from reclosing.

The gentle music has stopped, and the lights are at the same level of brightness as they were when I entered.

On the opposite side of the room, the white door slides open.

CHAPTER SIXTY-SEVEN

I walk into the final challenge. I can hardly hold my head up, and yet I'm one room away from the Cure. One room from saving my brother's life. I can't let myself believe I've been beaten by other Contenders. I am first. I have to be.

Four ecosystems.

Three months.

One remaining task.

Madox, Monster, and Oz are lying on a stark white-tiled floor. My legs carry me toward them, and I collapse in a dripping, half-naked mess, exhaustion switching to panic over my Pandoras. I reach Madox first, take his limp head in my hands.

Madox? Can you hear me?

When he doesn't move, I look to Monster and then Oz. The three Pandoras are completely out but not dead. The bear's sides rise and fall, soothing my alarm. The wall ahead is clear glass, with a glass door in the center. The others are white drywall, and together they form a room as large as a high school gymnasium. I turn and look toward the door I came in through. As it slides shut, my eyes land on a table much like the one that held the keys.

But this table holds something different.

I start to cross the area when I hear a stir from one of my Pandoras. Spinning around, I find Monster lifting his weary head.

"Monster!" I run toward him and drop to my knees. He groans like the great, lovable oaf he is, and I can't help but laugh as I stroke the thick fur behind his ear. He cranes his neck to look at me, his eyes dull with sleep. "You're okay," I whisper to him. "You're safe."

And then Monster does something I don't expect.

He growls.

CHAPTER SIXTY-EIGHT

At first, I think it's because he was drugged. He's confused. But when the hair on the back of his neck rises and he pushes himself up, every muscle in his body tensed with aggression, I know he realizes what he's doing.

I stumble backward and slam into the table. It rattles, and I look down. My fingers brush a small gun. Next to it are three others like it, and around those are other weapons: axes, knives, swords, rifles. Understanding washes over me. A thousand possibilities rush through my mind, but they all end with this: Three Pandoras, one Contender who loves them, a table full of weapons, and the Cure on the other side of that glass door.

I shake my head.

No.

In a war between man and beast, beast will win every time. But between modern weaponry and beast? Well, that's not war. That's extermination.

After all this, it can't end this way. I won't do it. I won't hurt them. I want to say my brother's life is worth anything — but he wouldn't want this, either, would he?

The alligator wakes next, his yellow eyes sharpening as if he hasn't seen a meal in weeks and here I am, a ready-made Snack Pack.

This is a test, I remind myself. I only have to remind the Pandoras that we're on the same team. *That's the obstacle,* I tell myself. *I won't have to hurt them,* I lie.

Madox raises his head, staggers to his feet. He sees me, and when he does, a vicious snarl rumbles low in his chest. This time, there's no holding back the tears. I weep openly, my hands flying across the table out of some primal instinct.

The three Pandoras stalk toward me, snapping their teeth, sniffing the air, anticipating the scent of my blood. Like Titus, I collected Pandoras during this race. But, for me, it was done out of love. I couldn't stand the thought of leaving them behind when their Contenders were gone. So here I am, alone in this room with one, two, three predators. I understand now why they allowed Oz to come along even though his Contender didn't enter him into the Pandora Wars. And I understand why they let me keep Rose, too.

A memory flashes through my mind: Braun holding his dead Pandora in his arms.

"It was in my Pandora's head. What is it?"

He pulled a silver chip from his Pandora's skull. It blinked on and off, green. We never figured that mystery out. But we didn't need to. It's unfolding now, in a grand finale at the exact right time. Ta-da!

Surprisingly, the alligator is the first to reach me. He scrambles across the floor and snaps at my left leg with inconceivable crushing power.

I fall backward onto the table, sobs drowning my screams. "Please, no!"

When Monster rises up on his back legs and roars, I fumble for a weapon. I only have time to grab a knife before Madox shifts to take the lion's shape and rushes forward. I slide to the right, fall off the table and onto my hands and knees. Then I'm up, flying across the room.

Monster rushes toward me, and I stand my ground, tossing the knife to my right hand. As much as I don't want to hurt him, survival instincts won't let me be eaten. Mankind has fought too long to overcome being prey. My ancestors, my blood, they all survived so that today I could stand here, shaking, with a blade in my hand.

AK-7 swipes a paw toward my body, and I leap back. As soon as his claws are out of reach, I throw my arms over my head and scream. It's not a normal scream. It's not a *there's a spider in my bathroom* scream. It's an intimidation tactic. A weapon of defense.

It works. He comes down on all fours.

It's all the time I need.

I slice the air between us. I can't bring myself to hurt him, not unless I absolutely have to, but I can show him I'm capable of inflicting harm. The bear eyes the knife, and I hold my breath. Now that I'm on the offense, he'll either lunge or fall back. The question is which.

He falls back.

With the bear out of the way, the alligator scurries forward, hissing. I leap to the right, and the alligator follows my steps, jaws open. He snaps once at my ankle, but this time I don't scream. I'm afraid if I scream again, I'll lose what limited control I have on this situation. So I roar instead. I roar like I'm furious and isn't he going to regret it when he finds out who he messed with.

He shouldn't be afraid. As much as my instincts demand I defend myself, my heart holds my blade back. I tell myself I don't want to die, but I also can't wrap my mind around the alternative:

Killing my Pandoras.

Thinking quick, I race across the room, barely escaping Madox when he swings a lion paw at my bare waist. I jump onto the table like a champ, as if I was born to fight for my life after having every ounce of energy leached from my body. I snatch a sword I noticed earlier and rip the leather binding off the handle. Once again, my eyes fall on the guns. As I lunge for one, Monster dives toward the table.

No time.

I had one chance to grab a second weapon, and I chose a length of leather. This is why I'll die. Because when I had the opportunity to pick up a gun for the second time, I didn't. I race across the room, Madox bounding after me. I jump onto the alligator's back, and Monster and Madox both stop to see what I'll do.

As the alligator thrashes, I wrap the leather band over his eyes and under his jaw, nearly losing my blade and my left hand in the process. I've almost got the strap secure when the alligator switches on his heat. He radiates hotter than he did in the mountains, and my fingers burn against his skin. I let go, and he throws me off like a bucking bronco. V-5 scurries in his blindness and slams his snout into the wall. After that, he lies still, afraid to move.

Monster rises up on his back legs again. I jump to my feet and raise my arms over my head, matching his pose.

"Roarrrrr!" I yell.

The bear opens his mouth and releases his own roar. It rattles the walls. It rattles the mountain. Wind fires out of his paws and slams into my body. I tumble across the floor and crash against the wall. I right myself, ready for his next attack. But the bear pauses when he sees Madox changing shapes. The yellowish fur pulls in, and a silky black skin replaces it. Two ivory horns stretch from the sides of his head and end in forward-facing points.

His right front leg kicks at the ground, though there's nothing to kick.

My Pandora, my Madox, lowers his head.

He snorts once through his ringed nose.

A warning.

CHAPTER SIXTY-NINE

Madox rushes forward, and I scream. I can't help it. Terror lashes at my body like a flaming whip. I dodge the bull but slip on water I trailed into the room. Madox's horn is a hand away from tearing into my abdomen, and I think of how ironic it is that he'll spear me in the same place Titus's knife did on top of that desert formation.

But then he slips, too. The bull's legs slide out, one to either side, as if he's a gymnast in training. I right myself and run toward the table. I'm halfway across the room when I'm blindsided. Pain rips through my side, and I'm thrown ten feet. My blade flies out of my hand and lands near Oz. When I sit up, blood is seeping through four shallow gashes.

Monster's claws are stained the same color, and fresh tears spring to my eyes. His name, Monster, isn't so funny anymore.

The cuts aren't deep, but my side throbs all the same. "AK," I whisper. "You hurt me."

His nose twitches, and for a second I wonder if he's heard me, if there's still a loyal part of him deep down that the people in charge of this race haven't perverted with their chips and blinking lights. But he catches the scent of my blood, and he roars again. When I hear that murderous sound, I realize there's no chance I can reverse the things that have snapped in their minds. I am the enemy. I must be destroyed, or they must die trying.

I grip my side and, biting down against the searing agony, I race back toward the table. Madox drops his head and sniffs the bright red droplets I leave behind. Slowly, he follows my trail. I crash onto the table, and this time, I don't form a plan. I don't hesitate. I just close my hand around the cold barrel of a gun, and I take aim at Madox.

He charges toward me.

I pull the trigger.

CHAPTER SEVENTY

At the sound of the gun, AK-7 runs to the other side of the room and V-5 pushes himself against the wall. And Madox, my sweet Pandora, he stumbles. The bull with glowing green eyes is on bended knees, stunned by what just happened.

My arm remains outstretched, fingers curled around the weapon, the bullet lodged into drywall. I didn't know I was going to pull to the right until I did. Somewhere deep down, I prayed the glass would crack. But of course the bullet only ricocheted off and implanted itself elsewhere. It could have ended up in any of us.

I move the gun to the left and position the barrel between my Pandora's eyes.

Back up, I think.

He does.

Two of my Pandoras, Madox and Monster, are on the other side of the enormous room. The other hasn't made a sound in several minutes. "If any of you approach me," I say. "I will shoot to kill."

I repeat the message to Madox using my mind.

I'm not sure what I think this will accomplish. Already, Monster is edging toward me, snarling. He's taking small steps, but it won't take long before the grizzly bear decides to chance an attack. There's something in their heads telling them to end me. It's a command, and they were built to obey.

I've bought myself precious time, but it's in vain. Nothing will happen between now and the moment they cross the room. It's either me or them. When I understand this, when I truly accept that this is the final challenge, I crumble.

As Madox takes RX-13's shape and Monster inches ever closer, I wail with grief. Maybe because I won't kill them. Maybe because

I will. I try to picture my brother, to use Cody as support, but I can't. All I can think of are my Pandoras.

I remember the first time Madox changed shape in the jungle clearing to protect me. I remember the way Monster stood between me and his own Contender on hind legs, all eight feet of him, and warned Titus to back down. I remember when Oz, the alligator that couldn't swim, laid his head in my lap as a polished moon hung over our raft.

I remember Madox circling before falling asleep, warm beside me. I remember him prancing next to me in the desert, small footprints in the sand. I remember how brave he was to fight in that arena, to risk his *life*, to give me a day's advantage in the mountains. Looking at him, I remember that underneath his coat of feathers, he is my fox. My companion. My Pandora.

They all are.

Madox takes to the air, his eagle wings flapping, his talons directed toward my face. He'll use them to tear my eyes out the same way he did Titus's. Monster is below him, moving toward me with determination, realizing I'm hesitating and he's not the hesitating type. Not when he has killing to do.

I drop the gun.

I grab a blade.

It's a nice blade. A solid, clean blade. I know I must make a decision — me, or them. My brother, or my Pandoras. But I can't make this decision. I can't. Hot tears trickle down my face and drip onto my chest. I tilt my head, begging my Pandoras to back down.

In the end, it's Monster who forces me into action.

He rushes at me, jaws open, eyes wide. I scream and fall back onto the table. Weapons clatter to the floor. Heat spreads through my body, and my head throbs, and Monster closes the distance between us. He lifts up at the last minute as if to take me into his arms. I'll die like this, the blade shaking in my uncertain hand, and maybe that's okay. Maybe this means that after all I've been through, my reluctance to kill something I care about means I'm still human.

Monster is a handbreadth away. I can feel the warmth of his breath on my exposed skin and fury rolling off his massive body.

Good-bye, Cody, I think.

My mind has given up, but when I look down, I notice the knife is still in my outstretched hand. And so when Oz barrels across the ground, surprising Monster and me both, the binding long gone from his eyes — I am able to defend myself.

The reptilian beast knocks me to the floor and snaps his jaws once, twice. A third of his body weight is laid over my legs, and his deadly teeth are dangerously close to my bare stomach. But that's not what causes me to cry out. I'm not afraid of being hurt by Oz, because it was I who hurt him.

My knife protrudes from the underside of his head. I drove it in so quickly, before I could even think about what I was doing. But now . . . now Oz moans, and his eyes close, and I scream for someone to help him.

Monster has stopped.

Madox has touched back down.

And my sweet Pandora, Oz, collapses onto his side.

I manage to pull my legs out from beneath him and then lay my body next to his. I stroke his thick skin and whisper in his ear and try to control the flood of emotion in my head. Because Oz is dying, his blood oozing onto the clean, white floor, and I'm the one who struck him down. It may have been a reflex reaction, but it's my fault all the same.

"You are the very best Pandora," I tell Oz, no longer caring if Monster or Madox will attack me while I'm vulnerable. "You are *my* Pandora, and I love you."

More and more blood flows from the wound beneath Oz's head, creating a circle of red around our bodies. He groans once more from deep in his chest and fills his lungs. And then he closes his eyes, and his body goes limp. When I realize he's gone and that I won't ever get him back, I release a cry that tears me apart from the inside. I curl myself over his lifeless form and let my tears fall onto his back, and I squeeze him hard.

Finally, I stand up, my chin quivering, my hands curled into fists. "I'm a good horse," I yell to the ceiling, knowing they're watching. What a great show I'm putting on, huh? Worth every penny! "But I don't want to race anymore. I'm done."

CHAPTER SEVENTY-ONE

Monster and Madox slump to the floor, and I hear the click of a door opening, louder than a gunshot in the sudden silence. The first thing I do is creep toward Madox. He's back in fox form and fast asleep. Blood runs down my leg and side, but the Pandoras aren't eager to taste it anymore. Hurting Oz did it — it stopped the test — and I feel sick to my stomach for doing what they wanted. There were guns on the table, for crying out loud. Guns. They didn't want us dead. They just wanted a last bit of torture. One last hoorah before they decided we were dedicated enough.

I touch each of my Pandoras in turn, sobbing at the sight of Oz, and stride toward the exit. In the doorway, I glance back at Madox.

I'll be back for you. For all of you.

Outside the glass wall, there's a white hallway that leads to my right. I trudge down it but perk when I see another glass wall. Inside, I see something that causes my steps to falter. If I had any heart left, this scene would steal the very last piece. But I'm all used up, and so when I see Guy Chambers holding M-4's head in his lap, crying as a child would, I am numb.

I am numb as Guy rocks over the lion's lifeless body. I am numb when I see the bloodied blade near Guy's leg. I am numb as I realize this person I worship hurts in a way I can't touch.

His door is open. I go in and attempt to pull him up despite my injuries, despite the pain ripping through my body. He won't come. I yank on his arm harder, amazed at the sobs that explode from my throat, because I can't feel, can I? I thought I couldn't feel.

"We have to go," I tell him. "It's all for nothing if we don't go."

Guy looks up at me, his eyes red, his face streaked with tears. Pain slams into me like a wrecking ball. I thought I was numb, but really all my anger and hurt was being pressed down, compacted, so that when I saw Guy Unbreakable Chambers crying, all that tension could explode in a mushroom cloud of anguish.

His body shudders and he buries his face into his lion's side. "He was going to die anyway. Willow's rat . . . it injected him with something in the arena." He raises his face. "I had to do it, Tella. Right? I had to."

If he keeps crying like this, I won't be able to stand. As it is, I can barely control this tornado of fury. I drop down beside him, and when I see M-4 unmoving, when I see that he's actually gone, I lose what little composure I had left. My hands run through the lion's thick mane, and I clench my eyes shut.

"He loved you," I tell Guy, my voice breaking. "M-4 truly loved you."

Guy gasps for air and pulls me to him. He cries into my hair and holds me to his chest for several long seconds. When I lean back, I see that he's a bit calmer. So I say, "Your Pandora's job was to ensure you win. The best way you can honor him now is to stick by your plan."

"To win," he mumbles.

I nod, even though that's not the plan at all. "To win . . . *in the end.*"

His eyes fall to my side, and when he sees that I'm wounded, he's on his feet. "You're hurt," he says. "We have to get you help."

When I take his hands and stand up, I realize he's right. I feel funny, as if I'm in the dentist chair and they asked if I wanted laughing gas and I said, "What do *you* think?"

Guy looks back at M-4, and his brow furrows as if he might break down again. Then he grabs my hand, and we turn down the hallway and run. As we jog, we pass several more glass walls on our right. All are empty. We turn left at the end of the hallway and keep going. My heart pounds inside my chest when I understand this is it. I'm done with the tasks. I'm done with the race. I left a part of myself back there with my Pandoras, but I also can't wait to finish this. The wounds on my side feel as if they're opening farther with every step, and I have to stop. I have . . . to stop.

There's a door at the end of this hallway. It's blue and solid and has a brass handle. Guy and I race toward it, and I wonder what will happen if we go through it at the exact same time. Will they split the Cure between the two of us? Could they do that?

Guy reaches the door first, and my excitement wanes, but something in my head says, *This is good. He needs this.*

Guy swings the door open and grabs my arms. He shoves me through the open doorway. As soon as I stumble into the room, an alarm sounds. It's a buzzer like the one in the pool area. I glance around the room. It looks like every doctor's waiting room I've ever seen. There are navy blue chairs and a check-in window. The carpet is brown, and the fluorescent lighting overhead is infuriating. It smells like formaldehyde. It smells like death.

Seated in one of the chairs is Harper.

Her hands are folded in her lap, smeared with blood. When she hears the buzzer go off, she rises.

"I won," she says. "I'm the first to arrive."

I throw my arms around my friend as best I can, thankful she's unharmed.

Harper whispers in my ear. "You climbed that desert formation for me, Tella. You saved my Pandora so I could win, and you put your life on the line to do it. I didn't know Titus would be up there." She pauses. "It doesn't matter. You did that for me. And I did this for you."

She leans back and takes my face in her hands. When she drops them, I can feel the stickiness she leaves behind. Harper gazes down at her own hands.

"I didn't kill her," she says. "I only cut her a little, and the door opened."

Guy attempts to open the door on the other side of the room, but it doesn't budge. Then he taps on the glass where a receptionist would typically sit. No one comes. Guy sighs and sits down on one of the chairs. I can't handle seeing the sorrow on his face. I want to pull the numbness back over me like a warm blanket, but I can't remember how to do it.

We sit for a few minutes, unsure of what to do, until the door we came in through flies open, and the buzzer sounds.

"Olivia!" Harper yells, and the girl staggers toward her like her left knee might be blown.

I hug the two of them as Olivia cries. She doesn't have any blood on her, and Harper asks about this.

"I was going to," she sobs. "I was going to, but the door opened before I could. Oh God. I was going to hurt my Pandora."

Harper sits down and pulls the girl into her lap. "Don't cry. You're here now. I'll take care of everything."

I'm about to ask what she means when Braun appears through the door. He's sobbing, and when he sees that the four of us are already in the room, he drops to his knees. "No."

Unlike Harper, Braun is coated in blood. Soaked in it. His face is running with the stuff, and he's sleeved in scarlet like a surgeon who operated up to his elbows. All this time, I never thought about FDR-1, about the iguana that lit our way to the final base camp. But now . . .

"What happened to Rose?" I ask.

"I did what I had to do!" he yells. "For nothing. All of it was for nothing."

"You killed her?" Olivia asks.

"I killed M-4, too," Guy interjects, his face in his hands.

It's different, though, and we both know it. When Braun slumps to the ground and weeps, I slide down beside him, gripping my side. I allow myself to absorb this new heartbreak. It's my fault, in a way. If I had kept Rose instead of handing her off, maybe she'd still be alive. "It's okay," I say, trying to soothe his misery. "You didn't have a choice." Part of me doesn't understand why his door didn't open until the iguana was dead, but then again, I suppose I know exactly why. Rose had a red stripe down her back. So did Oz.

Marked Pandoras are disposable.

Guy sits up as if he's going to do something, and then his head falls again when he remembers his lion. He does this in sequence. Resolve — guilt — resolve — guilt. I crawl toward him and lay my head on his thigh, my body seeping blood like an overfilled sponge.

"Harper won?" Olivia asks the room.

"Tella won," Harper corrects.

When I hear that, *Tella won*, I raise my head. The suddenness with which I understand the meaning of this is staggering.

Cody will live.

I didn't win the race. Not me anyway. But I made friends, I helped Contenders and Pandoras alike, I thought about others. I finished the race second.

I finished the race first.

My brother is going to receive the Cure.

I break down, and Guy holds on to my head as if he can only breathe through the feel of my skin in his hands. Harper cries, too. Olivia and Braun sit next to each other. They are happy for me, I know. But they are devastated for their own loved ones.

"I'm sorry," I say to them through my joy, through my pain.

Neither responds. I don't blame them.

"We made it," Guy says suddenly. "All five of us. We're the first." The weight of his words settles over us, and Olivia and Braun seem comforted by this fact. Somehow, against incredible odds, we survived together. We proved that there is strength in numbers. That's there's strength in helping one another. "You know what this means," he adds.

We know what it means.

The five of us will receive invitations. In the end, though only Cody will be saved, we'll all have our chance to destroy this race.

The door on the opposite side of the room opens, and an older man strides into view. He has the look of a doctor, of someone who knows essential things others don't. His lashes are long and his beard heavy. He stands awkwardly, favoring his right side. In his left hand is a clipboard like the one the woman in orange held.

He glances down at it, his lashes bowing like a cast of characters at the end of a play. He reads something. "Harper?"

She stands. "That's me."

"You can come back now." He glances at the rest of us, and a smile parts his face. "Congratulations to all of you on completing the Brimstone Bleed. We'll be calling you back one by one." His eyes run over our bodies, inspecting our wounds. When he sees me, he says, "I'll be quick."

Harper comes to stand beside him. "Do you work for the race?"

He nods, his chest filling with pride.

In one swift movement, Harper withdraws a blade from her back waistband and puts it at his throat. She asks him one question, her voice so calm, it's terrifying.

"Tell me, are you afraid to die?"

CHAPTER SEVENTY-TWO

A half dozen people are in the room within seconds. They're dressed in blue scrubs and look like nurses. A woman with dark hair and a wide nose speaks softly to Harper, but Harper screams at her to shut up, shut up, *SHUT UP!*

"You took my daughter," she snarls. "All of you. I don't know what part each of you play in this race, but the day I put my daughter in the ground, I made a vow: two lives for one. One to save" — Harper nods toward me — "and one to take. I knew who I'd save; that was easy. And you know what? In the end, I decided who I killed wasn't such a big deal, either, as long as somebody died."

In the back, behind the locked door that is now held open by a nurse, I hear voices arguing.

"Harper," I say. "Don't do this. Remember what we said."

She pushes the knife closer to the man's throat, and sweat dots his forehead. That's when it hits me: I'm not concerned for the man's safety. I only want Harper to work with me inside headquarters. I'm pretty sure if she offs someone on their team, they'll revoke her invitation. Does this make me a monster? That I don't care if this man, who I've never met, drops dead?

A voice grows louder, and suddenly, I understand whose it is.

Cotton steps into view, appearing from the same door the doctor came through.

"Harper," he says gently. Behind him, two men are trying to pull him back, but he escapes their grasp.

Harper freezes, but she doesn't drop her arm.

"Harper," he repeats. "These people . . . they've done terrible things, *unspeakable* things, but you'll come to understand it —"

Harper screams with rage and knees the doctor in the groin. He slumps over, and she shoves the tip of the blade to his back. "Don't you dare. Don't you *dare* defend them. Why are you on *their* side?"

Cotton closes the distance between them as Guy tightens his grip on my hand. I can't breathe. I can't think. Harper is my best friend. I can't lose her, but I don't know how to take away her anger. There's too much inside me battling for the same release. I can practically feel the knife handle in my own hand, the thought of Oz's dying steady in my mind.

"I'm not on their side. I'm a Contender, same as you," Cotton says. "You and I, we're not so different. You lost your daughter. I lost my brother. I know how you feel. I *know*. So I can't stand by and watch you get hurt."

Tears escape Harper's eyes, and her bottom lip trembles. Her eyes, though . . . her eyes never lose their fury.

Cotton leans toward her. His lips touch her ear. He whispers quickly, saying things I can't hear. The nurses stand perfectly still. We all stand perfectly still.

A red dot appears on Harper's neck. It takes me too long to understand what it is.

Too long.

A sharp sound slices the air, and Harper drops to the ground.

"Harper!" I scream.

Braun and Guy are already charging toward the person who fired the bullet — the woman in orange from the desert base camp. Today, she wears pink, because shooting a gun doesn't have to be such a masculine thing.

"Stop, stop!" Cotton hollers at the two Contenders hurtling across the space. "She's okay. It's a dart." He looks at the woman. One arm is stretched toward her and one toward us, as if he can hold back the erupting tension with the flats of his hands. "She's asleep, right?"

The woman nods as if she's sorry for the way this unfolded.

She's not sorry.

I eye the knife on the floor.

The doctor grabs it and orders the nurses into the back. He follows them out but stops at the door. "I need to see her first." He nods toward me.

The woman opens her mouth to speak. She isn't wearing lipstick, even though she seems like a lipstick kind of girl. "I know this is a frustrating time, but trust me when I say we, *all* of us, have been in a similar position." She touches a hand to her hip bone. "You're angry. You have questions. And right now you'd probably like nothing better than to kill every last one of us." She sighs. "Trust me, I felt the same way. But, in time, you'll understand our reasoning for the Brimstone Bleed and all the challenges it entailed. For now all I ask, with complete respect as to what you've been through, is that you follow me."

Cotton gathers Harper into his arms.

"Wait," I tell him.

He looks at me, and when he does, I understand he's still with us, still a Contender and nothing more. Cotton has played his part of empathizer well, but I see the rage lying beneath it, hidden from the woman but not from me. He wants to destroy these people every bit as much as I do. So I say, "I'll help you carry Harper."

"No, you're hurt," he responds. "I've got her."

Olivia glances at me, and when I motion toward the door, she gets to her feet and follows after Cotton. We've come this far, why not a bit farther? Once it's clear Olivia won't stay behind and that Braun is getting up as well, I allow Guy to lead me into the hallway. The woman turns around.

"Oh, I'm sorry," she says to Braun. "I'll need you to stay in the waiting room. The doctor will be out to check on you in a few minutes."

"He stays with us," I snarl.

Her head falls to the side with mock sympathy. "Not anymore. We have a special message for the first five Contenders who finish the race, and unfortunately, he is number six."

I do a quick count, and when I realize she's right, I turn to Braun.

"It's okay," he says. "It doesn't matter now."

I let go of Guy's hand and throw myself at Braun. "I can't do this without you," I whisper in his ear.

He buries his head into my shoulder. "You can do anything without me."

Braun releases me and walks away.

"Braun," Olivia says. "Braun!"

He never turns around, and when the door slams behind him, no one speaks another word. Cotton appears almost guilty, holding Harper, and that's when a new, gut-wrenching thought occurs to me.

I wasn't first.

My brother won't receive the Cure.

Guy senses the moment I come to this realization, and he's there, wrapping his arm around my waist, telling me to keep walking, to stay awake, to stay focused. But my mind threatens to turn off anyway as the woman leads us into a room with five clean cots. As the doctor gives me pain medication and stitches up my wounds. As a new person, one I've never met but who seems unnervingly familiar, enters the room and delivers five crisp green envelopes. She stares at the feather in my hair as if it's the most remarkable thing she's ever seen.

My rational thought is gone.

Good riddance.

When Guy Chambers crawls into my cot, though, against the nurses' advisement, I snap to attention. "You're here," I say through the drug's fog.